ACCLAIM FOR WALKER PERCY'S *THE MOVIEGOER*

"Clothed in originality, intelligence and a fierce regard for man's fate ... handled with just the right degree of seriousness and humor, of rancor and indifference. Percy has a rare talent for making his people look and sound as though they were being seen and heard for the first time by anyone."

Time

"A truthful novel with shocks of recognition and spasms of nostalgia for every—or nearly every—American."

Citation for the National Book Award

"Mr. Percy's writing has a lyric quality. It is honest and it can be bluntly humorous. ... It is a rewarding book and Mr. Percy has turned in a memorable performance."

St. Louis Post-Dispatch

Also by Walker Percy:

Fiction
THE LAST GENTLEMAN★
LOVE IN THE RUINS★
LANCELOT★
THE SECOND COMING
THE THANATOS SYNDROME★

Nonfiction
THE MESSAGE IN THE BOTTLE
LOST IN THE COSMOS

★Published by Ivy Books

THE MOVIEGOER

Walker Percy

IVY BOOKS • NEW YORK

Ivy Books
Published by Ballantine Books
Copyright © 1960, 1961 by Walker Percy

A small section of this book originally appeared in FORUM in slightly different form as "Carnival in Gentilly."

Library of Congress Catalog Card Number: 61-7754

ISBN: 0-8041-0290-2

This edition published by arrangement with Alfred A. Knopf, Inc.

Manufactured in the United States of America

First Ballantine Books Edition: May 1988
Seventh Printing: February 1990

in gratitude to
W. A. P.

. . . the specific character of
despair is precisely this: it
is unaware of being despair.

SØREN KIERKEGAARD,
The Sickness Unto Death

What follows is a work of the imagination. Every character, except movie stars, and every event without exception are fictitious. No resemblance to real persons is intended or should be inferred. When movie stars are mentioned, it is not the person of the actor which is meant but the character he projects upon the screen. The geography of New Orleans and the bayous has been changed slightly. As for "Feliciana Parish," there are parishes named East Feliciana and West Feliciana, but I know not a soul in either place.

1

1. THIS MORNING I GOT A NOTE FROM MY AUNT ASK-
ing me to come for lunch. I know what this means.
Since I go there every Sunday for dinner and today is
Wednesday, it can mean only one thing: she wants to
have one of her serious talks. It will be extremely grave,
either a piece of bad news about her stepdaughter Kate
or else a serious talk about me, about the future and what
I ought to do. It is enough to scare the wits out of anyone, yet I confess I do not find the prospect altogether
unpleasant.

I remember when my older brother Scott died of pneumonia. I was eight years old. My aunt had charge of me
and she took me for a walk behind the hospital. It was
an interesting street. On one side were the power plant
and blowers and incinerator of the hospital, all humming
and blowing out a hot meaty smell. On the other side
was a row of Negro houses. Children and old folks and
dogs sat on the porches watching us. I noticed with pleasure that Aunt Emily seemed to have all the time in the
world and was willing to talk about anything I wanted to
talk about. Something extraordinary had happened all
right. We walked slowly in step. "Jack," she said,
squeezing me tight and smiling at the Negro shacks, "you

1

and I have always been good buddies, haven't we?" "Yes ma'am." My heart gave a big pump and the back of my neck prickled like a dog's. "I've got bad news for you, son." She squeezed me tighter than ever. "Scotty is dead. Now it's all up to you. It's going to be difficult for you but I know you're going to act like a soldier." This was true. I could easily act like a soldier. Was that all I had to do?

It reminds me of a movie I saw last month out by Lake Pontchartrain. Linda and I went out to a theater in a new suburb. It was evident somebody had miscalculated, for the suburb had quit growing and here was the theater, a pink stucco cube, sitting out in a field all by itself. A strong wind whipped the waves against the seawall; even inside you could hear the racket. The movie was about a man who lost his memory in an accident and as a result lost everything: his family, his friends, his money. He found himself a stranger in a strange city. Here he had to make a fresh start, find a new place to live, a new job, a new girl. It was supposed to be a tragedy, his losing all this, and he seemed to suffer a great deal. On the other hand, things were not so bad after all. In no time he found a very picturesque place to live, a houseboat on the river, and a very handsome girl, the local librarian.

After the movie Linda and I stood under the marquee and talked to the manager, or rather listened to him tell his troubles: the theater was almost empty, which was pleasant for me but not for him. It was a fine night and I felt very good. Overhead was the blackest sky I ever saw; a black wind pushed the lake toward us. The waves jumped over the seawall and spattered the street. The manager had to yell to be heard while from the sidewalk speaker directly over his head came the twittering conversation of the amnesiac and the librarian. It was the part where they are going through the newspaper files in search of some clue to his identity (he has a vague recollection of an accident). Linda stood by unhappily. She was unhappy for the same reason I was happy—because here we at a neighborhood theater out in the sticks and without a car (I have a car but I prefer to ride buses and streetcars). Her idea of happiness is to drive downtown and have supper at the Blue Room of the Roosevelt Hotel. This I am obliged to do from time to time. It is worth it, however. On these occasions Linda becomes as exalted as I am now. Her eyes glow, her lips become moist, and when we dance she brushes her fine long legs against mine. She actually loves me at these times—and not as a reward for being taken to the Blue Room. She loves me because she feels exalted in this romantic place and not in a movie out in the sticks.

But all this is history. Linda and I have parted company. I have a new secretary, a girl named Sharon Kincaid.

For the past four years now I have been living uneventfully in Gentilly, a middle-class suburb of New Orleans. Except for the banana plants in the patios and the curlicues of iron on the Walgreen drugstore one would never guess it was part of New Orleans. Most of the houses are either old-style California bungalows or new-style Daytona cottages. But this is what I like about it. I can't stand the old-world atmosphere of the French Quarter or the genteel charm of the Garden District. I lived in the Quarter for two years, but in the end I got tired of Birmingham businessmen smirking around Bourbon Street and the homosexuals and patio connoisseurs on Royal Street. My uncle and aunt live in a gracious house in the Garden District and are very kind to me. But whenever I try to live there, I find myself first in a rage during which I develop strong opinions on a variety of subjects and write letters to editors, then in a depression during which I lie rigid as a stick for hours staring straight up at the plaster medallion in the ceiling of my bedroom.

Life in Gentilly is very peaceful. I manage a small branch office of my uncle's brokerage firm. My home is the basement apartment of a raised bungalow belonging to Mrs Schexnaydre, the widow of a fireman. I am a model tenant and a model citizen and take pleasure in doing all that is expected of me. My wallet is full of identity cards, library cards, credit cards. Last year I purchased a flat olive-drab strongbox, very smooth and heavily built with double walls for fire protection, in which I placed my birth certificate, college diploma, honorable discharge, G.I. insurance, a few stock certificates, and my inheritance: a deed to ten acres of a defunct duck club down in St Bernard Parish, the only relic of my father's many enthusiasms. It is a pleasure to carry out the duties of a citizen and to receive in return a receipt or a neat styrene card with one's name on it certifying, so to speak, one's right to exist. What satisfaction I take in appearing the first day to get my auto tag and brake sticker! I subscribe to *Consumer Reports* and as a consequence I own a first-class television set, an all but silent air conditioner and a very long lasting deodorant. My armpits never stink. I pay attention to all spot announcements on the radio about mental health, the seven signs of cancer, and safe driving—though, as I say, I usually prefer to ride the bus. Yesterday a favorite of mine, William Holden, delivered a radio announcement on litterbugs. "Let's face it," said Holden. "Nobody can do anything about it—but you and me." This is true. I have been careful ever since.

In the evenings I usually watch television or go to the movies. Weekends I often spend on the Gulf Coast. Our neighborhood theater in Gentilly has permanent lettering on the front of the marquee reading: Where Happiness Costs So Little. The fact is I am quite happy in a movie, even a bad movie. Other people, so I have read, treasure memorable moments in their lives: the time one climbed the Parthenon at sunrise, the summer night one met a lonely girl in Central Park and achieved with her a sweet and natural relationship, as they say in books. I too once met a girl in Central Park, but it is not much to remember. What I remember is the time John Wayne killed three men with a carbine as he was falling to the dusty street in *Stagecoach*, and the time the kitten found Orson Welles in the doorway in *The Third Man*.

My companion on these evening outings and weekend trips is usually my secretary. I have had three secretaries, girls named Marcia, Linda, and now Sharon. Twenty years ago, practically every other girl born in Gentilly must have been named Marcia. A year or so later it was Linda. Then Sharon. In recent years I have noticed that the name Stephanie has come into fashion. Three of my acquaintances in Gentilly have daughters named Stephanie. Last night I saw a TV play about a nuclear test explosion. Keenan Wynn played a troubled physicist who had many a bad moment with his conscience. He took solitary walks in the desert. But you could tell that in his heart of hearts he was having a very good time with his soul-searching. "What right have we to do what we are doing?" he would ask his colleagues in a bitter voice. "It's my four-year-old daughter I'm really thinking of," he told another colleague and took out a snapshot. "What kind of future are we building for her?" "What is your daughter's name?" asked the colleague, looking at the picture. "Stephanie," said Keenan Wynn in a gruff voice. Hearing the name produced a sharp tingling sensation on the back of my neck. Twenty years from now I shall perhaps have a rosy young Stephanie perched at my typewriter.

Naturally I would like to say that I had made conquests of these splendid girls, my secretaries, casting them off one after the other like old gloves, but it would not be strictly true. They could be called love affairs, I suppose. They started off as love affairs anyway, fine careless raptures in which Marcia or Linda (but not yet Sharon) and I would go spinning along the Gulf Coast, lie embracing in a deserted cove of Ship Island, and hardly believe our good fortune, hardly believe that the world could contain such happiness. Yet in the case of Marcia and Linda the affair ended just when I thought our relationship was coming into its best phase. The air in the office would begin to grow thick with silent reproaches. It would become impossible to exchange a single word or glance that was not freighted with a thousand hidden meanings. Telephone conversations would take place at all hours of the night, conversations made up mostly of long silences during which I would rack my brain for something to say while on the other end you could hear little else but breathing and sighs. When these long telephone silences come, it is a sure sign that love is over. No, they were not conquests. For in the end my Lindas and I were so sick of each other that we were delighted to say good-by.

I am a stock and bond broker. It is true that my family was somewhat disappointed in my choice of a profession. Once I thought of going into law or medicine or even pure science. I even dreamed of doing something great. But there is much to be said for giving up such grand ambitions and living the most ordinary life imaginable, a life without the old longings; selling stocks and bonds and mutual funds; quitting work at five o'clock like everyone else; having a girl and perhaps one day settling down and raising a flock of Marcias and Sandras and Lindas of my own. Nor is the brokerage business as uninteresting as you might think. It is not a bad life at all.

We live, Mrs Schexnaydre and I, on Elysian Fields, the main thoroughfare of Faubourg Marigny. Though it was planned to be, like its namesake, the grandest boulevard of the city, something went amiss, and now it runs an undistinguished course from river to lake through shopping centers and blocks of duplexes and bungalows and raised cottages. But it is very spacious and airy and seems truly to stretch out like a field under the sky. Next door to Mrs Schexnaydre is a brand new school. It is my custom on summer evenings after work to take a shower, put on shirt and pants and stroll over to the deserted playground and there sit on the ocean wave, spread out the movie page of the *Times-Picayune* on one side, phone book on the other, and a city map in my lap. After I have made my choice, plotted a route—often to some remote neighborhood like Algiers or St Bernard—I stroll around the schoolyard in the last golden light of day and admire the building. Everything is so spick-and-span: the aluminum sashes fitted into the brick wall and gilded in the sunset, the pretty terrazzo floors and the desks molded like wings. Suspended by wires above the door is a schematic sort of bird, the Holy Ghost I suppose. It gives me a pleasant sense of the goodness of creation to think of the brick and the glass and the aluminum being extracted from common dirt—though no doubt it is less a religious sentiment than a financial one, since I own a few shares of Alcoa. How smooth and well-fitted and thrifty the aluminum feels!

But things have suddenly changed. My peaceful existence in Gentilly has been complicated. This morning, for the first time in years, there occurred to me the possibility of a search. I dreamed of the war, no, not quite dreamed but woke with the taste of it in my mouth, the queasy-quince taste of 1951 and the Orient. I remembered the first time the search occurred to me. I came to myself under a chindolea bush. Everything is upside-down for me, as I shall explain later. What are generally considered to be the best times are for me the worst times, and that worst of times was one of the best. My shoulder didn't hurt but it was pressed hard against the ground as if somebody sat on me. Six inches from my nose a dung beetle was scratching around under leaves. As I watched, there awoke in me an immense curiosity. I was onto something. I vowed that if I ever got out of this fix, I would pursue the search. Naturally, as soon as I recovered and got home, I forgot all about it. But this morning when I got up, I dressed as usual and began as usual to put my belongings into my pockets: wallet, notebook (for writing down occasional thoughts), pencil, keys, handkerchief, pocket slide rule (for calculating percentage returns on principal). They looked both unfamiliar and at the same time full of clues. I stood in the center of the room and gazed at the little pile, sighting through a hole made by thumb and forefinger. What was unfamiliar about them was that I could see them. They might have belonged to someone else. A man can look at this little pile on his bureau for thirty years and never once see it. It is as invisible as his own hand. Once I saw it, however, the search became possible. I bathed, shaved, dressed carefully, and sat at my desk and poked through the little pile in search of a clue just as the detective on television pokes through the dead man's possessions, using his pencil as a poker.

The idea of a search comes to me again as I am on my way to my aunt's house, riding the Gentilly bus down Elysian Fields. The truth is I dislike cars. Whenever I drive a car, I have the feeling I have become invisible. People on the street cannot see you; they only watch your rear fender until it is out of their way. Elysian Fields is not the shortest route to my aunt's house. But I have my reasons for going through the Quarter. William Holden, I read in the paper this morning, is in New Orleans shooting a few scenes in the Place d'Armes. It would be interesting to catch a glimpse of him.

It is a gloomy March day. The swamps are still burning at Chef Menteur and the sky over Gentilly is the color of ashes. The bus is crowded with shoppers, nearly all women. The windows are steamed. I sit on the lengthwise seat in front. Women sit beside me and stand above me. On the long back seat are five Negresses so black that the whole rear of the bus seems darkened. Directly next to me, on the first cross seat, is a very fine-looking girl. She is a strapping girl but by no means too big, done up head to toe in cellophane, the hood pushed back to show a helmet of glossy black hair. She is magnificent with her split tooth and her Prince Val bangs split on her forehead. Gray eyes and wide black brows, a good arm and a fine swell of calf above her cellophane boot. One of those solitary Amazons one sees on Fifty-seventh Street in New York or in Nieman Marcus in Dallas. Our eyes meet. Am I mistaken or does the corner of her mouth tuck in ever so slightly and the petal of her lower lip curl out ever so richly? She is smiling—at me! My mind hits upon half a dozen schemes to circumvent the terrible moment of separation. No doubt she is a Texan. They are nearly always bad judges of men, these splendid Amazons. Most men are afraid of them and so they fall victim to the first little Mickey Rooney that comes along. In a better world I should be able to speak to her: come, darling, you can see that I love you. If you are planning to meet some little Mickey, think better of it. What a tragedy it is that I do not know her, will probably never see her again. What good times we could have! This very afternoon we could go spinning along the Gulf Coast. What consideration and tenderness I could show her! If it were a movie, I would have only to wait. The bus would get lost or the city would be bombed and she and I would tend the wounded. As it is, I may as well stop thinking about her.

Then it is that the idea of the search occurs to me. I become absorbed and for a minute or so forget about the girl.

What is the nature of the search? you ask.

Really it is very simple, at least for a fellow like me; so simple that it is easily overlooked.

The search is what anyone would undertake if he were not sunk in the everydayness of his own life. This morning, for example, I felt as if I had come to myself on a strange island. And what does such a castaway do? Why, he pokes around the neighborhood and he doesn't miss a trick.

To become aware of the possibility of the search is to be onto something. Not to be onto something is to be in despair.

The movies are onto the search, but they screw it up. The search always ends in despair. They like to show a fellow coming to himself in a strange place—but what does he do? He takes up with the local librarian, sets about proving to the local children what a nice fellow he is, and settles down with a vengeance. In two weeks' time he is so sunk in everydayness that he might just as well be dead.

What do you seek—God? you ask with a smile.

I hesitate to answer, since all other Americans have settled the matter for themselves and to give such an answer would amount to setting myself a goal which everyone else has reached—and therefore raising a question in which no one has the slightest interest. Who wants to be dead last among one hundred and eighty million Americans? For, as everyone knows, the polls report that 98% of Americans believe in God and the remaining 2% are atheists and agnostics—which leaves not a single percentage point for a seeker. For myself, I enjoy answering polls as much as anyone and take pleasure in giving intelligent replies to all questions.

Truthfully, it is the fear of exposing my own ignorance which constrains me from mentioning the object of my search. For, to begin with, I cannot even answer this, the simplest and most basic of all questions: Am I, in my search, a hundred miles ahead of my fellow Americans or a hundred miles behind them? That is to say: Have 98% of Americans already found what I seek or are they so sunk in everydayness that not even the possibility of a search has occurred to them?

On my honor, I do not know the answer.

As the bus ascends the overpass, a concrete hill which affords a fine view of New Orleans, I discover that I am frowning and gazing at a noble young calf clad in gunmetal nylon. Now beyond question she is aware of me: she gives her raincoat a sharp tug and gives me a look of annoyance—or do I imagine this? I must make sure, so I lift my hat and smile at her as much as to say that we might still become friends. But it is no use. I have lost her forever. She flounces out of the bus in a loud rustle of cellophane.

I alight at Esplanade in a smell of roasting coffee and creosote and walk up Royal Street. The lower Quarter is the best part. The ironwork on the balconies sags like rotten lace. Little French cottages hide behind high walls. Through deep sweating carriageways one catches glimpses of courtyards gone to jungle.

Today I am in luck. Who should come out of Pirate's Alley half a block ahead of me but William Holden!

Holden crosses Royal and turns toward Canal. As yet he is unnoticed. The tourists are either browsing along antique shops or snapping pictures of balconies. No doubt he is on his way to Galatoire's for lunch. He is an attractive fellow with his ordinary good looks, very suntanned, walking along hands in pockets, raincoat slung over one shoulder. Presently he passes a young couple, who are now between me and him. Now we go along, the four of us, not twenty feet apart. It takes two seconds to size up the couple. They are twenty, twenty-one, and on their honeymoon. Not Southern. Probably Northeast. He wears a jacket with leather elbow patches, pipestem pants, dirty white shoes, and affects the kind of rolling seafaring gait you see in Northern college boys. Both are plain. He has thick lips, cropped reddish hair and skin to match. She is mousy. They are not really happy. He is afraid their honeymoon is too conventional, that they are just another honeymoon couple. No doubt he figured it would be fun to drive down the Shenandoah Valley to New Orleans and escape the honeymooners at Niagara Falls and Saratoga. Now fifteen hundred miles from home they find themselves surrounded by couples from Memphis and Chicago. He is anxious; he is threatened from every side. Each stranger he passes is a reproach to him, every doorway a threat. What is wrong? he wonders. She is unhappy for a different reason, because he is unhappy and she knows it but doesn't know why.

Now they spot Holden. The girl nudges her companion. The boy perks up for a second, but seeing Holden doesn't really help him. On the contrary. He can only contrast Holden's resplendent reality with his own shadowy and precarious existence. Obviously he is more miserable than ever. What a deal, he must be thinking, trailing along behind a movie star—we might just as well be rubbernecking in Hollywood.

Holden slaps his pockets for a match. He has stopped behind some ladies looking at iron furniture on the sidewalk. They look like housewives from Hattiesburg come down for a day of shopping. He asks for a match; they shake their heads and then recognize him. There follows much blushing and confusion. But nobody can find a match for Holden. By now the couple have caught up with him. The boy holds out a light, nods briefly to Holden's thanks, then passes on without a flicker of recognition. Holden walks along between them for a second; he and the boy talk briefly, look up at the sky, shake their heads. Holden gives them a pat on the shoulder and moves on ahead.

The boy has done it! He has won title to his own existence, as plenary an existence now as Holden's, by refusing to be stampeded like the ladies from Hattiesburg. He is a citizen like Holden; two men of the world they are. All at once the world is open to him. Nobody threatens from patio and alley. His girl is open to him too. He puts his arm around her neck, noddles her head. She feels the difference too. She had not known what was wrong nor how it was righted but she knows now that all is well.

Holden has turned down Toulouse shedding light as he

goes. An aura of heightened reality moves with him and all who fall within it feel it. Now everyone is aware of him. He creates a regular eddy among the tourists and barkeeps and B-girls who come running to the doors of the joints.

I am attracted to movie stars but not for the usual reasons. I have no desire to speak to Holden or get his autograph. It is their peculiar reality which astounds me. The Yankee boy is well aware of it, even though he pretends to ignore Holden. Clearly he would like nothing better than to take Holden over to his fraternity house in the most casual way. "Bill, I want you to meet Phil. Phil, Bill Holden," he would say and go sauntering off in the best seafaring style.

It is lunch hour on Canal Street. A parade is passing, but no one pays much attention. It is still a week before Mardi Gras and this is a new parade, a women's krewe from Gentilly. A krewe is a group of people who get together at carnival time and put on a parade and a ball. Anyone can form a krewe. Of course there are the famous old krewes like Comus and Rex and Twelfth Night, but there are also dozens of others. The other day a group of Syrians from Algiers formed a krewe named Isis. This krewe today, this must be Linda's krewe. I promised to come to see her. Red tractors pulled the floats along; scaffoldings creak, paper and canvas tremble. Linda, I think, is one of half a dozen shepherdesses dressed in short pleated skirts and mercury sandals with thongs crisscrossed up bare calves. But they are masked and I can't be sure. If she is, her legs are not so fine after all. All twelve legs are shivery and goosepimpled. A few businessmen stop to watch the girls and catch trinkets.

A warm wind springs up from the south piling up the clouds and bearing with it a far-off rumble, the first thunderstorm of the year. The street looks tremendous. People on the far side seem tiny and archaic, dwarfed by the great sky and the windy clouds like pedestrians in old prints. Am I mistaken or has a fog of uneasiness, a thin gas of malaise, settled on the street? The businessmen hurry back to their offices, the shoppers to their cars, the tourists to their hotels. Ah, William Holden, we already need you again. Already the fabric is wearing thin without you.

The mystery deepens. For ten minutes I stand talking to Eddie Lovell and at the end of it, when we shake hands and part, it seems to me that I cannot answer the simplest question about what has taken place. As I listen to Eddie speak plausibly and at length of one thing and another—business, his wife Nell, the old house they are redecorating—the fabric pulls together into one bright texture of investments, family projects, lovely old houses, little theater readings and such. It comes over me: this is how one lives! My exile in Gentilly has been the worst kind of self-deception.

Yes! Look at him. As he talks, he slaps a folded newspaper against his pants leg and his eye watches me and at the same time sweeps the terrain behind me, taking note of the slightest movement. A green truck turns down Bourbon Street; the eye sizes it up, flags it down, demands credentials, waves it on. A businessman turns in at the Maison Blanche building; the eye knows him, even knows what he is up to. And all the while he talks very well. His lips move muscularly, molding words into pleasing shapes, marshalling arguments, and during the slight pauses are held poised, attractively everted in a Charles Boyer pout—while a little web of saliva gathers in a corner like the clear oil of a good machine. Now he jingles the coins deep in his pocket. No mystery here!—he is as cogent as a bird dog quartering a field. He understands everything out there and everything out there is something to be understood.

Eddie watches the last float, a doubtful affair with a squashed cornucopia.

"We'd better do better than that."

"We will."

"Are you riding Neptune?"

"No."

I offer Eddie my four call-outs for the Neptune ball. There is always the problem of out-of-town clients, usually Texans, and especially their wives. Eddie thanks me for this and for something else.

"I want to thank you for sending Mr Quieulle to me. I really appreciate it."

"Who?"

"Old man Quieulle."

"Yes, I remember." Eddie has sunk mysteriously into himself, eyes twinkling from the depths. "Don't tell me—"

Eddie nods.

"—that he has already set up his trust and up and died?"

Eddie nods, still sunk into himself. He watches me carefully, hanging fire until I catch up with him.

"In Mrs Quieulle's name?"

Again a nod; his jaw is shot out.

"How big?"

The same dancing look, now almost malignant. "Just short of nine hundred and fifty thou." His tongue curves around and seeks the hollow of his cheek.

"A fine old man," I say absently, noticing that Eddie has become as solemn as a bishop.

"I'll tell you one thing, Binx. I count it a great privilege to have known him. I've never known anyone, young or old, who possessed a greater fund of knowledge. That man spoke to me for two hours about the history of the crystallization of sugar and it was pure romance. I was fascinated."

Eddie tells me how much he admires my aunt and my cousin Kate. Several years ago Kate was engaged to marry Eddie's brother Lyell. On the very eve of the wedding Lyell was killed in an accident, the same accident

15

which Kate survived. Now Eddie comes around to face me, his cottony hair flying up in the breeze. "I have never told anybody what I really think of that woman—" Eddie says "woman" as a deliberate liberty to be set right by the compliment to follow. "I think more of Miss Emily—and Kate—than anyone else in the world except my own mother—and wife. The good that woman has done."

"That's mighty nice, Eddie."

He murmurs something about how beautiful Kate is, that next to Nell etc.—and this is a surprise because my cousin Nell Lovell is a plain horsy old girl. "Will you please give them both my love?"

"I certainly will."

The parade is gone. All that is left is the throb of a drum.

"What do you do with yourself?" asks Eddie and slaps his paper against his pants leg.

"Nothing much," I say, noticing that Eddie is not listening.

"Come see us, fellah! I want you to see what Nell has done." Nell has taste. The two of them are forever buying shotgun cottages in rundown neighborhoods and fixing them up with shutterblinds in the bathroom, saloon doors for the kitchen, old bricks and a sugar kettle for the backyard, and selling in a few months for a big profit.

The cloud is turning blue and pressing down upon us. Now the street seems closeted; the bricks of the buildings glow with a yellow stored-up light. I look at my watch: one is not late at my aunt's house. In an instant Eddie's hand is out.

"Give the bride and groom my best."

"I will."

"Walter is a wonderful fellow."

"He is."

16

Before letting me go, Eddie comes one inch closer and asks in a special voice about Kate.

"She seems fine now, Eddie. Quite happy and secure."

"I'm so damn glad. Fellah!" A final shake from side to side, like a tiller. "Come see us!"

"I will!"

2. MERCER LETS ME IN. "LOOK OUT NOW! UH OH." He carries on in a mock astonishment and falls back limberkneed. Today he does not say "Mister Jack" and I know that the omission is deliberate, the consequence of a careful weighing of pros and cons. Tomorrow the scales might tip the other way (today's omission will go into the balance) and it will be "Mister Jack."

For some reason it is possible to see Mercer more clearly today than usual. Ordinarily it is hard to see him because of the devotion. He worked for my grandfather in Feliciana Parish before Aunt Emily brought him to New Orleans. He is thought to be devoted to us and we to him. But the truth is that Mercer and I are not at all devoted to each other. My main emotion around Mercer is unease that in threading his way between servility and presumption, his foot might slip. I wait on Mercer, not he on me.

"Didn't nobody tell me you was coming!" cries Mercer, feeling the balance tilt against me. "I was just commencing to make a fire."

Mercer is a chesty sand-colored Negro with a shaved head and a dignified Adolph Menjou mustache. Behind the mustache, his face, I notice, is not at all devoted but is as sulky as a Pullman porter's. My aunt brought him down from Feliciana, but he has changed much since then. Not only is he a city man now; he is also Mrs

17

Cutrer's butler and as such presides over a shifting ménage of New Orleans Negresses, Jamaicans and lately Hondurians. He is conscious of his position and affects a clipped speech, pronouncing his *R*s and *ing*s and dipthonging his *I*s Harlem-style.

Despite the gray day outside, the living room is bright, but it is not snug. The windows are open to the ceiling and the gray sky comes pouring in.

Mercer puts coal on the blazing kindling. His white coat, starched stiff as armor, creaks and rustles. A welt and a tuck form at the base of his skull. He places the coals carefully, his hand passing slowly and imperviously through the flame. Head thrown back, he breathes heavily through his mouth, holding his breath as he places a coal, then expelling it in a hiss.

We might be back in Feliciana. Here is the very sound of winter mornings in Feliciana twenty years ago when cold dark dawns were announced by the clatter of the handle on the scuttle and Mercer's strangled breathing.

The room is a beautiful room and by every right a cheerful room, with its walls of books, its bokhara glowing like a jewel, its blackening portraits. The prisms of the chandelier wink red in the firelight. Scattered over the satinwood table is the usual litter of quarterlies and rough-paper weeklies and, as always, the great folio *The Life of the Buddha*. My aunt likes to say she is an Episcopalian by emotion, a Greek by nature and a Buddhist by choice.

Mercer is speaking to me.

"—but they still hasn't the factories and the—ah—producing setup we has."

So Mercer wants to talk about current events. I do so willingly though I am certain he knows more about the subject than I do. He stands facing neither me nor the fire but in a kind of limbo. He holds the coal scuttle and puts one foot toward the door but neither quite stays nor leaves.

Mercer has dissolved somewhat in recent years. It is not so easy to say who he is anymore. My aunt truly loves him and sees him as a faithful retainer, a living connection with a bygone age. She tells about Mercer's devotion to Dr Wills, how he went around for days after Dr Wills's death, his face streaming with tears. I do not doubt this. Yet I know for a fact that Mercer steals regularly from her by getting kickbacks from the servants and tradespeople. But you can't call him a thief and let it go at that. Mercer has aspirations. How does he see himself? When he succeeds in seeing himself, it is as a remarkable sort of fellow, a man who keeps himself well-informed in science and politics. This is why I am always uneasy when I talk to him. I hate it when his vision of himself dissolves and he sees himself as neither, neither old retainer nor expert in current events. Then his eyes get muddy and his face runs together behind his mustache. Last Christmas I went looking for him in his rooms over the garage. He wasn't there but on his bed lay a well-thumbed volume put out by the Rosicrucians called *How to Harness Your Secret Powers*. The poor bastard.

While Mercer speaks of current events, I edge closer to the mantelpiece. There are the Cutrers in their "grand slam" year. Uncle Jules was Rex, Kate was queen of Neptune, Aunt Emily won the *Picayune* cup for her work with the Home Service. Everyone said that Kate was a lovely queen, but she wasn't. When Kate gets her hair waved and puts on an evening gown, she looks frumpy; the face in the picture is plain as a pudding.

One picture I never tire looking at. For ten years I have looked at it on this mantelpiece and tried to understand it. Now I take it down and hold it against the light from the darkening sky. Here are the two brothers, Dr Wills and Judge Anse with their arms about each other's shoulders, and my father in front, the three standing on a mountain trail against a dark forest. It is the Schwarz-wald. A few years after the first war they had gotten

19

together for once and made the grand tour. Only Alex Bolling is missing—he is in the third frame: an astonishingly handsome young man with the Rupert Brooke-Galahad sort of face you see so often in pictures of World War I soldiers. His death in the Árgonne (five years before) was held to be fitting since the original Alex Bolling was killed with Roberdaux Wheat in the Hood breakthrough at Gaines Mill in 1862. My father is wearing some kind of fraternity blazer and a hard katy straw. He looks different from the brothers. Alex too is much younger, yet he is still one of them. But not my father. It is hard to say why. The elder Bollings—and Alex—are serene in their identities. Each one coincides with himself, just as the larch trees in the photograph coincide with themselves: Judge Anse with his drooping mustache and thin cold cheeks, the hard-eyed one who is still remembered for having publicly described a Louisiana governor as a peckerwood son of a bitch; Dr Wills, the lion-headed one, the rumpled country genius who developed a gut anastomosis still in use; and Alex, serene in his dream of youth and of his hero's death to come. But my father is not one of them. His feet are planted wide apart, arms locked around an alpenstock behind him; the katy is pushed back releasing a forelock. His eyes are alight with an expression I can't identify; it is not far from what his elders might have called smart-alecky. He is something of a dude with his round head and tricky tab collar. Yet he is, by every right, one of them. He was commissioned in the RCAF in 1940 and got himself killed before his country entered the war. And in Crete. And in the wine dark sea. And by the same Boche. And with a copy of *The Shropshire Lad* in his pocket. Again I search the eyes, each eye a stipple or two in a blurred oval. Beyond a doubt they are ironical.

"Does you, Mister Jack?" asks Mercer, still in limbo, one foot toward the fire, the other on its way out.

THE MOVIEGOER

"Yes, I do. Unilateral disarmament would be a disaster."

"What drivel." My aunt comes in smiling, head to one side, hands outstretched, and I whistle with relief and feel myself smiling with pleasure as I await one of her special kind of attacks, attacks which are both playful and partly true. She calls me an ingrate, a limb of Satan, the last and sorriest scion of a noble stock. What makes it funny is that this is true. In a split second I have forgotten everything, the years in Gentilly, even my search. As always we take up again where we left off. This is where I belong after all.

My aunt has done a great deal for me. When my father was killed, my mother, who had been a trained nurse, went back to her hospital in Biloxi. My aunt offered to provide my education. As a consequence much of the past fifteen years has been spent in her house. She is really my great aunt. Yet she is younger by so many years than her brothers that she might easily be my father's sister—or rather the daughter of all three brothers, since it is as their favorite and fondest darling that she still appears in her own recollection, the female sport of a fierce old warrior gens and no doubt for this reason never taken quite seriously, even in her rebellion—as when she left the South, worked in a settlement house in Chicago and, like many well-born Southern ladies, embraced advanced political ideas. After years of being the sort of "bird" her brothers indulged her in being and even expected her to be—her career reached its climax when she served as a Red Cross volunteer in the Spanish civil war, where I cannot picture her otherwise than as that sort of fiercely benevolent demoniac Yankee lady most incomprehensible to Spaniards—within the space of six months she met and married Jules Cutrer, widower with child, settled down in the Garden District and became as handsome and formidable as her brothers. She is no longer a "bird." It is as if, with her illustrious brothers dead and gone, she might now at

21

last become what they had been and what as a woman had been denied her: soldierly both in look and outlook. With her blue-white hair and keen face and terrible gray eyes, she is somehow at sixty-five still the young prince.

It is just as I thought. In an instant we are off and away down the hall and into her office, where she summons me for her "talks." This much is certain: it is bad news about Kate. If it were a talk about me, my aunt would not be looking at me. She would be gazing into the hive-like recesses of her old desk, finger pressed against her lip. But instead she shows me something and searches my face for what I see. With her watching me, it is difficult to see anything. There is a haze. Between us there is surely a carton of dusty bottles—*bottles?*—yes, surely bottles, yet blink as I will I can't be sure.

"Do you see these whisky bottles?"

"Yes ma'am."

"And this kind?" She gives me an oblong brown bottle. "Yes."

"Do you know where they came from?"

"No'm."

"Mercer found them on top of the armoire. That armoire." She points mysteriously to the very ceiling above us. "He was setting out rat poison."

"In Kate's room?"

"Yes. What do you think?"

"Those are not whisky bottles."

"What are they?"

"Wine. Gipsy Rose. They make wine bottles flat like that."

"Read that." She nods at the bottle in my hand.

"Sodium pentobarbital. One and one-half grains. This is a wholesaler's bottle."

"Do you know where we found that?"

"In the box?"

"In the incinerator. The second in a week."

I am silent. Now my aunt does take her seat at the desk.

22

"I haven't told Walter. Or Jules. Because I'm not really worried. Kate is just fine. She is going to come through with flying colors. And she and Walter are going to be happy. But as time grows short, she is getting a little nervous."

"You mean you think she is afraid of another accident?"

"She is afraid of a general catastrophe. But that is not what worries me."

"What worries you?"

"I don't want her moping around the house again."

"She's not working downtown with you?"

"Not for two weeks."

"Does she feel bad?"

"Oh no. Nothing like that. But she's a little scared."

"Is she seeing Dr Mink?"

"She refuses. She thinks that if she goes to see a doctor she'll get sick."

"What do you want me to do?"

"She will not go to the ball. Now that's all right. But it is very important that she not come to the point where it becomes more and more difficult to meet people."

"She's seen no one?"

"No one but Walter. Now all in the world I want you to do is take her to the Lejiers and watch the parade from the front porch. It is not a party. There will be no question of making an entrance or an exit. There is nothing to brace for. You will drop in, speak or not speak, and leave."

"She is that bad?"

"She is not bad at all. I mean to take care that she won't be."

"What about Walter?"

"He's krewe captain. He can't possibly get away. And I'm glad he can't, to tell the truth. Do you know what I really want you to do?"

"What?"

"I want you to do whatever it was you did before you

walked out on us, you wretch. Fight with her, joke with her—the child doesn't laugh. You and Kate always got along, didn't you? Sam too. You knew Sam will be here Sunday to speak at the Forum?''

"Yes.''

"I want Sam to talk to Kate. You and Sam are the only people she'd ever listen to.''

My aunt is generous with me. What she really means is that she is sure Sam can set things right and that she hopes I can hold the fort till Sam arrives.

3. IT IS A SURPRISE TO FIND UNCLE JULES AT LUNCH. Last fall he suffered a serious heart attack from which, however, he recovered so completely that he has dispensed with his nap since Christmas. He sits between Kate and Walter and his manner is so pleasant and easy that even Kate is smiling. It is hard to believe anything is wrong; the bottles, in particular, seem grotesque. Uncle Jules is pleased to see me. During the past year I discovered my sole discernible talent: the trick of making money. I manage to sell a great many of the stocks which Uncle Jules underwrites. He is convinced, moreover, that I predicted the January sell-off and even claims that he advanced a couple of issues on my say-so. This he finds pleasing, and he always greets me with a tremendous wink as if we were in cahoots and might get caught any minute.

He and Walter talk football. Uncle Jules's life ambition is to revive the fortunes of the Tulane football team. I enjoy the talk because I like football myself and especially do I like to hear Uncle Jules tell about the great days of Jerry Dalrymple and Don Zimmerman and Billy Banker. When he describes a goal-line stand against L.S.U. in

1932, it is like King Arthur standing fast in the bloodred sunset against Sir Modred and the traitors. Walter was manager of the team and so he and Uncle Jules are thick as thieves.

Uncle Jules is as pleasant a fellow as I know anywhere. Above his long Creole horseface is a crop of thick gray hair cut short as a college boy's. His shirt encases his body in a way that pleases me. It fits him so well. My shirts always have something wrong with them; they are too tight in the collar or too loose around the waist. Uncle Jules's collar fits his dark neck like a tape; his cuffs, folded like a napkin, just peep out past his coatsleeve; and his shirt front: the impulse comes over me at times to bury my nose in that snowy expanse of soft finespun cotton. Uncle Jules is the only man I know whose victory in the world is total and unqualified. He has made a great deal of money, he has a great many friends, he was Rex of Mardi Gras, he gives freely of himself and his money. He is an exemplary Catholic, but it is hard to know why he takes the trouble. For the world he lives in, the City of Man, is so pleasant that the City of God must hold little in store for him. I see his world plainly through his eyes and I see why he loves it and would keep it as it is: a friendly easy-going place of old-world charm and new-world business methods where kind white folks and carefree darkies have the good sense to behave pleasantly toward each other. No shadow ever crosses his face, except when someone raises the subject of last year's Tulane-L.S.U. game.

I mention seeing Eddie Lovell and deliver his love.

"Poor Eddie," my aunt sighs as she always does, and as always she adds: "What a sad thing that integrity, of itself, should fetch such a low price in the market place."

"Has she gone to Natchez again?" asks Uncle Jules, making his lip long and droll.

Walter Wade cocks an ear and listens intently. He has not yet caught on to the Bollings' elliptical way of talking. "She" is Eddie's sister Didi, and "Going to Natchez" is our way of referring to one of Didi's escapades. Several years ago, while Didi was married to her first husband, she is said to have attended the Natchez Pilgrimage with several other couples and "swapped husbands."

"Oh yes," says my aunt grimly. "Several times."

"I didn't think the Pilgrimage came until April," says Walter, smiling warily.

Kate frowns at her hands in her lap. Today Kate has her brown-eyed look. Sometimes her irises turn to discs. I remember another time when my aunt asked me to "talk" to Kate. When Kate was ten and I was fifteen, my aunt became worried about her. Kate was a good girl and made good grades, but she had no friends. Instead of playing at recess, she would do her lessons and sit quietly at her desk until class began. I made up the kind of spiel I thought my aunt had in mind. "Kate," I said in my aunt's Socratic manner, "you think you are the only person in the world who is shy. Believe me, you are not. Let me tell you something that happened to me," etc. But Kate only watched me with the same brown-eyed look, irises gone to discs.

Mercer passes the corn sticks, holding his breath at each place and letting it out with a strangling sound.

Walter and Uncle Jules try to persuade me to ride Neptune. My aunt looks at me in disgust—with all her joking, she has a solid respect for the Carnival krewes, for their usefulness in business and social life. She shifts over into her Lorenzo posture, temple propped on three fingers.

"What a depraved and dissolute specimen," she says as usual. She speaks absently. It is Kate who occupies her. "Grown fat-witted from drinking of old sack."

"What I am, Hal, I owe to thee," say I as usual and drink my soup.

Kate eats mechanically, gazing about the room vacantly like someone at the automat. Walter is certain of himself now. He gets a raffish gleam in the eye.

"I don't think we ought to let him ride, do you, Mrs

26

Cutrer? Here we are doing the work of the economy and there he is skimming off his five percent like a pawnbroker on Dryades Street.''

My aunt turns into herself another degree and becomes Lorenzo himself.

''Now here's a distinguished pair for you,'' she tells Kate and watches her carefully; she is not paying any attention to us. ''The barbarians at the inner gate and who defends the West? Don John of Austria? No, Mr Bolling the stockbroker and Mr Wade the lawyer. Mr Bolling and Mr Wade, defenders of the faith, seats of wisdom, mirrors of justice. God, I wouldn't mind if they showed a little spirit in their debauchery, but look at them. Rosenkranz and Guildenstern.''

It comes to me again how formidable Walter was in college, how much *older* he seemed then. Walter is a sickly-looking fellow with a hollow temple but he is actually quite healthy. He has gray sharklike skin and lidded eyes and a lock of hair combed across his forehead in the MacArthur style. Originally from Clarksburg, West Virginia, he attended Tulane and settled in New Orleans after the war. Now at thirty-three he is already the senior partner of a new firm of lawyers, Wade & Molyneux, which specializes in oil-lease law.

''Mr Wade,'' my aunt asks Walter. ''Are you a seat of wisdom?''

''Yes ma'am, Mrs Cutrer.''

I have to grin. What is funny is that Walter always starts out in the best brilliant-young-lawyer style of humoring an old lady by letting her get the better of him, whereas she really does get the better of him. Old ladies in West Virginia were never like this. But strangely, my aunt looks squarely at Kate and misses the storm warnings. Kate's head lowers until her brown shingled hair falls along her cheek. Then as Walter's eyes grow wider and warier, his smile more wolfish—he looks like a recruit picking his way through a minefield—Kate utters a clicking sound in her teeth and abruptly leaves the room.

Walter follows her. My aunt sighs. Uncle Jules sits easy. He has the gift of believing that nothing can really go wrong in his household. There are household-ups and household-downs but he smiles through them without a flicker of unease. Even at the time of Kate's breakdown, it was possible for him to accept it as the sort of normal mishap which befalls sensitive girls. It is his confidence in Aunt Emily. As long as she is mistress of his house, the worst that can happen, death itself, is nothing more than seemly.

Presently Uncle Jules leaves for the office. My aunt speaks to Walter in the hall. I sit in the empty dining room thinking of nothing. Walter joins me for dessert. Afterwards, as Mercer clears the table, Walter goes to the long window and stands looking out, hands in his pockets. I am prepared to reassure him about Kate, but it turns out that it is the Krewe of Neptune, not Kate, which is on his mind.

"I wish you would reconsider, Binx." There is an exhilaration in his voice which carries over from his talk with Uncle Jules. "We've got a damn good bunch of guys now." Ten years ago he would have said "ace gents"; that was what we called good guys in the 1940s "You may not agree with me, but in my opinion it is the best all-around krewe in Carnival. We're no upstarts and on the other hand we're not a bunch of old farts—and—," he adds hastily as he thinks of Uncle Jules, "our older men are among the ten wealthiest and most prominent families in New Orleans." Walter would never never say "rich"; and indeed the word "wealthy," as he says it, is redolent of a life spiced and sumptuous, a tapestry thick to the touch and shot through with the bright thread of freedom. "You'd really like it now, Jack. I mean it. You really would. I can give you positive assurance that every last one of us would be delighted to have you back."

"I certainly appreciate it, Walter."

Walter still dresses as well as he did in college and sits and stands and slouches with the same grace. He still wears thick socks summer and winter to hide his thin veined ankles and still crosses his legs to make his calf look fat. In college he was one of those upperclassmen freshmen spot as a model: he was Phi Beta Kappa without grinding for it and campus leader without intriguing for it. But most of all he was arbiter of taste. We pledges would see him in the fraternity house sitting with his hat on and one skinny knee cocked up, and so the style was set for sitting and wearing hats. The hat had to be a special kind of narrow-brim brown felt molded to a high tricornered peak and then only passable after much fingering had worn the peak through. He liked to nickname the new pledges. One year he fancied "head" names. He lined them up and sat back with his knee cocked up, pushed up his hat with his thumbnail. "You over there, you look to me like Pothead; you talking, you're Blowhead; you're Meathead; you're Sackhead; you're Needlehead." For a year after I joined the fraternity I lived in the hope of pleasing him by hitting upon just the right sour-senseless rejoinder, and so of gaining admission to his circle, the fraternity within the fraternity. So when he stopped before the last pledge, a boy from Monroe with a bulging forehead and eyes set low in his face, he paused. "And you, you're—" "That's Whalehead," I said. Walter raised an eyebrow and pulled down his mouth and nodded a derisive nod to his peers of the inner circle. I was in.

A pledge too felt the privilege of his company and felt the strain too. For one lived only to walk the tightrope with him, to be sour yet affable, careless but in a certain style of carelessness, sardonic yet likable, as popular with men as with women. But strain or no strain, I was content to be his friend. One night I walked home with him after he had been tapped for Golden Fleece—which was but the final honor of a paragraph of honors beneath his picture in the annual. "Binx," he said—with me he had at last dropped his sour-senseless way of talking. "I'll let you in on a secret. That business back there—believe it or not, that doesn't mean anything to me." "What does, Walter?" He stopped and we looked back at the twinkling campus as if the cities of the world had been spread out at our feet. "The main thing, Binx, is to be humble, to make Golden Fleece and be humble about it." We both took a deep breath and walked back to the Delta house in silence.

When I was a freshman, it was extremely important to me to join a good fraternity. But what if no fraternity invited me to join? During rush week I was invited to the Delta house so the brothers could look me over. Another candidate, Boylan "Sockhead" Bass from Bastrop, and I sat together on a leather sofa, hands on our knees while the brothers stood around courting us like virgins and at the same time eying us like heifers. Presently Walter beckoned to me and I followed him upstairs where we had a confidential talk in a small bedroom. Walter motioned to me to sit on the bed and for a long moment he stood, as he is standing now: hands in pockets, rocking back on his heels and looking out the window like Samuel Hinds in the movies. "Binx," he said. "We know each other pretty well, don't we?" (We'd both gone to the same prep school in New Hampshire.) "That's right, Walter," I said. "You know me well enough to know I wouldn't hand you the usual crap about this fraternity business, don't you?" "I know you wouldn't, Walter." "We don't go in for hot boxes around here, Binx. We don't have to." "I know you don't." He listed the good qualities of the SAEs, the Delta Psis, the Dekes, the KAs. "They're all good boys, Binx. I've got friends in all of them. But when it comes to describing the fellows here, the caliber of the men, the bond between us, the meaning of this little symbol—" he turned back his lapel to show the pin and I wondered if it was true that Deltas held their pins in their mouths when they

30

took a shower—"there's not much I can say, Binx." Then Walter took his hat off and stood stroking the tricornered peak. "As a matter of fact, I'm not going to say anything at all. Instead, I'll ask you a single question and then we'll go down. Did you or did you not feel a unique something when you walked into this house? I won't attempt to describe it. If you felt it, you already know exactly what I mean. If you didn't—!" Now Walter stands over me, holding his hat over his heart. "Did you feel it, Binx?" I told him straight off that nothing would make me happier than to pledge Delta on the spot, if that was what he was getting at. We shook hands and he called in some of the brothers. "Fellows, I want you to meet Mister John Bickerson Bolling. He's one of those broken-down Bollings from up in Feliciana Parish—you may have heard the name. Binx is a country boy and he's full of hookworm but he ought to have some good stuff in him. I believe he'll make us a good man." We shook hands all around. They were good fellows.

As it turned out, I did not make them a good man at all. I managed to go to college four years without acquiring a single honor. When the annual came out, there was nothing under my picture but the letters $\Delta\Psi\Delta$—which was appropriate since I had spent the four years propped on the front porch of the fraternity house, bemused and dreaming, watching the sun shine through the Spanish moss, lost in the mystery of finding myself alive at such a time and place—and next to $\Delta\Psi\Delta$ my character summary: "Quiet but a sly sense of humor." Boylan Bass of Bastrop turned out to be no less a disappointment. He was a tall farm boy with a long neck and an Adam's apple who took pharmacy and for four years said not a word and was not known even to his fraternity brothers. His character line was: "A good friend."

Walter is at ease again. He turns away from the window and once more stands over me and inclines his narrow hollowed-out temple.

"You know most of the krewe, don't you?"

"Yes. As a matter of fact I still belong—"

"It's the same bunch that go down to Tigre au Chenier. Why didn't you come down last month?"

"I really don't like to hunt much."

Walter seems to spy something on the table. He leans over and runs a thumb along the grain. "Just look at that wood. It's all one piece, by God." Since his engagement, I have noticed that Walter has begun to take a proprietary interest in the house, tapping on walls, measuring floorboards, hefting vases. He straightens up. "I don't know what's gotten into you. All I can figure is that you've got me on your list."

"It's not that."

"What is it then?"

"What is what?"

"Why in the hell don't you give me a call sometime?"

"What would we talk about?" I say in our sour-senseless style of ten years ago.

Walter gives my shoulder a hard squeeze. "I'd forgotten what a rare turd you are. No, you're right. What would we talk about," says Walter elegiacally. "Oh Lord. What's wrong with the goddamn world, Binx?"

"I am not sure. But something occurred to me this morning. I was sitting on the bus—"

"What do you do with yourself out there in Gentilly?" People often ask me what is wrong with the world and also what I do in Gentilly, and I always try to give an answer. The former is an interesting question. I have noticed, however, that no one really wants to listen to an answer.

"Not much. Sell mutual funds to widows and dagos."

"Is that right?" Walter drops his shoulder and feels the muscle in his back. Squatting down on his heels, he runs an eye along the baseboard calculating the angle of settle.

After the war some of us bought a houseboat on Vermilion Bay near Tigre au Chenier. Walter got everything organized. It was just like him to locate a cook-caretaker living right out there in the swamp and to line up some real boogalee guides. But to me the venture was not a success. It was boring, to tell the truth. Actually there was very little fishing and hunting and a great deal of poker and drinking. Walter liked nothing better than getting out in that swamp on weekends with five or six fellows, quit shaving and play poker around the clock. He really enjoyed it. He would get up groaning from the table at three o'clock in the morning and pour himself a drink and, rubbing his beard, stand looking out into the darkness. "Goddamn, this is all right, isn't it? Isn't this a terrific setup, Binx? Tomorrow we're going to have duck Rochambeau right here. Tell me honestly, have you ever tasted better food at Galatoire's?" "No, it's very good, Walter." "Give me your honest opinion, Binx." "It's very good." He got Jake the caretaker out of trouble once and liked having him around. Jake would sit in close to the poker game. "Jake, what do you think of that fellow over there?" Walter would ask him, nodding toward me or one of the others. He liked to think that Negroes have a sixth sense and that his Negro had an extra good one. Jake would cock his head as if he were fathoming me with his sixth sense. "You got to watch *him*! That Mister Binx is all right now!" And in some fashion, more extraordinary than a sixth sense, Jake would manage to oblige Walter without disobliging me. The houseboat seemed like a good idea, but as it worked out I became depressed. To tell the truth I like women better. All I could think about in that swamp was how much I'd like to have my hands on Marcia or Linda and be spinning along the Gulf Coast.

To tell the absolute truth, I've always been slightly embarrassed in Walter's company. Whenever I'm with him, I feel the stretch of the old tightrope, the necessity of living up to the friendship of friendships, of cultivating an intimacy beyond words. The fact is we have little to say to each other. There is only this thick sympathetic silence between us. We are comrades, true, but somewhat embarrassed comrades. It is probably my fault. For years now I have had no friends. I spend my entire time working, making money, going to movies and seeking the company of women.

The last time I had friends was eight years ago. When I returned from the Orient and recovered from my wound, I took up with two fellows I thought I should like. I did like them. They were good fellows both. One was an ex-Lieutenant like me, a University of Cal man, a skinny impoverished fellow who liked poetry and roaming around the countryside. The other was a mad eccentric from Valdosta, a regular young Burl Ives with beard and guitar. We thought it would be a good thing to do some hiking, so we struck out from Gatlinburg in the Smokies, headed for Maine on the Appalachian Trail. We were all pretty good drinkers and talkers and we could spiel about women and poetry and Eastern religion in pretty good style. It seemed like a fine idea, sleeping in shelters or under the stars in the cool evergreens, and later hopping freights. In fact this was what I was sure I wanted to do. But in no time at all I became depressed. The times we did have fun, like sitting around a fire or having a time with some girls, I had the feeling they were saying to me: "How about this, Binx? This is really it, isn't it, boy?", that they were practically looking up from their girls to say this. For some reason I sank into a deep melancholy. What good fellows they were, I thought, and how much they deserved to be happy. If only I could make them happy. But the beauty of the smoky blue valleys, instead of giving us joy, became heartbreaking. "What's the matter with you, Binx?" they said at last. "My dear friends," I said to them. "I will say good-by and wish you well. I think I will go back to New Orleans and live in Gentilly." And there I have lived ever since, solitary and in wonder. Now and then my friends stop by, all gotten up as young eccentrics with their beards and bicycles, and down they go into the Quarter to hear some music and find some whores and still I wish them well. As for me, I stay home with Mrs Schexnaydre and turn on TV. Not that I like TV so much, but it doesn't distract me from the wonder. That is why I can't go to the trouble they go to. It is distracting, and not for five minutes will I be distracted from the wonder.

4. WALTER OFFERS TO DRIVE UNCLE JULES TO TOWN. Through the living-room doors I can see my aunt sitting by the fire, temple propped on her fingers. The white light from the sky pours into her upturned face. She opens her eyes and, seeing me, forms a soundless word with her lips.

I find Kate in the ground-level basement, rubbing an iron fireplace. Since Christmas she and Walter have taken to cleaning things, removing a hundred years' accumulation of paint from old walls and cupboards to expose the cypress and brick underneath. As if to emphasize her sallowness and thinness, she has changed into shirt and jeans. She is as frail as a ten year old, except in her thighs. Sometimes she speaks of her derrière, sticks it out Beale Street style and gives it a slap and this makes me blush because it is a very good one, marvelously ample and mysterious and nothing to joke about.

To my relief she greets me cheerfully. She clasps one leg, rests her cheek on a knee and rubs an iron welt with steel wool. She has the advantage of me, sitting at her ease in a litter of summers past, broken wicker, split croquet balls, rotting hammocks. Now she wipes the welt with solvent; it begins to turn pale. "Well? Aren't you supposed to tell me something?"

"Yes, but I forget what it was."

"Binx Binx. You're to tell me all sorts of things."

"That's true."

"It will end with me telling you."

"That would be better."

"How do you make your way in the world?"

"Is that what you call it? I don't really know. Last month I made three thousand dollars—less capital gains."

"How did you get through a war without getting killed?"

"It was not through any doing of yours."

"Anh anh anh." It is an old passage between us, more of a joke now than a quarrel. "And how do you appear so reasonable to Mother?"

"I feel reasonable with her."

"She thinks you're one of her kind."

"What kind is that?"

"A proper Bolling. Jules thinks you're a go-getter. But you don't fool me."

"You know."

"Yes."

"What kind?"

"You're like me, but worse. Much worse."

She is in tolerable good spirits. It is not necessary to pay too much attention to her. I spy the basket-arm of a broken settee. It has a presence about it: the ghost of twenty summers in Feliciana. I perch on a bony spine of wicker and prop hands on knees.

"I remember what I came for. Will you go to Lejiers and watch the parade?"

Kate stretches out a leg to get at her cigarettes. Her ritual of smoking stands her in good stead. She extracts the wadded pack, kneads the warm cellophane, taps a cigarette violently and accurately against her thumbnail, lights it with a Zippo worn smooth and yellow as a pocket watch. Pushing back her shingled hair, she blows out a plume of gray lung smoke and plucks a grain from her tongue. She reminds me of college girls before the war, how they would

sit five and six in a convertible, seeming old to me and
sullen-silent toward men and toward their own sex, how
they would take refuge in their cigarettes: the stripping of
cellophane, the clash of Zippos, the rushing plume of lung
smoke expelled up in a long hissing sigh.

"Her idea?"

"Yes."

Kate begins to nod and goes on nodding. "You must
have had quite a powwow."

"Not much of one."

"You've never understood Mother's dynamics."

"Her dynamics?"

"What do you suppose she and I talk about?"

"What?"

"You. I'm sick of talking about you."

Now I do look at her. Her voice has suddenly taken on
its "objective" tone. Since she started her social work,
Kate has spells of talking frankly in which she recites case
histories in a kind of droning scientific voice: "—and all
the while it was perfectly obvious that the poor woman
had never experienced an orgasm." "Is such a thing possible!" I would cry and we would shake our heads in the
strong sense of our new camaraderie, the camaraderie of
a science which is not too objective to pity the follies and
ignorance of the world.

There is nothing new in her tack against her stepmother.
Nor do I object, to tell the truth. It seems to serve her
well enough, this discovery of the possibilities of hatred.
She warms under its influence. It serves to make the basement a friendlier place. Her hatred is a consequence of a
swing of her dialectic. She has, in the past few months,
swung back to her father (the basement is to be a TV room
for him). In the beginning she had been her father's child.
Then, as a young girl, the person of her stepmother, this
quick, charming and above all intelligent woman, had appeared at a critical time in her rebellion. Her stepmother
became for her the rallying point of all those forces which,

until then, had been hardly felt as more than formless
discontents. If she hadn't much use for her father's ways,
his dogged good nature, his Catholic unseriousness, his
little water closet jokes, his dumbness about his God, the
good Lord; the everlasting dumb importuning of her just
to be good, to mind the sisters, and to go his way, his
dumb way of inner faith and outer good spirits—if she
hadn't much use for this, she hardly knew how little until
she found herself in the orbit of this enchanting person.
Her stepmother had taken her in charge and set her free.
In the older woman, older than a mother and yet something of a sister, she found the blithest gayest fellow rebel
and comrade. The world of books and music and art and
ideas opened before her. And if later her stepmother was
to take alarm at Kate's political activities—a spiritual rebellion was one thing, the soaring of the spirit beyond the
narrow horizons of the parochial and into the lofty regions
of Literature and Life; nor was there anything wrong with
the girlish socialism of Sarah Lawrence; but political con-
spiracy here and now in New Orleans with the local dirty
necks of the bookshops and a certain oracular type of social worker my aunt knew only too well—that was something else. But even so, now that it was in the past, it was
not really so bad. In fact, as time went on, it might even
take on the flavor of one's *Studententage*. How well I remember, her stepmother told her, the days when we Wag-
nerians used to hiss old Brahms—O for the rapturous
rebellious days of youth. But now it is she, my aunt herself, who falls prey to Kate's dialectic of hatreds. It was
inevitable that Kate should catch up with and "see into"
her stepmother, just as she caught up with her father, and
that she should, in the same swing of the dialectic, redis-
cover her father as the authentic Louisiana businessman
and, if not go to Mass with him, build him a TV room. It
was inevitable that she should give up the Philharmonic
upstairs and take up the Gillette Cavalcade in the basement. It is, as I say, all the same to me which parent she

presently likes or dislikes. But I am uneasy over the mea-
gerness of her resources. Where will her dialectic carry
her now? After Uncle Jules what? Not back to her stepmother, I fear, but into some kind of deadend where she
must become aware of the dialectic. "Hate her then," I
feel like telling her, "and love Jules. But leave it at that.
Don't try another swing."

I say: "Then you're not going to the Lejiers."

She puts her cigarette on a potsherd and goes back to
her rubbing.

"And you're not going to the ball?" I ask.

"No."

"Don't you want to see Walter as krewe captain?"

Kate swings around and her eyes go to discs. "Don't
you dare patronize Walter."

"I wasn't."

"Do you think I didn't see the two of you upstaging
him at lunch? What a lovely pair you are."

"I thought you and I were the pair."

"You and I are not a pair of any sort."

I consider this.

"Good day," says Kate irritably.

5. WE TALK, MY AUNT AND I, IN OUR OLD WAY OF
talking, during pauses in the music. She is playing
Chopin. She does not play very well; her fingernails click
against the keys. But she is playing one of our favorite
pieces, the E flat Étude. In recent years I have become
suspicious of music. When she comes to a phrase which
once united us in a special bond and to which once I opened
myself as meltingly as a young girl, I harden myself.

She asks not about Kate but about my mother. My aunt

does not really like my mother; yet, considering the circumstances, that my father was a doctor and my mother was his nurse and married him, she likes her as well as she can. She has never said a word against her and in fact goes out of her way to be nice to her. She even says that my father was "shot with luck" to get such a fine girl, by which she means that my father did, in a sense, leave it to luck. All she really holds against my mother, and not really against her but against my father, is my father's lack of imagination in marrying her. Sometimes I have the feeling myself that who my mother was and who I am depended on the chance selection of a supervisor of nurses in Biloxi. When my father returned from medical school and his surgical residency in Boston to practice with my grandfather in Feliciana Parish, he applied for a nurse. The next day he waited (and I too waited) to see who would come. The door opened and in walked the woman who, as it turned out, would, if she were not one-legged or downright ugly, be his wife and my mother. My mother is a Catholic, what is called in my aunt's circle a "devout Catholic," which is to say only that she is a practicing Catholic since I do not think she is devout. This accounts for the fact that I am, nominally at least, also a Catholic.

After my father's death my aunt sent me off to prep school; during my years in college I lived in her house. After returning to work in a Biloxi hospital, my mother remarried and now lives on the Gulf Coast where her husband is a Western Auto dealer. I have six half-brothers and sisters named Smith. Sometimes during the summer I drop in at their fishing camp on Bayou des Allemands with my Marcia or my Linda.

Now Aunt Emily, fingernails clicking over the keys, comes back to the tune, the sweet sad piping of the nineteenth century, good as it can be but not good enough. To protect myself, I take one of the photographs from the mantel.

"Is she coming?" asks my aunt during the pause.

"Kate? No."

"Well. No matter."

Again I hold the picture to the light. The sky is darkening and a fresh wind has sprung up.

"Why didn't you get into the picture, Sweetie?" I ask her. "Weren't you there?"

"No indeed. Do you know what they wanted to do?"

"What?"

"Go gallivanting off to Hungary to shoot quail. I said, My God, you can shoot quail in Feliciana Parish. Anyhow I heard that something queer was going on in München. There was some kind of putsch and I didn't like the smell of it. So off they went to hunt quail in Hungary and off I went to my putsch." She watches me replace the picture. "We'll not see their like again. The age of the Catos is gone. Only my Jules is left. And Sam Yerger. Won't it be good to see Sam again?"

This is absurd of course. Uncle Jules is no Cato. And as for Sam Yerger: Sam is only a Cato on long Sunday afternoons and in the company of my aunt. She transfigures everyone. Mercer she still sees as the old retainer. Uncle Jules she sees as the Creole Cato, the last of the heroes—whereas the truth is that Uncle Jules is a canny Cajun straight from Bayou Lafourche, as canny as a Marseilles merchant and a very good fellow, but no Cato. All the stray bits and pieces of the past, all that is feckless and gray about people, she pulls together into an unmistakable visage of the heroic or the craven, the noble or the ignoble. So strong is she that sometimes the person and the past are in fact transfigured by her. They become what she sees them to be. Uncle Jules has come to see himself as the Creole member of the gens, the Beauregard among the Lees. Mercer is on occasions not distinguishable from an old retainer. Truthfully I do not know, and Mercer does not know, what Mercer really is.

The storm which has been brewing since noon now breaks over our heads. Thunder rattles the panes. We walk

out on the gallery to watch it. A rushing Gulf wind slashes
the banana leaves into ribbons and blows dead camellia
blooms across the yard. Veils of rain, parted for a second
by the house, rush back together again. Trash from the
camphor trees rattles on the roof. We stroll arm in arm up
and down the lee gallery like passengers on a promenade.

"After Germany I insisted on going back to England. I
wanted to see the Lake Country again."

"Did Father go?"

"Jack? Heavens no. He met two of his buddies from
Charlottesville and Princeton and they took off helter-
skelter up the Rhine. Off he went with a bottle of Lieb-
fraumilch under one arm and *Wilhelm Meister* under the
other." (But they do not fit, I think for the hundredth time:
your student prince and the ironic young dude on the mantel.)

"Jack," she says in a different voice and immediately the
Black Forest is two thousand miles away and forty years ago.

"Yes, ma'am." My neck begins to prickle with a
dreadful-but-not-unpleasant eschatological prickling.

We take up our promenade. My aunt steps carefully,
lining up her toe with the edge of the boards. She presses
a finger against her lip, but it is not possible to tell whether
she is smiling or grimacing.

"I had a brainstorm last night. It still looked reasonably
good this morning. How does this strike you?"

"What?" My neck prickles like a bull terrier.

"Last week at Great Books I had a chat with old Dr
Minor. I didn't bring your name up. He did. He asked me
what you were doing with yourself. When I told him, he
said it was a shame because—and there was no reason for
him to say this if it weren't true—you have a keen mind
and a natural scientific curiosity."

I know what she is going to say. My aunt is convinced
I have a "flair for research." This is not true. If I had a
flair for research, I would be doing research. Actually I'm
not very smart. My grades were average. My mother and

my aunt think I am smart because I am quiet and absent-minded—and because my father and grandfather were smart. They think I was meant to do research because I am not fit to do anything else—I am a genius whom ordinary professions can't satisfy. I tried research one summer. I got interested in the role of the acid-base balance in the formation of renal calculi; really, it's quite an interesting problem. I had a hunch you might get pigs to form oxalate stones by manipulating the pH of the blood, and maybe even to dissolve them. A friend of mine, a boy from Pittsburg named Harry Stern, and I read up the literature and presented the problem to Minor. He was enthusiastic, gave us everything we wanted and turned us loose for the summer. But then a peculiar thing happened. I became extraordinarily affected by the summer afternoons in the laboratory. The August sunlight came streaming in the great dusty fanlights and lay in yellow bars across the room. The old building ticked and creaked in the heat. Outside we could hear the cries of summer students playing touch football. In the course of an afternoon the yellow sunlight moved across old group pictures of the biology faculty. I became bewitched by the presence of the building; for minutes at a stretch I sat on the floor and watched the motes rise and fall in the sunlight. I called Harry's attention to the presence but he shrugged and went on with his work. He was absolutely unaffected by the singularities of time and place. His abode was anywhere. It was all the same to him whether he catheterized a pig at four o'clock in the afternoon in New Orleans or at midnight in Transylvania. He was actually like one of those scientists in the movies who don't care about anything but the problem in their heads—now here is a fellow who does have a "flair for research" and will be heard from. Yet I do not envy him. I would not change places with him if he discovered the cause and cure of cancer. For he is no more aware of the mystery which surrounds him than a fish is aware of the water it swims in. He could do research for a thousand years and never have an inkling of it. By the middle of August I could not see what difference it made whether the pigs got kidney stones or not (they didn't, incidentally), compared to the mystery of those summer afternoons. I asked Harry if he would excuse me. He was glad enough to, since I was not much use to him sitting on the floor. I moved down to the Quarter where I spent the rest of the vacation in quest of the spirit of summer and in the company of an attractive and confused girl from Bennington who fancied herself a poet.

But I am mistaken. My aunt is not suggesting that I go into research.

"I want you to think about entering medical school this fall. You know you've always had it in the back of your mind. Now I've fixed up your old *garçonnière* in the carriage house. Wait till you see it—I've added a kitchenette and some bookshelves. You will have absolute privacy. We won't even allow you in the house. No—it is not I doing something for you. We could use you around. Kate is going through something I don't understand. Jules, my dear Jules won't even admit anything is wrong. You and Sam are the only ones she'd ever listen to."

We come to the corner of the gallery and a warm spray blows in our faces. One can smell the islands to the south. The rain slackens and tires hiss on the wet asphalt.

"Here's what we'll do. As soon as hot weather comes, we'll all go up to Flat Rock, the whole family, Walter included. He's already promised. We'll have a nice long summer in the mountains and come back here in September and buckle down to work."

Two cars come racing abreast down Prytania; someone shouts an obscenity in a wretched croaking voice. Our footsteps echo like pistol shots in the basement below.

"I don't know."

"You think about it."

"Yes ma'am."

She does not smile. Instead she stops me, holds me off.

"What is it you want out of life, son?" she asks with a sweetness that makes me uneasy.

"I don't know'm. But I'll move in whenever you want me."

"Don't you feel obliged to use your brain and to make a contribution?"

"No'm."

She waits for me to say more. When I do not, she seems to forget about her idea. Far from holding my refusal against me, she links her arm in mine and resumes the promenade.

"I no longer pretend to understand the world." She is shaking her head yet still smiling her sweet menacing smile. "The world I knew has come crashing down around my ears. The things we hold dear are reviled and spat upon." She nods toward Prytania Street. "It's an interesting age you will live in—though I can't say I'm sorry to miss it. But it should be quite a sight, the going under of the evening land. That's us all right. And I can tell you, my young friend, it is evening. It is very late."

For her too the fabric is dissolving, but for her even the dissolving makes sense. She understands the chaos to come. It seems so plain when I see it through her eyes. My duty in life is simple. I go to medical school. I live a long useful life serving my fellowman. What's wrong with this? All I have to do is remember it.

"—you have too good a mind to throw away. I don't quite know what we're doing on this insignificant cinder spinning away in a dark corner of the universe. That is a secret which the high gods have not confided in me. Yet one thing I believe and I believe it with every fiber of my being. A man must live by his lights and do what little he can and do it as best he can. In this world goodness is destined to be defeated. But a man must go down fighting. That is the victory. To do anything less is to be less than a man."

She is right. I will say yes. I will say yes even though I do not really know what she is talking about.

But I hear myself saying: "As a matter of fact I was planning to leave Gentilly soon, but for a different reason. There is something—" I stop. My idea of a search seems absurd.

To my surprise this lame reply is welcomed by my aunt.

"Of course!" she cries. "You're doing something every man used to do. When your father finished college, he had his *Wanderjahr*, a fine year's ramble up the Rhine and down the Loire, with a pretty girl on one arm and a good comrade on the other. What happened to you when you finished college? War. And I'm so proud of you for that. But that's enough to take it out of any man."

Wanderjahr. My heart sinks. We do not understand each other after all. If I thought I'd spent the last four years as a *Wanderjahr*, before "settling down," I'd shoot myself on the spot.

"How do you mean, take it out of me?"

"Your scientific calling, your love of books and music. Don't you remember how we used to talk—on the long winter evenings when Jules would go to bed and Kate would go dancing, how we used to talk! We tired the sun with talking and sent him down the sky. Don't you remember discovering Euripides and Jean-Christophe?"

"You discovered them for me. It was always through you that—" All at once I am sleepy. It requires an effort to put one foot in front of the other. Fortunately my aunt decides to sit down. I wipe off an iron bench with my handkerchief and we sit, still arm in arm. She gives me a pat.

"Now. I want you to make me a promise."

"Yes ma'am."

"Your birthday is one week from today."

"Is that right?"

"You will be thirty years old. Don't you think a thirty-

46

year-old man ought to know what he wants to do with his life?"

"Yes."

"Will you tell me?"

"Then?"

"Yes. Next Wednesday afternoon—after Sam leaves. I'll meet you here at this spot. Will you promise to come?"

"Yes ma'am." She expects a great deal from Sam's visit.

Pushing up my sleeve to see my watch, she sucks in her breath. "Back to the halt and the lame and the generally no 'count."

"Sweetie, lie down first and let me rub your neck." I can tell from her eyes when she has a headache.

Later, when Mercer brings the car around to the front steps, she lays a warm dry cheek against mine. "M-m! You're such a comfort to me. You remind me so much of your father."

"I can't seem to remember him."

"He was the sweetest old thing. So gay. And did the girls fall over him. And a mind! He had a mind like a steel trap, an analytical mind like yours." (She always says this, though I have never analyzed anything.) "He had the pick of New Orleans."

(And picked Anna Castagne.)

Mercer, who has changed to a cord coat and cap, holds the door grudgingly and cranes up and down the street as much as to say that he may be a chauffeur but not a footman.

She has climbed into the car but she does not release my hand.

"He would have been much happier in research," she says and lets me go.

6. THE RAIN HAS STOPPED. KATE CALLS FROM UNDER the steps.

She is in the best of spirits. She shows me the brick she found under linoleum and the shutters Walter bought in a junkyard. It bothers her that when the paint was removed the shutters came somewhat frayed from the vat. "They will form a partition here. The fountain and planter will go out here." By extending the partition into the garden, a corner of the wall will be enclosed to form a pleasant little nook. I can see why she is so serious: truthfully it seems that if she can just hit upon the right *place*, a shuttered place of brick and vine and flowing water, her very life can be lived. "I feel wonderful."

"What made you feel wonderful?"

"It was the storm." Kate clears the broken settee and pulls me down in a crash of wicker. "The storm cut loose, you and Mother walked up and down, up and down, and I fixed myself a big drink and enjoyed every minute of it."

"Are you ready to go to Lejiers?"

"Oh, I couldn't do that," she says, plucking her thumb. "Where are you going?" she asks nervously, hoping that I will leave.

"To Magazine Street." I know she isn't listening. Her breathing is shallow and irregular, as if she were giving thought to each breath. "Is it bad this time?"

She shrugs.

"As bad as last time?"

"Not as bad." She gives her knee a commonplace slap. After a while she says: "Poor Walter."

"What's the matter with Walter?"

48

"Do you know what he does down here?"

"No."

"He measures the walls. He carries a little steel tape in his pocket. He can't get over how thick the walls are."

"Are you going to marry him?"

"I don't know."

"Your mother thought it was the accident that still bothered you."

"Did you expect me to tell her otherwise?"

"That it did not bother you?"

"That it gave me my life. That's my secret, just as the war is your secret."

"I did not like the war."

"Because afterwards everyone said: what a frightful experience she went through and doesn't she do remarkably well. So then I did very well indeed. I would have made a good soldier."

"Why do you want to be a soldier?"

"How simple it would be to fight. What a pleasant thing it must be to be among people who are afraid for the first time when you yourself for the first time in your life have a proper flesh-and-blood enemy to be afraid of. What a lark! Isn't that the secret of heroes?"

"I couldn't say. I wasn't a hero."

Kate muses. "Can you remember the happiest moment of your life?"

"No. Unless it was getting out of the army."

"I can. It was in the fall of 1955. I was nineteen years old and I was going to marry Lyell and Lyell was a fine fellow. We were driving from Pass Christian to Natchez to see Lyell's family and the next day we were going up to Oxford to see a game. So we went to Natchez and the next day drove to Oxford and saw the game and went to the dance. Of course Lyell had to drive home after the dance. We got almost to Port Gibson and it was after dawn but there was a ground fog. The Trace was still dark in low spots. Lyell passed a car in one of the dips. It was a

coupe with the word Spry painted on the door.'' Kate tells
this in her wan analytic voice and with something of a
relish for the oddness of it. "Spry was the last thing I saw.
Lyell ran head on into a truckful of cotton-pickers. I must
have been slumped down so low that I rolled up into a
ball. When I woke up I was lying on the front porch of a
shack. I wasn't even scratched. I heard somebody say that
the white man had been killed. I could only think of one
thing: I didn't want to be taken to Lyell's family in
Natchez. Two policemen offered to drive me to a hospital.
But I felt all right—somebody had given me a shot. I went
over and looked at Lyell and everybody thought I was an
onlooker. He had gravel driven into his cheek. There were
twenty or thirty cars stopped on the road and then a bus
came along. I got on the bus and went into Natchez. There
was some blood on my blouse, so when I got to a hotel,
I sent it out to be cleaned, took a bath and ordered a big
breakfast, ate every crumb and read the Sunday paper. (I
can still remember what good coffee it was.) When the
blouse came back, I put it on, walked over to the station
and caught the Illinois Central for New Orleans. I slept
like a log and got off at Carrollton Avenue early in the
evening and walked home.''

"When was the happiest moment?"

"It was on the bus. I just stood there until the door
opened, then I got on and we went sailing along from
bright sunshine down through deep clefts as cool and dark
as a springhouse.''

Kate frowns and drums her fingers on the wicker. A
diesel horn blows on the river. Overhead a motor labors.
Mercer thinks he has to bear down on the waxer—I have
noticed that Negroes do not have an affection for motors.
"Pardon," says Kate, rising abruptly and leaving. The
little Yankee word serves her well: she leaves in disguise.
A water pipe sings and stops with a knock. When Kate
returns, she cranes around and smacks her arm cowboy

style. The light glimmers in the courtyard and the empty house above roars like a seashell.

"Does this mean you're not going to marry Walter?"

"Probably not," says Kate, yawning at a great rate.

"Are you going to see him tonight?"

"No."

"Why don't you come with me?"

"No," she says, smacking her arm. "I'll stay here."

7. SHE COMES UP SO QUIETLY THAT I THINK AT FIRST it is the Negro boy who wheels the cans of shells into the street and from time to time spreads the whole oysters into the shaved ice. The oyster bar is between the restaurant and the kitchen, a kind of areaway through which waitresses pass. A yellow bulb hangs from the rafters but the service door is open and the areaway is filled with the darkness of the evening.

Kate drums her fingers on the zinc bar and gazes abstractedly as the Negro sweeps oyster grime along the tile floor. The opener begins to set oysters before her.

"I can't go to Lejiers and I can't marry Walter."

I drink beer and watch her.

"I didn't tell you the truth. It's bad."

"This very moment?"

"Yes."

"Do you want to stay here or go outside?"

"Tell me," she says, abstracted. A stranger, seeing her, would notice nothing wrong.

"Do you want me to call Merle?"

"No. The other."

The "other" is a way we found of getting through it before. It has to do with her becoming something of a small boy and my not paying much attention to her. She eats a brown cock oyster, as cold and briny as the sea. She is not so bad. I have seen her worse.

"We'll go over to St Charles and watch the parade. Then there's a movie I want to see."

She nods and presently begins to notice the waitresses, watching with her lips parted and drying, like a boy who has come into a place with his father or brother and so is given leave to see without being seen.

We are in time for the downtown swing of Neptune. The crowd has already moved from the lake side to the river side of St Charles. It is quite dark now. The streetlights make golden spaces inside the wet leaves of the live oaks. A south wind carries the smell of coffee from the Tchoupitoulas docks. Mounted police shoulder the crowd over the curb. To the dark neutral ground come Negroes from Louisiana Avenue and Claiborne; some Negro men carry children astride their necks to see over the crowd.

Here is the public service truck with its tower, measuring the clearance under the oak limbs and cutting some wet drooping branches. We wait to see the flambeaux bearers and now here they come, a vanguard of half a dozen extraordinary Negroes dressed in dirty Ku Klux Klan robes, each bearing aloft a brace of pink and white flares. The flambeaux create a sensation. The bearers stride swiftly along the very edge of the crowd, showering sparks on everyone. They look angrily at each other to keep abreast, their fierce black faces peeping sidewise from their soiled hoods. Kate laughs at them. The Negro onlookers find them funny, but their bold manner, their contemptuous treatment of the crowd, excites them too. "Ah now!" they cry. "Look at *him*! Ain't he something though!"

The floats rumble along under the leaves. Some fathers have brought ladders with orange crates, big enough for three children, nailed to the top. These lucky ones gaze openmouthed at the maskers who pass them at eye level and almost within reach. The maskers look like crusaders with their nosepieces and their black eye sockets. Yet these specters are strangely good-natured, leaning forward and dropping whole bunches of necklaces and bracelets or sailing them over to the colored folk in the neutral ground. High school bands from North Louisiana and Texas follow the floats. Negro boys run along behind the crowd to keep up with the parade and catch the trinkets that sail too high.

The krewe captain and a duke come toward us on horeseback.

I ask Kate whether she wants to see Walter.

"No."

"We'd better go then."

Panic in the Streets with Richard Widmark is playing on Tchoupitoulas Street. The movie was filmed in New Orleans. Richard Widmark is a public health inspector who learns that a culture of cholera bacilli has gotten loose in the city. Kate watches, lips parted and dry. She understands my moviegoing but in her own antic fashion. There is a scene which shows the very neighborhood of the theater. Kate gives me a look—it is understood that we do not speak during the movie.

Afterwards in the street, she looks around the neighborhood. "Yes, it is certified now."

She refers to a phenomenon of moviegoing which I have called certification. Nowadays when a person lives somewhere, in a neighborhood, the place is not certified for him. More than likely he will live there sadly and the emptiness which is inside him will expand until it evacuates the entire neighborhood. But if he sees a movie which shows his very neighborhood, it becomes possible for him to live, for a time at least, as a person who is Somewhere and not Anywhere.

She sounds better but she is not. She is trapping herself, this time by being my buddy, best of all buddies and privy to my little researches. In spite of everything she finds herself, even now, playing out the role. In her long nightmare, this our old friendship now itself falls victim to the grisly transmogrification by which she unfailingly turns everything she touches to horror.

II

1. THE LAST WEEKEND OF CARNIVAL BEFORE MARDI Gras; business is very slow. But this morning I awoke with a strong feeling about American Motors. I sell my Ford common and buy American Motors at 26½.

Again this morning the dream of war, not quite a dream but the simulacrum of a dream, and again there visits the office the queasy-quince smell of 1951 and the Orient. It is not fear but the smell of fear and so it is peevish-pleasant, like a sore tooth which offers itself to the tongue. It attaches itself to everything in the office. An earnings analysis reminds me of it; a lady came in to pick up her AT & T debentures and she smelled of it.

Only my secretary does not smell of it. Her name is Sharon Kincaid and she comes from Eufala, Alabama. Although she has been working for me two weeks, I have not asked her for a date nor spoken of anything other than business. Yet the fact is that for two weeks I have thought of little else. She seems quite indifferent so far; and she is not really beautiful. She is a good-sized girl, at least five feet six and a hundred and thirty-five pounds—as big as a majorette—and her face is a little too short and pert, like one of those Renoir girls, and her eyes a little too yellow. Yet she has the most fearful soap-clean good looks.

Her bottom is so beautiful that once as she crossed the room to the cooler I felt my eyes smart with tears of gratitude. She is one of those village beauties of which the South is so prodigal. From the sleaziest house in the sleaziest town, from the loins of redneck pa and rockface ma spring these lovelies, these rosy-cheeked Anglo-Saxon lovelies, by the million. They are commoner than sparrows, and like sparrows they are at home in the streets, in the parks, on doorsteps. No one marvels at them; no one holds them dear. They flush out of their nests first thing and alight in the cities to stay, and no one misses them. Even their men pay no attention to them, anyhow far less attention than they pay to money. But I marvel at them; I miss them; I hold them dear.

I speak several times by telephone with my aunt and with Kate. Kate seems better and my aunt is pleased and gives me the credit. She has made an appointment for Kate with Dr Mink and Kate has consented to go. When Kate calls me, she takes her analytic tone. It is something of a strain for both of us. For some reason or other she feels obliged to keep one jump ahead of the conventional. When I answer the phone, instead of hearing "Hello, this is Kate," there comes into my ear a low-pitched voice saying something like: "Well, the knives have started flying," which means that she and her mother have been aggressive toward each other; or: "What do you know? I'm celebrating the rites of spring after all," which turns out to mean that she has decided, in her ironic and reflected way, to attend the annual supper given for former queens of the Neptune ball. This is something of a strain for both of us, as I say, but I am glad to hear from her. To tell the truth, I am somewhat worried about her, more so than her stepmother is. Kate is trapping herself too often: hitting upon a way out, then slamming the door upon herself. She has broken her engagement with Walter. But her stepmother understands, and Walter too, it seems. He stands by loyally to do what he can—it is none other than Walter, in fact, who will drive her to the hotel for the queens' supper. All seems well, but Kate is uneasy. "They think they're helping me, but they aren't," comes the low voice in my ear. "How much better it would be if they weren't so damn understanding—if they kicked me out of the house. To find yourself out in the street with two dollars to your name, to catch the streetcar downtown and get a job, perhaps as an airline stewardess. Think how wonderful it would be to fly to Houston and back three times a week for the next twenty years. You think I'm kidding? I'm not. It would be wonderful." "Then why don't you walk out of the house and get yourself a job?" I ask her. There comes a silence, then a click. But this doesn't mean anything. Abrupt hang-ups are a part of our analytic way of talking.

Sharon seems to pay no attention to these alexandrine conversations, even though we occupy the same small office and she is close enough to touch. Today she wears a sleeveless dress of yellow cotton; her arms come out of the armholes as tenderly as a little girl's. But when she puts her hand to her hair, you see that it is quite an arm. The soft round muscle goes slack of its own weight. Once she slapped a fly with her bare hand and set my Artmetal desk ringing like a gong. Her back is turned to me, but obliquely, so that I can see the line of her cheek with its whorl of down and the Slavic prominence under the notch of her eye and the quick tender incurve, shortening her face like a little mignon. There is on her desk a snapshot of her father and it is this very crowding of the cheekbone into the eye socket, narrowing the eye into a squint-eyed almost Chinese treacherousness, which is so ugly in him and so beautiful in her. As she types, the little kidney-shaped cushion presses against the small of her back in a nice balance of thrusts.

I am in love with Sharon Kincaid. She knows nothing of this, I think. I have not asked her for a date nor even been specially friendly. On the contrary: I have been aloof and correct as a Nazi officer in occupied Paris. Yet when she came in this morning unshouldering her Guatemalan bag and clearing her hair from her short collar, I heard a soughing sound in my ears like a desert wind. The Guatemalan bag contains *Peyton Place*, I happen to know. She had it when she applied for the job, a drugstore-library copy which she held under her purse. Ever since, the bag has been heavy with it—I can tell by the swing of it. She reads it at her lunch in the A & G cafeteria. Her choice in literature I took to be a good omen at the time, but I have changed my mind. My Sharon should not read this kind of stuff.

Her person has acquired a priceless value to me. For the first time I understand the conceits of the old poets: how I envy thee, little kidney-shaped cushion! Oh, to take thy place and press in thy stead against the sweet hollow of her back, etc. The other day Frank Hebert from Savings & Loan next door was complaining about his overhead: his rent was so much, his office girl such and such. To think of it: Sharon Kincaid as an item on a list, higher than the janitor, lower than the rent. Yet I dare not raise her salary, though before long I shall and with reason. She is a first-class secretary, quicker to learn than either Marcia or Linda. Only this much do I know from the interview: she comes from Barbour County, Alabama; she attended Birmingham Southern for two years; her mother and father left the farm and are divorced; her mother sells Real Silk hosiery and often visits Sharon but does not live with her. Sharon lives in a rooming house on Esplanade. Her roommate works for Alcoa. One night I drove by the house, a tall narrow pile with blue windows and a display of plumbing fixtures on the ground floor.

Toward her I keep a Gregory Peckish sort of distance. I am a tall black-headed fellow and I know as well as he how to keep to myself, make my eyes fine and my cheeks spare, tuck my lip and say a word or two with a nod or two.

It is just as well I keep my distance. Today it is louder than ever, this mistral whistling in my ears. I am nearly sick with it. Desire for her is like a sorrow in my heart. Ten minutes ago she rolled backwards in her little chair to hand me a letter and did not even touch me, but there singing about me was Rosenkavalier and here was the yellow-cotton smell of her and of the summer to come. Once she did touch my hand with the warm ventral flesh of her forearm: sparks flew past the corner of my eye and I actually became dizzy.

Today I read *Arabia Deserta* enclosed in a Standard & Poor binder. She conceals *Peyton Place*; I conceal *Arabia Deserta*.

> Pleasant, as the fiery heat of the daylight is done, is our homely evening fire. The sun goes down upon a highland steppe of Arabia, whose common altitude is above three thousand feet, the thin dry air is presently refreshed, the sand is soon cold; wherein yet at three fingers' depth is left the sunny warmth of the past day's heat until the new sunrise. After a half hour it is the blue night, and a clear hoary starlight in which there shines the girdle of the milky way, with a marvelous clarity. As the sun is setting, the nomad housewife brings in a truss of sticks and dry bushes, which she has pulled or hoed with a mattock (a tool they have seldom) in the wilderness; she casts down this provision by our hearthside, for the sweet-smelling evening fire.

There was a time when this was the last book on earth I'd have chosen to read. Until recent years, I read only "fundamental" books, that is, key books on key subjects, such as *War and Peace*, the novel of novels; *A Study of History*, the solution of the problem of time; Schroedinger's *What is Life?*, Einstein's *The Universe as I See It*, and such. During those years I stood outside the universe and sought to understand it. I lived in my room as an Anyone living Anywhere and read fundamental books and only for diversion took walks around the neighborhood and saw an occasional movie. Certainly it did not matter to me where I was when I read such a book as *The Expanding Universe*. The greatest success of this enterprise, which I call my vertical search, came one night when I sat in a hotel room in Birmingham and read a book called *The Chemistry of Life*. When I finished it, it seemed to me that the main goals of my search were reached or were in principle reachable, whereupon I went out and saw a movie called *It Happened One Night* which was itself very good. A memorable night. The only difficulty was that though the universe had been disposed of, I myself was left over. There I lay in my hotel room with my search over yet still obliged to draw one breath and then the next. But now I have undertaken a different kind of search, a horizontal search. As a consequence, what takes place in my room is less important. What is important is what I shall find when I leave my room and wander in the neighborhood. Before, I wandered as a diversion. Now I wander seriously and sit and read as a diversion.

Sharon turns not one hair as I talk with my aunt about Kate in our old Feliciana style of talking and as I talk to Kate in our analytic style of talking. Yet she recognizes each voice and passes the phone back with a "Miz Cutrer" or a "Miss Cutrer." Now, as she answers the phone again, it crosses my mind that she may not be entirely unselfconscious: she tilts her head and puts her pencil to her cheek like the secretary in the Prell commercial. She presses the mouthpiece against her chest.

"Mr Sartalamaccia called earlier. I forgot."

"Is that he?"

She nods. Her agate eyes watch me. I think it over Gregory-Peckishly and hold out a hand with no time for her.

It is a matter of no importance. Mr Sartalamaccia wants

to buy some land, my patrimony in fact, a worthless parcel of swamp in St Bernard Parish. He offers eight thousand dollars. It is enough to say yes here and now, but a Gregorish Peckerish idea pops into my head. I propose to Mr Sartalamaccia that he meet me on the site at ten thirty tomorrow morning. He sounds disappointed.

"Miss Kincaid, I'll want you to come down with me to St Bernard Parish tomorrow and copy a title in the courthouse." In truth it would be interesting to see how much my father paid for it. Any doings of my father, even his signature, is in the nature of a clue in my search.

"St Bernard Parish?" To my Sharon, fresh from Eufala, I might just as well have said Mont Saint Michel.

"We'll be back here by one."

"Just as long as I get back uptown by seven thirty tomorrow night."

Now I am Gregory-grim and no fooling this time. What the devil. Three weeks in New Orleans and she's already having dates?

2. CUSTOMERS COME IN AFTER HOURS AND IT IS LATE evening when I leave the office. Unlike the big downtown brokers, most of our clients are storekeepers and employed people. It is a source of satisfaction to me to make money. Not even Sharon or *Arabia Deserta* interferes with this. Another idea occurred to me yesterday as I read about Khalil in the high plateau country of the Negd. What gives it merit is that it should not only make money; it should also bring me closer to Sharon. I shall discuss it with her tomorrow. My first idea was the building itself. It looks like a miniature bank with its Corinthian pilasters, portico and iron scrolls over the windows. The firm's name, Cutrer, Klostermann & Lejier, is lettered in Gothic and below in smaller letters, the names of the Boston mutual funds we represent. It looks far more conservative than the modern banks in Gentilly. It announces to the world: modern methods are no doubt excellent but here is good old-fashioned stability, but stability with imagination. A little bit of old New England with a Creole flavor. The Parthenon façade cost twelve thousand dollars but commissions have doubled. The young man you see inside is clearly the soul of integrity; he asks no more than to be allowed to plan your future. This is true. This is all I ask.

The sun has set but the sky is luminous and clear and apple green in the east. Nothing is left of the smog but a thumb-smudge over Chef Menteur. Bullbats hawk the insects in the warm air next to the pavement. They dive and utter their thrumming *skonk-skonk* and go sculling up into the bright upper air. I stop at the corner of Elysian Fields to buy a paper from Ned Daigle. Ned is a former jockey and he looks quite a bit like Leo Carroll but older and more dried-up. "What seh, Jackie," he calls in his hoarse bass, as hoarse as the bullbats, and goes humping for the cars, snapping the papers into folds as he goes. He catches the boulevard traffic at the stoplight and often sells half a dozen papers before the light changes. Ned knows everybody at the Fairgrounds including all the local hoods and racketeers. During racing season he often brings them around to my office. For some reason or other he thinks my brokerage business is a virtuous and deserving institution, something like a church. The gangsters too; quite a few of them buy growth funds for their children. Uncle Jules would be astonished if he knew some of his customers who own Massachusetts Investors Trust.

"Is it going to be clear for Carnival, Jackie?"

We stand on the concrete island between the double streams of traffic. The light changes and off Ned goes again.

Evening is the best time in Gentilly. There are not so

many trees and the buildings are low and the world is all sky. The sky is a deep bright ocean full of light and life. A mare's tail of cirrus cloud stands in high from the Gulf. High above the Lake a broken vee of ibises points for the marshes; they go suddenly white as they fly into the tilting salient of sunlight. Swifts find a windy middle reach of sky and come twittering down so fast I think at first gnats have crossed my eyelids. In the last sector of apple green a Lockheed Connie lowers from Mobile, her running lights blinking in the dusk. Station wagons and Greyhounds and diesel rigs rumble toward the Gulf Coast, their fabulous taillights glowing like rubies in the darkening east. Most of the commercial buildings are empty except the filling stations where attendants hose down the concrete under the glowing discs and shells and stars.

On the way home I stop off at the Tivoli. It is a Jane Powell picture and I have no intention of seeing it. However, Mr Kinsella the manager sees me and actually pulls me in by the coatsleeve for a sample look. He says it is a real pleaser and he means it. There go Jane and some fellow walking arm in arm down the street in a high wide and handsome style and doing a wake up and sing number. The doorman, the cop on the corner, the taxi driver, each sunk in his own private misery, smile and begin to tap their feet. I am hardly ever depressed by a movie and Jane Powell is a very nice-looking girl, but the despair of it is enough to leave you gone in the stomach. I look around the theater. Mr Kinsella has his troubles too. There are only a few solitary moviegoers scattered through the gloom, the afternoon sort and the most ghostly of all, each sunk in his own misery, Jane or no Jane. On the way out I stop at the ticket window and speak to Mrs de Marco, a dark thin worried lady who has worked here ever since I moved to Gentilly. She does not like the movies and takes no pleasure in her job (though she could see most of the last show every night). I tell her that it is a very fine job and that I would like nothing better than sitting out here night after night and year after year and watch the evenings settle over Elysian Fields, but she always thinks I am kidding and we talk instead about her son's career in the air force. He is stationed in Arizona and he hates the desert. I am sorry to hear this because I would like it out there very much. Nevertheless I am interested in hearing about it. Before I see a movie it is necessary for me to learn something about the theater or the people who operate it, to touch base before going inside. That is the way I got to know Mr Kinsella: engaging him in conversation about the theater business. I have discovered that most people have no one to talk to, no one, that is, who really wants to listen. When it does at last dawn on a man that you really want to hear about his business, the look that comes over his face is something to see. Do not misunderstand me. I am no do-gooding Jose Ferrer going around with a little whistle to make people happy. Such do-gooders do not really want to listen, are not really selfish like me; they are being nice fellows and boring themselves to death, and their listeners are not really cheered up. Show me a nice Jose cheering up an old lady and I'll show you two people existing in despair. My mother often told me to be unselfish, but I have become suspicious of the advice. No, I do it for my own selfish reasons. If I did not talk to the theater owner or the ticket seller, I should be lost, cut loose metaphysically speaking. I should be seeing one copy of a film which might be shown anywhere and at any time. There is a danger of slipping clean out of space and time. It is possible to become a ghost and not know whether one is in downtown Loews in Denver or suburban Bijou in Jacksonville. So it was with me.

Yet it was here in the Tivoli that I first discovered place and time, tasted it like okra. It was during a re-release of *Red River* a couple of years ago that I became aware of the first faint stirrings of curiosity about the particular seat I sat in, the lady in the ticket booth . . . As Montgomery Clift was whipping John Wayne in a fistfight, an absurd scene, I made a mark on my seat arm with my thumbnail. Where, I wondered, will this particular piece of wood be twenty years from now, 543 years from now? Once as I was travelling through the Midwest ten years ago I had a layover of three hours in Cincinnati. There was time to go see Joseph Cotten in *Holiday* at a neighborhood theater called the Altamont—but not before I had struck up an acquaintance with the ticket seller, a lady named Mrs Clara James, and learned that she had seven grandchildren all living in Cincinnati. We still exchange Christmas cards. Mrs James is the only person I know in the entire state of Ohio.

When I get back to my apartment, the first thing I see is a letter from my aunt stuck behind the aluminum seagull on the screen door. I know what it is. It is not a letter actually but a memo. Often when we have had one of our serious talks, she has second thoughts which she is anxious to communicate. Sometimes I get a memo out of a clear sky. She takes a great deal of trouble with me. I wish I were able to please her better.

But before I can read the letter, Mrs Schexnaydre comes down and lends me her copy of *Reader's Digest*.

Mrs Schexnaydre is a vigorous pony-size blond who wears sneakers summer and winter. She is very good to me and sees to it that everything is kept spick-and-span. The poor woman is quite lonely; she knows no one except the painters and carpenters and electricians who are forever working on her house. She has lived in New Orleans all her life and knows no one. Sometimes I watch television with her and share a bottle of Jax and talk about her years at MacDonough No. 6 school, the happiest period of her life. It is possible to do this because her television will bring in channel 12 and mine won't. She watches the quiz programs faithfully and actually feels she knows the contestants. Sometimes I even persuade her to go to the movies with me. Her one fear in life is of Negroes. Although one seldom sees Negroes in this part of

Gentilly, our small yard is enclosed by a hurricane fence eight feet high; every window is barred. Over the years she has acquired three dogs, each for the reason that it had been reputed to harbor a special dislike for Negroes. I have no particular objection to this trait in a dog—for all I know, Mrs Schexnaydre's fears may be quite justified. However, these are miserable curs and to make matters worse, they also dislike me. One I especially despise, an orange-colored brute with a spitz face and a plume of a tail which curves over his back exposing a large convoluted anus. I have come to call him old Rosebud. He is usually content to eye me and raise his lip, but one foggy night he slipped out of an azalea bush and sank his teeth in my leg. Now and then when I know Mrs Schexnaydre is out, I will give him a tremendous kick in the ribs and send him yowling.

"I marked a real cute article for you," she says briskly and makes a point of leaving immediately to show she is not one of those landladies who intrude upon their tenants.

I am happy to have the magazine. The articles are indeed cute and heartwarming. People who are ordinarily understood to dislike each other or at least to be indifferent toward each other discover that they have much in common. I seem to recall an article about a subway breaking down in New York. The passengers who had their noses buried in newspapers began to talk to each other. They discovered that their fellow passengers were human beings much like themselves and with the same hopes and dreams; people are much the same the world over, even New Yorkers, the article concluded, and given the opportunity will find more to like than to dislike about each other. A lonely old man found himself talking excitedly to a young girl about his hobby of growing irises in a window box, she to him about her hopes and dreams for a career in art. I have to agree with Mrs Schexnaydre: such an episode is indeed heartwarming. On the other hand, it would make me nervous to be present at such a gathering. To tell the truth, if I were a young girl, I would have nothing to do with kindly old philosophers such as are portrayed by Thomas Mitchell in the movies. These birds look fishy to me.

But I can't read the article now. My aunt's letter makes a stronger demand upon me. She thinks constantly of other people—she is actually unselfish, the only person I know who is. When she reads something or thinks of something which may be useful to others, she is likely as not to write it down on the spot and mail it to them. Yes, it is a memo. There is no salutation or signature, only a single fat paragraph in a bold backslanted hand.

Every moment think steadily as a Roman and a man, to do what thou hast in hand with perfect and simple dignity, and a feeling of affection and freedom and justice. These words of the Emperor Marcus Aurelius Antoninus strike me as pretty good advice, for even the orneriest young scamp.

My apartment is as impersonal as a motel room. I have been careful not to accumulate possessions. My library is a single book, *Arabia Deserta*. The television set looks as if it took coins. On the wall over the bed hang two Currier and Ives prints of ice skaters in Central Park. How sad the little figures seem, skimming along in step! How sad the city seems!

I switch on television and sit directly in front of it, bolt upright and hands on knees in my ladder-back chair. A play comes on with Dick Powell. He is a cynical financier who is trying to get control of a small town newspaper. But he is baffled by the kindliness and sincerity of the town folk. Even the editor whom he is trying to ruin is nice to him. And even when he swindles the editor and causes him to have a heart attack from which he later dies, the editor is as friendly as ever and takes the occasion to give Powell a sample of his homespun philosophy. ''We're no great shakes as a town," says the editor on his deathbed, teetering on the very brink of eternity. "But we're friendly." In the end Powell is converted by these good folk and instead of trying to control the paper, applies to the editor's daughter for the job of reporter so he can fight against political corruption.

It is time to pick up Kate.

3. TONIGHT, THURSDAY NIGHT, I CARRY OUT A SUC-cessful experiment in repetition.

Fourteen years ago, when I was a sophomore, I saw a western at a moviehouse on Freret Street, a place frequented by students and known to them as the Armpit. The movie was *The Oxbow Incident* and it was quite good. It was about this time of year I saw it, for I remember the smell of privet when I came out and the camphor berries popping underfoot. (All movies smell of a neighborhood and a season: I saw *All Quiet on the Western Front*, one of my first, in Arcola, Mississippi, in August of 1941, and the noble deeds were done, not merely fittingly but inevitably, in the thick singing darkness of Delta summer and in the fragrance of cottonseed meal.) Yesterday evening I noticed in the *Picayune* that another western was playing at the same theater. So up I went, by car to my aunt's house, then up St Charles in a streetcar with Kate so we can walk through the campus.

Nothing had changed. There we sat, I in the same seat I think, and afterwards came out into the smell of privet. Camphor berries popped underfoot on the same section of broken pavement.

A successful repetition.

What is a repetition? A repetition is the re-enactment

of past experience toward the end of isolating the time segment which has lapsed in order that it, the lapsed time, can be savored of itself and without the usual adulteration of events that clog time like peanuts in brittle. Last week, for example, I experienced an accidental repetition. I picked up a German-language weekly in the library. In it I noticed an advertisement for Nivea Creme, showing a woman with a grainy face turned up to the sun. Then I remembered that twenty years ago I saw the same advertisement in a magazine on my father's desk, the same woman, the same grainy face, the same Nivea Creme. The events of the intervening twenty years were neutralized, the thirty million deaths, the countless torturings, uprootings and wanderings to and fro. Nothing of consequence could have happened because Nivea Creme was exactly as it was before. There remained only time itself, like a yard of smooth peanut brittle.

How, then, tasted my own fourteen years since *The Oxbow Incident*?

As usual it eluded me. There was this: a mockery about the old seats, their plywood split, their bottoms slashed, but enduring nevertheless as if they had waited to see what I had done with my fourteen years. There was this also: a secret sense of wonder about the enduring, about all the nights, the rainy summer nights at twelve and one and two o'clock when the seats endured alone in the empty theater. The enduring is something which must be accounted for. One cannot simply shrug it off.

"Where to now?" asks Kate. She stands at my shoulder under the marquee, plucking at her thumb and peering into the darkness.

"Wherever you like."

"Go on about your business."

"Very well."

She saw Merle Mink this afternoon and seems to feel better for it. He approved her breaking her engagement with Walter and set up a not very rigorous schedule of office visits. Most important, she no longer feels she is coming near the brink of an abyss. "But the trouble is," she said gloomily as we sat in the theater waiting for the lights to go out, "I am always at my best with doctors. They are charmed with me. I feel fine when I'm sick. It is only when I'm well that—" Now in the shadow of the camphor tree she stops suddenly, takes my arm in both hands. "Have you noticed that only in time of illness or disaster or death are people real? I remember at the time of the wreck—people were so kind and helpful and *solid*. Everyone pretended that our lives until that moment had been every bit as real as the moment itself and that the future must be real too, when the truth was that our reality had been purchased only by Lyell's death. In another hour or so we had all faded out again and gone our dim ways."

We wander along the dark paths of the campus and stop off at my weedy stoop behind the laboratory. I sit on the concrete step and think of nothing. Kate presses her bleeding thumb to her mouth. "What is this place?" she asks. A lamp above the path makes a golden sphere among the tree-high shrubs.

"I spent every afternoon for four years in one of those laboratories up there."

"Is this part of the repetition?"

"No."

"Part of the search?"

I do not answer. She can only believe I am serious in her own fashion of being serious: as an antic sort of seriousness, which is not seriousness at all but despair masquerading as seriousness. I would as soon not speak to her of such things, since she is bound to understand it as a cultivated eccentricity, like the eccentricity of the roommate she used to talk about: "A curious girl, BoBo. Do you know what she liked to do? Collect iron deer. She located every iron deer in Westchester County and once a month she'd religiously make her rounds and pay them a visit—just park and look at them. She had names for each one: Tertullian, Archibald MacLeish, Alf Landon—she was quite serious about it.'' I have no use at all for girls like BoBo nor for such antic goings as collecting iron deer in Westchester County.

"Why don't you sit down?" I ask her irritably.

"Now the vertical search is when—''

(Am I irritable because, now that she mentions it, I do for a fact sound like BoBo and her goddamn iron deer?)

"If you walk in the front door of the laboratory, you undertake the vertical search. You have a specimen, a cubic centimeter of water or a frog or a pinch of salt or a star.''

"One learns general things?''

"And there is excitement to the search.''

"Why?" she asks.

"Because as you get deeper into the search, you unify. You understand more and more specimens by fewer and fewer formulae. There is the excitement. Of course you are always after the big one, the new key, the secret leverage point, and that is the best of it.''

"And it doesn't matter where you are or who you are.''

"No.''

"And the danger is of becoming no one nowhere.''

"Never mind.''

Kate parses it out with the keen male bent of her mind and yet with her woman's despair. Therefore I take care to be no more serious than she.

"On the other hand, if you sit back here and take a little carcass out of the garbage can, a specimen which has been used and discarded, there remains something left over, a clue?''

"Yes, but let's go.''

"You're a cold one, dear.''

"As cold as you?''

"Colder. Cold as the grave.'' She walks about tearing shreds of flesh from her thumb. I say nothing. It would take very little to set her off on an attack on me, one of her "frank" appraisals. "It is possible, you know, that you are overlooking something, the most obvious thing of all. And you would not know it if you fell over it."

"What?"

She will not tell me. Instead, in the streetcar, she becomes gay and affectionate toward me. She locks her arms around my waist and gives me a kiss on the mouth and watches me with brown eyes gone to discs.

4. IT IS TWO O'CLOCK BEFORE I GET BACK TO GENtilly. Yet sometime before dawn I awake with a violent start and for the rest of the night lie dozing yet wakeful and watchful. I have not slept soundly for many years. Not since the war when I was knocked out for two days have I really lost consciousness as a child loses consciousness in sleep and wakes to a new world not even remembering when he went to bed. I always know where I am and what time it is. Whenever I feel myself sinking toward a deep sleep, something always recalls me: "Not so fast now. Suppose you should go to sleep and it should happen. What then?" What is this that is going to happen? Clearly nothing. Yet there I lie, wakeful and watchful as a sentry, ears tuned to the slightest noise. I can even hear old Rosebud turning round and round in the azalea bushes before settling down.

At dawn I dress and slip out so quietly that the dogs do not stir. I walk toward the lake. It is almost a summer night. Heavy warm air has pushed up from the Gulf, but the earth has memories of winter and lies cold and sopping wet from dew.

It is good to walk in the suburbs at this hour. No one

ever uses the sidewalks anyhow and now there are not even children on tricycles and miniature tractors. The concrete is virginal, as grainy as the day it was poured; weeds sprout in the cracks.

The closer you get to the lake, the more expensive the houses are. Already the bungalows and duplexes and tiny ranch houses are behind me. Here are the fifty and sixty thousand dollar homes, fairly big moderns with dagger plants and Australian pines planted in brick boxes, and reproductions of French provincial and Louisiana colonials. The swimming pools steam like sleeping geysers. These houses look handsome in the sunlight; they please me with their pretty colors, their perfect lawns and their clean airy garages. But I have noticed that at this hour of dawn they are forlorn. A sadness settles over them like a fog from the lake.

My father used to suffer from insomnia. One of my few recollections of him is his nighttime prowling. In those days it was thought that sleeping porches were healthful, so my father stuck one onto the house, a screen box with canvas blinds that pulled up from below. Here Scott and I slept on even the coldest nights. My father had trouble sleeping and moved out with us. He tossed like a wounded animal, or slept fitfully, his breath whistling musically through the stiff hairs of his nose—and went back inside before morning, leaving his bed tortured and sour, a smell which I believed to be caused by a nasal ailment known then as "catarrh." The porch did not work for him and he bought a Saskatchewan sleeping bag from Abercrombie and Fitch and moved out into the rose garden. Just at this hour of dawn I would be awakened by a terrible sound: my father crashing through the screen door, sleeping bag under his arm, his eyes crisscrossed by fatigue and by the sadness of these glimmering dawns. My mother, without meaning to, put a quietus on his hopes of sleep even more effectively than this forlorn hour. She had a way of summing up his doings in a phrase that took the heart out of him. He dreamed, I know, of a place of quiet breathing and a deep sleep under the stars and next to the sweet earth. She agreed. "Honey, I'm all for it. I think we all ought to get back to nature and I'd be right with you, Honey, if it wasn't for the chiggers. I'm chigger bait." She made him out to be another Edgar Kennedy (who was making shorts then) thrashing around in the bushes with his newfangled camping equipment. To her it was better to make a joke of it than be defeated by these chilly dawns. But after that nothing more was said about getting back to nature.

He made a mistake. He was trying to sleep. He thought he had to sleep a certain number of hours every night, breathe fresh air, eat a certain number of calories, evacuate his bowels regularly and have a stimulating hobby (it was the 1930s and everybody believed in science and talked about "ductless glands"). I do not try to sleep. And I could not tell you the last time my bowels moved; sometimes they do not move for a week but I have no interest in such matters. As for hobbies, people with stimulating hobbies suffer from the most noxious of despairs since they are tranquillized in their despair. I muse along as quietly as a ghost. Instead of trying to sleep I try to fathom the mystery of this suburb at dawn. Why do these splendid houses look so defeated at this hour of the day? Other houses, say a 'dobe house in New Mexico or an old frame house in Feliciana, look much the same day or night. But these new houses look haunted. Even the churches out here look haunted. What spirit takes possession of them? My poor father. I can see him, blundering through the patio furniture, the Junior Jets and the Lone Ranger pup tents, dragging his Saskatchewan sleeping bag like the corpse of his dead hope.

When I return, the sun is warm on my back. I stretch out in a snug little cul de sac between the garage and the house, under the insolent eye of Rosebud, and doze till nine o'clock when the market opens.

5. AWAKENED BY ROSEBUD'S GROWLING. IT IS THE postman. Rosebud feels my eye on him, cocks an eyebrow around to see me and is discomfited to meet my eye; he looks away, pretends to settle his mouth, but his lip is dry and snags high on a tooth. Now he is actively embarrassed.

School children across the street line up in ragged platoons before the storklike nuns, the girls in little blue bell-shaped skirts and suspenders, the boys a bit dreary in their khaki. In they march, under the schematic dove. The morning sunlight winks on the polished metal of ocean wave and the jungle gym. How shiny and strong and well-set are the steel pipes, polished to silver by thousands of little blue-skirted and khaki-clad butts.

The postman has a letter from Harold Graebner in Chicago. It is a note and a birth announcement. Harold asks me to be godfather to his new baby. The enclosed card announces the birth in the following way:

> 1 C.O.D. PACKAGE
> SHIPPING WEIGHT: 7 LB. 4 OZ.
> HANDLE WITH TENDER LOVING CARE, ETC.

Harold Graebner probably saved my life in the Orient and for this reason he loves me. When I get a letter, it is almost certain to be from Harold Graebner. I no longer write or receive letters, except Harold's. When I was in the army I wrote long, sensitive and articulate letters to my aunt, giving my impressions of countries and peoples. I wrote such things as

Japan is lovely this time of year. How strange to think of going into combat! Not so much fear—since my chances are very good—as wonder, wonder that everything should be so full of expectancy, every tick of the watch, every rhododendron blossom. Tolstoy and St Exupery were right about war, etc.

A regular young Rupert Brooke was I, "—full of expectancy." Oh the crap that lies lurking in the English soul. Somewhere it, the English soul, received an injection of romanticism which nearly killed it. That's what killed my father, English romanticism, that and 1930 science. A line for my notebook:

Explore connection between romanticism and scientific objectivity. Does a scientifically minded person become a romantic because he is a leftover from his own science?

I must reply to Harold, but it is almost more than I can do to write two sentences in a row. The words are without grace.

Dear Harold: Thank you for asking me to be godfather to your baby. Since, however, I am not a practical Catholic, I doubt if I could. But I certainly appreciate—

Certainly appreciate. Tear it up.

 6. AN ODD THING. EVER SINCE WEDNESDAY I HAVE become acutely aware of Jews. There is a clue here, but of what I cannot say. How do I know? Because whenever I approach a Jew, the Geiger counter in my head starts rattling away like a machine gun; and as I go past with the utmost circumspection and with every sense alert—the Geiger counter subsides.

There is nothing new in my Jewish vibrations. During the years when I had friends my Aunt Edna, who is a theosophist, noticed that all my friends were Jews. She knew why moreover: I had been a Jew in a previous incarnation. Perhaps that is it. Anyhow it is true that I am Jewish by instinct. We share the same exile. The fact is, however, I am more Jewish than the Jews I know. They are more at home than I am. I accept my exile.

Another evidence of my Jewishness: the other day a sociologist reported that a significantly large percentage of solitary moviegoers are Jews.

Jews are my first real clue.

When a man is in despair and does not in his heart of hearts allow that a search is possible and when such a man passes a Jew in the street, he notices nothing.

When a man becomes a scientist or an artist, he is open to a different kind of despair. When such a man passes a Jew in the street, he may notice something but it is not a remarkable encounter. To him the Jew can only appear as a scientist or artist like himself or as a specimen to be studied.

But when a man awakes to the possibility of a search and when such a man passes a Jew in the street for the first time, he is like Robinson Crusoe seeing the footprint on the beach.

7. A BEAUTIFUL FRIDAY MORNING AND A SUCCESSFUL excursion into St Bernard Parish with Sharon.

Sharon eyes my MG narrowly. After she has gotten in, she makes it plain that MG or no MG there is to be no monkey business. How does she make such a thing plain and in an MG sitting thigh to thigh and knee to knee? By her Southern female trick of politeness. "This is the cutest little *car*!" she sings and goes trailing off in a fit of absent-mindedness, hands to the nape of her neck and tilting her head forward so that she surveys the street through her eyebrows and with a cold woman's eye; then seeming to rouse herself apologetically: "This sure beats typing. Mhm-M"—as singsongy and shut off to herself as her mammy in Eufala. Southern girls learn a lot from their nurses.

We meet Mr Sartalamaccia and a queer thing happens.

First, some kind of reversal takes place and it becomes natural for Mr Sartalamaccia to show me the place he wants to buy. He becomes the guide to my property and even points out the good features. A far cry from a duck club now, my patrimony is hemmed in on one side by a housing development and on the other by a police pistol range. In fact, my estate puts me in mind of the pictures in detective magazines of the scene where a crime was committed: a bushy back lot it is, tunnelled through by hog trails and a suspicious car track or two. Every inch of open ground sprouts new green shoots and from the black earth there seems to arise a green darkness. It is already like summer here. Cicadas drone in the weeds and the day seems long.

We leave the MG in a glade (a good hard-used creature

78

of red metal and fragrant worn leather; I run a hand over its flank of stout British steel as if it were a mare) and stand on a hummock with Mr Sartalamaccia between us; Mr Sartalamaccia: wagging a limp panama behind him and giving off a bitter cotton smell. He is less an Italian than a Southern country man, haggard and clean as an Alabama farmer come to church.

"The lodge was here, Roaring Camp they called it," I tell Sharon. She stands blinking and inviolate, a little rared back and entrenched within herself. Not for her the thronging spirit-presence of the place and the green darkness of summer come back again and the sadness of it. She went to Eufala High School and it is all the same to her where she is (so she might have stood in the Rotunda during her school trip to Washington) and she is right, for she is herself sweet life and where is the sadness of that? "I came here once with my father and great uncle. They wouldn't have beds, so we slept on the floor. I slept between them and I had a new Ingersoll watch and when I went to bed, I took it out and put it on the floor beside my head. During the night my uncle rolled over on it and broke it. It became a famous story and somehow funny, the way he rolled over on my watch, and they would all laugh—haw haw haw—like a bunch of Germans. Then at Christmas he gave me another watch which turned out to be a gold Hamilton." Sharon stands astraddle, as heavy of leg as a Wac. "I remember when my father built the lodge. Before that he had read the works of Fabre and he got the idea of taking up a fascinating scientific hobby. He bought a telescope and one night he called us outside and showed us the horsehead nebula in Orion. That was the end of the telescope. After that he began to read Browning and saw himself in need of a world of men. That was when he started the duck club."

"Grow old along with me. The best is yet to be," says Sharon.

"That's right."

Mr Sartalamaccia has become restless; he works his hat behind him. His fingernails are large and almost filled with white moons. "Your father didn't build it. Judge Anse was the one that built it."

"Is that right? You knew them? I didn't know you—"

Mr Sartalamaccia tells it forlornly, without looking up—knowing no more than the facts pure and simple and hardly believing that we don't know. Everybody knows. "I built it for him."

"How did you know him?"

"I didn't. One morning before Christmas I was just about finished with my store over there and Judge Anse come in and started talking to me. He said—uh—" Mr Sartalamaccia smiles a secret little smile and his head sinks even lower as he makes bold to recall the very words. "—what's your name? Yes: *what's your name?* I told him. He said—uh: *you built this store?* I said, yessir. We talked. So he looked at me and he said—uh: *I'm going tell you what I want you to do.* He writes this check. He said—uh: *Here's a check for a thousand dollars. I want you to build me a lodge and come on, I'll show you where.* So I said, all right. So he said—uh—" Mr Sartalamaccia waits until the words, the very words, speak themselves—"*Let's go, Vince*, like him and me, we were going to have us a big time. He never saw me before in his life and he walks in my store and writes me a check on the Canal Bank for a thousand dollars. And he didn't come back for six weeks."

"Did he like the lodge?"

"I mean he liked it."

"I see." I see. There was such a time and there were such men (and Mr Sartalamaccia smiles to remember it), men who could say to other men, *here do this*, and have it done and done with pleasure and remembered with pleasure. "Have you always been here?"

"Me?" Mr Sartalamaccia looks up for the first time. "I had only been here three weeks! Since November."

"Where are you from?"

"I was raised in Ensley, near Birmingham, but in nineteen thirty-two times was so hard I started moving around. I visited forty-six states, all but Washington and Oregon, just looking around and I never went hungry. In nineteen thirty-four I come to stay with my brother in Violet and started trapping."

It turns out that Mr Sartalamaccia is a contractor and owns the housing development next door. He has done well and he wants my duck club for an addition. I ask about the houses.

"You want to see one?"

We follow him along a hog trail to a raw field full of pretty little flat-topped houses. He must show us one abuilding. I take pleasure in watching him run a thumb over the sawn edges of the sheathing. Sharon does not mind. She stands foursquare, eyes rolled back a little, showing white. She is sleepy-eyed and frumpy; she looks like snapshots of Ava Gardner when she was a high school girl in North Carolina.

"You know what's in this slab?" The concrete is smooth as silk.

"No."

"Chance number six copper pipe. Nobody will ever know it's there but it will be there a long time." I see that with him it is not purely and simply honesty; it is his own pleasure at thinking a good pipe in a good slab.

Back at the hummock, Mr Sartalamaccia takes me aside and holds his hat away to the east. "You see that ditcher and doozer?"

"Yes."

"You know what that's going to be?"

"No."

"That's the tidewater canal to the Gulf. You know how much our land is going to be worth?"

"How much?"

"Fifty dollars a foot." Mr Sartalamaccia draws me close.

81

Again he tells it as the veriest piece of news. Deal or no deal, this is a piece of news that bears telling.

Later Sharon tells me I was smart to trick him into revealing the true value of my duck club. But she is mistaken. It came about from the moment I met him that thenceforward it pleased him to speak of the past, of his strange odyssey in 1932 when he gazed at Old Faithful in Yellowstone Park and worked on the causeway to Key West and did not go hungry—it pleased him to speak with me of the past and to connive with me against the future. He speaks from his loneliness and together we marvel at the news of the canal and enjoy the consolation of making money. For money is a great joy.

Mr Sartalamaccia has become possessed by a secret hilarity. He gives me a poke in the ribs. "I'll tell you what we can do, Mr Bolling. You keep your land! I'll develop it for you. You make the offsite improvements. I'll build the houses. We'll make us some money." He shrinks away in some kind of burlesque.

"How much do you think we can make?"

"Well I don't know. But I can tell you this." Mr Sartalamaccia is hopping in a sort of goat dance and Sharon stands dreaming in the green darkness of the glade. "I'll give you fifteen thousand for it right now!"

Our name is Increase.

Sharon and I spin along the River Road. The river is high and the booms and stacks of ships ride up and down the levee like great earth engines.

In the Shell station and in a drift of honeysuckle sprouting through the oil cans and standing above Sharon with a Coke balanced on her golden knee, I think of flattening my hummock with bulldozers and it comes back to me how the old Gable used to work at such jobs: he knew how to seem to work and how to seem to forget about women: stand asweat with his hands in his back pockets.

It is a great joy to be with Sharon and to make money

at it and to seem to pay no attention to her. As for Sharon: she finds nothing amiss in sitting in the little bucket seat with her knees doubled up in the sunshine, dress tucked under. An amber droplet of Coca-Cola meanders along her thigh, touches a blond hair, distributes itself around the tiny fossa.

"Aaauugh," I groan aloud.

"What's the matter?"

"It is a stitch in the side." It is a sword in the heart.

Sharon holds a hand against the sun to see me." Mr Bolling?"

"Yes."

"Do you remember the price Mr Sartalamaccia first mentioned?"

"Eight thousand dollars."

"He was really gon mess you up."

"No he wasn't. But if it hadn't been for you, I'd have taken the eight thousand."

"Me?"

"You got me to come down here."

She assents doubtfully, casting back in her mind with one eye screwed up.

"Do you know how much you saved me, or rather made for me? At least seven thousand dollars and probably a great deal more. I'm obliged to give you ten percent."

"You're not giving me any money, son."

I have to laugh. "Why not?"

"Ain't nobody giving me any money." (Now she catches herself and speaks broadly on purpose.) "I got plenty money."

"How much money do you have?"

"Ne'mind."

By flexing her leg at a certain angle, she can stand the Coke on a facet of her knee. What a structure it is, tendon and bone, facet and swell, and gold all over.

I go home as the old Gable, asweat and with no thought for her and sick to death with desire. She is pleased because, for one thing, she can keep quiet. I notice that it makes her uneasy to keep up a conversation.

She says only one more thing, tilting her head, eyes alight. "What about the courthouse?"

"It's too late. You didn't have to come. I'm sorry."

"Listen!" she cries, as far away as Eufala itself. "I had a wonderful time!"

8. ONCE A WEEK, ON FRIDAYS, ALL CUTRER SALESmen return to the main office for a lunch conference with the staff. The week's business is reviewed, sales reports made, talks given on market conditions and coming issues presented by the underwriter. But today there is not much talk of business. Carnival is in full swing. Parades and balls go on night and day. A dozen krewes have already had their hour, and Proteus, Rex and Comus are yet to come. Partners and salesmen alike are red-eyed and abstracted. There is gossip about the identity of the king and queen of Iberia tonight (most of the staff of Cutrer, Klostermann and Lejier are members either of the Krewe of Neptune or the Krewe of Iberia). It is generally conceded that the king of Iberia will be James (Shorty) Jones, president of Middle Gulf Utilities, and the queen Winky Ouillibert, the daughter of Plauche Ouillibert of Southern Mutual. The choice is a popular one—I can testify that both men are able, likable and unassuming fellows.

Some Fridays, Uncle Jules likes to see me in his office after lunch. When he does, he so signifies by leaving his door open to the corridor so that I will see him at his desk and naturally stop by to say hello. Today he seems particularly glad to see me. Uncle Jules has a nice way of making you feel at home. Although he has a big office with an antique desk and a huge portrait of Aunt Emily, and although he is a busy man, he makes you feel as if you and he had come upon this place in your wanderings; he is no more at home than you. He sits everywhere but in his own chair and does business everywhere but at his own desk. Now he takes me into a corner and stands feeling the bones of my shoulder like a surgeon.

"Ravaud came in to see me this morning." Uncle Jules falls silent and throws his head straight back. I know enough to wait. "He said, Jules, I've got a little bad news for you—you know the conversation of the open-ends, the one you never miss? I said, sure, I know about it." Now Uncle Jules puts his head down to my chest as if he were listening to my heart. I wait. "Do you know when it is? Why yes, along the middle of March, I told him. Along about Tuesday, says Ravaud. Carnival day." Uncle Jules presses my shoulder to keep me quiet. "Is that right, Ravaud? Oh, that reminds me. Here are your tickets. Have a good trip." Uncle Jules is bent way over and I can't tell whether he is laughing, but his thumb presses deep into the socket of my shoulder.

"That's pretty good."

"But then he said something that stuck in my mind. He said, I don't mind going if you want me to, Jules, but you got the man right in your own family. Why that scoun'l beast Jack Bolling knows more about selling open-ends than anybody on Carondelet Street. So. You don't really care about Carnival, do you?" He does not really believe I do not. As for himself, he could not conceive being anywhere on earth Mardi Gras morning but the Boston Club.

"No sir."

"So. You take the ten-thirty plane Tuesday morning," says Uncle Jules in his gruff way of conferring favors.

"Where to?"

"Where to! Why goddam, Chicago!"

Chicago. Misery misery son of a bitch of all miseries.

Not in a thousand years could I explain it to Uncle Jules, but it is no small thing for me to make a trip, travel hundreds of miles across the country by night to a strange place and come out where there is a different smell in the air and people have a different way of sticking themselves into the world. It is a small thing to him but not to me. It is nothing to him to close his eyes in New Orleans and wake up in San Francisco and think the same thoughts on Telegraph Hill that he thought on Carondelet Street. Me, it is my fortune and misfortune to know how the spirit-presence of a strange place can enrich a man or rob a man but never leave him alone, how, if a man travels lightly to a hundred strange cities and cares nothing for the risk he takes, he may find himself No one and Nowhere. Great day in the morning. What will it mean to go mosying down Michigan Avenue in the neighborhood of five million strangers, each shooting out his own personal ray? How can I deal with five million personal rays?

"I want you to make a few more contacts." Uncle Jules lays back his head and we wait ten seconds. "Then when you get back, I think we might have something for you downtown." The gruffest voice and so the greatest favor of all.

"Yes sir," say I, looking pleased as punch and even prickling in the hairline to do justice to his gruffest favor. Oh sons of all bitches and great beast of Chicago lying in wait. There goes my life in Gentilly, my Little Way, my secret existence among the happy shades in Elysian Fields.

9. FOR SOME TIME NOW THE IMPRESSION HAS BEEN growing upon me that everyone is dead.

It happens when I speak to people. In the middle of a

sentence it will come over me: yes, beyond a doubt this is death. There is little to do but groan and make an excuse and slip away as quickly as one can. At such times it seems that the conversation is spoken by automatons who have no choice in what they say. I hear myself or someone else saying things like: "In my opinion the Russian people are a great people, but—" or "Yes, what you say about the hypocrisy of the North is unquestionably true. However—" and I think to myself: this is death. Lately it is all I can do to carry on such everyday conversations, because my cheek has developed a tendency to twitch of its own accord. Wednesday as I stood speaking to Eddie Lovell, I felt my eye closing in a broad wink.

After the lunch conference I run into my cousin Nell Lovell on the steps of the library—where I go occasionally to read liberal and conservative periodicals. Whenever I feel bad, I go to the library and read controversial periodicals. Though I do not know whether I am a liberal or a conservative, I am nevertheless enlivened by the hatred which one bears the other. In fact, this hatred strikes me as one of the few signs of life remaining in the world. This is another thing about the world which is upside down: all the friendly and likable people seem dead to me; only the haters seem alive.

Down I plunk myself with a liberal weekly at one of the massive tables, read it from cover to cover, nodding to myself whenever the writer scores a point. Damn right, old son, I say, jerking my chair in approval. Pour it on them. Then up and over to the rack for a conservative monthly and down in a fresh cool chair to join the counterattack. Oh ho, say I, and hold fast to the chair arm: that one did it: eviscerated! And then out and away into the sunlight, my neck prickling with satisfaction.

Nell Lovell, I was saying, spotted me and over she comes brandishing a book. It seems she has just finished reading a celebrated novel which, I understand, takes a somewhat gloomy and pessimistic view of things. She is angry.

"I don't feel a bit gloomy!" she cries. "Now that Mark and Lance have grown up and flown the coop, I am having the time of my life. I'm taking philosophy courses in the morning and working nights at Le Petit Theatre. Eddie and I have re-examined our values and found them pretty darn enduring. To our utter amazement we discovered that we both have the same life-goal. Do you know what it is?"

"No."

"To make a contribution, however small, and leave the world just a little better off."

"That's very good," I say somewhat uneasily and shift about on the library steps. I can talk to Nell as long as I don't look at her. Looking into her eyes is an embarrassment.

"—we gave the television to the kids and last night we turned on the hi-fi and sat by the fire and read *The Prophet* aloud. I don't find life gloomy!" she cries. "To me, books and people and things are endlessly fascinating. Don't you think so?"

"Yes." A rumble has commenced in my descending bowel, heralding a tremendous defecation.

Nell goes on talking and there is nothing to do but shift around as best one can, take care not to fart, and watch her in a general sort of way: a forty-year-old woman with a good open American face and another forty years left in her; and eager, above all, eager, with that plaintive lost eagerness American college women get at a certain age. I get to thinking about her and old Eddie re-examining their values. Yes, true. Values. Very good. And then I can't help wondering to myself: why does she talk as if she were dead? Another forty years to go and dead, dead, dead.

"How is Kate?" Nell asks.

I jump and think hard, trying to escape death. "To tell you the truth, I don't know."

"I am so devoted to her! What a grand person she is."

"I am too. She is."

"Come see us, Binx!"

"I will!"

We part laughing and dead.

10. AT FOUR O'CLOCK I DECIDE IT IS NOT TOO early to set in motion my newest scheme conceived in the interests of money and love, my love for Sharon. Everything depends on a close cooperation between business and love. If ever my business should suffer because of my admiration for Sharon, then my admiration for Sharon would suffer too. Never never will I understand men who throw over everything for some woman. The trick, the joy of it, is to prosper on all fronts, enlist money in the service of love and love in the service of money. As long as I am getting rich, I feel that all is well. It is my Presbyterian blood.

At four fifteen I sit on the edge of her desk, fold my arms and look troubled.

"Miss Kincaid. I have a favor to ask of you."

"Yes sir, Mr Bolling."

As she looks up at me, I think how little we know each other. She is really a stranger. Her yellow eyes are quite friendly and opaque. She is very nice and very anxious to be helpful. My heart sinks. Love, the very possibility of love, vanishes. Our sexes vanish. We are a regular little team.

"Do you know what these names are?"

"Customers' files."

"They are also portfolios, individual listings of stocks and bonds and so forth. Now I tell you what we do every

year about this time. In a few weeks income taxes must
be filed. Now we usually mail our customers a lot of book-
lets and charts and whatnot to help them with their returns. This year we're going to do something different. I'm
going to go through each portfolio myself, give the tax
status of each transaction and make specific recommen-
dations to every customer in a personal letter, recommen-
dations about capital gains, and losses, stock rights and
warrants, dates of involuntary conversions, stock divi-
dends and so on. You'd be amazed how many otherwise
shrewd businessmen will take long term gains and losses
the same year.''

She listens closely, her yellow eyes snapping with intelligence.

"Now I'm already familiar with the accounts, so that's
no problem. But it's going to mean a lot of letters. And
we don't have much time.'' Why I must have been crazy;
this girl is a good little sister.

"When would we start?''

"Can you work an hour later this afternoon and Saturday morning?''

"I'd like to make a phone call,'' she says in the brusque-
kindly manner of country folk who grant favors with an
angry willingness.

A moment later she is standing at my desk stroking the
beige plastic with two scarlet nails.

"Is it all right for someone to pick me up at five for a
few minutes?''

Someone. How ancient is her wisdom. I am nothing to
her, yet by the surest of instincts she labels her date a
neuter person. She knows I do not believe there is such a
person. But she knows what she does. Despite myself I
believe a someone will pick her up, a shadowy and incon-
sequential person of neuter gender.

"I hope I'm not interfering with anything too serious.''

"Are you kidding?''

"Why no.''

She surprises me. I said "serious" ambiguously and perhaps purposely so. But she is quick to give it its court-ship meaning.

Here is an unexpected advantage. It could be useful to me to see what sort of fellow her friend is. But I needn't worry about managing a glimpse of him. A few minutes before five he walks right into the office. He is much to my liking—I could throw my arms around him. A sharp character—no youth as I feared—a Faubourg Marigny type, Mediterranean, big-nosed, lumpy-jawed, a single stitched-in wrinkle over his eyebrows from just above which there springs up a great pompadour of wiry bronze hair. His face aches with it. He has no use for me at all. I nod at him with the warmest feelings, and he appears to nod at me but keeps on nodding, nods past me and at the office as if he were appraising it. Now and then his lip draws back along his teeth admitting a suck of air as sharp as a steam blast. As he waits for Sharon, he swings his fist into an open hand and snaps his knee back and forth inside his wide pants.

The Faubourg Marigny fellow leaves at last and we work steadily until seven. I dictate some very sincere letters. Dear Mr Hebert: I happened to be looking over your port-folio this morning and it occurred to me that you might realize a substantial tax saving by unloading your holding of Studebaker-Packard. Naturally I am not acquainted with your overall tax picture, but if you do have a problem taxwise, I suggest taking a capital loss for the following reasons . . .

It is good to have both Mr Hebert and Sharon on my mind. To be thinking of only one of them would make me nervous.

We work hard and as comrades, swept along by a part-nership so strong that the smallest overture of love would be brushed aside by either of us as foolishness. *Peyton Place* would embarrass both of us now.

By six o'clock I become aware that it is time to modulate the key ever so slightly. From now on everything I do must exhibit a certain value in her eyes, a value, moreover, which she must begin to *recognize*.

Thus we send out for sandwiches and drink coffee as we work. Already the silences between us have changed in character, become easier. It is possible to stand at the window, loosen my collar and rub the back of my neck like Dana Andrews. And to become irritable with her: "No no no no, Kincaid, that's not what I meant to say. Take five." I go to the cooler, take two aspirins, crumple the paper cup. Her friend, old "someone," turns out to be invaluable. In my every tactic he is the known quantity. He is my triangulation point. I am all business to his monkey business.

Already she has rolled a fresh sheet into the platen. "Try it again," and she looks at me ironically and with lights in her eyes.

I stretch out both hands to her desk, put my head down between my arms.

"All right. Take it this way . . ." O Rory Rory Rory.

She is getting it. She is alert: there is something afoot. Now when she looks up between sentences, it is through her eyebrows and with her head cocked and still, still as a little partridge.

She watches closely now, her yellow agate-eyes snapping with interest. We are, all at once, on our way. We are like two children lost in a summer afternoon who, hardly aware of each other, find a door in a wall and enter an enchanted garden. Now we might join hands. She is watchful to see whether I see this too.

But this is no time to take chances. Although Baron Ochs's waltz sings in my ears and although I could grab her up out of her chair and kiss her smack on the mouth— we go back to work.

"Dear Mr Fontenot: Glancing over your portfolio, it struck me that you are not in the best position to take advantage of the dawning age of missiles . . ."

* * *

The Faubourg Marigny fellow does not return and at seven thirty it seems natural for me to drive Sharon home.

A line of squalls is due from Texas and we drive down to Esplanade in a flicker of summer lightning. The air presses heavily over Elysian Fields; earlier in the evening lake swallows took alarm and went veering away to the swamps. The Quarter is teeming. It is good to put behind us the green fields and the wide sky of Gentilly and to come into a narrow place pressed in upon by decrepit buildings and filled by man-smells and man-sounds. No thrush flutings and swallow cries in here. At twilight it is good to come away from the open sky and into a yellow-lit place and sit next to a warm thigh. I almost violate my resolution and ask Sharon if she will have a drink. But I don't. Instead I watch her up into her house. She ascends a new flight of concrete steps which soars like a gangplank into a dim upper region.

11. TONIGHT IS KATE'S SUPPER WITH THE QUEENS and I shall not see her. I drink beer and watch television, but every minute or so thoughts of Sharon, my big beautiful majorette from Alabama, come crowding into my head and my hands begin to sweat. The air is heavy and still. It is a time to be on guard. At such times there is the temptation to behave without prudence, to try to see Sharon tonight, or even park on Esplanade and spy on her and run the risk of ruining everything. Then at last the storm breaks, a real Texas rattler. Gradually the malaise lets up and it becomes possible to sit without perturbation and at heart's ease, hands on knees in my ladder-back chair and watch television.

The marshal traps some men in an Indian hogan. The squaw has been killed, leaving a baby. In an unexpected turn of events the killers get the upper hand and hold the marshal in a line shack as a hostage. The marshal reminds them of the baby in the hogan. This is no ordinary marshal. He is also a humanist. "It ain't nothing but a stinking Indian," says one of the killers. "You're wrong," says the marshal. "It is a human being." In the end he prevails upon the killers to spare the baby and even to have it baptized. The killers go out in a gruff manner and fetch the padre, a fellow who looks as much like the late H. B. Warner as it is possible for a man to look.

I go to bed cozy and dry in the storm, snug as a larva in a cocoon, wrapped safe and warm in loving Christian kindness. From chair to bed and from TV to radio for one little nightcap of a program. Being a creature of habit, as regular as a monk, and taking pleasure in the homeliest repetitions, I listen every night at ten to a program called "This I Believe." Monks have their compline, I have "This I Believe." On the program hundreds of the highest-minded people in our country, thoughtful and intelligent people, people with mature inquiring minds, state their personal credos. The two or three hundred I have heard so far were without exception admirable people. I doubt if any other country or any other time in history has produced such thoughtful and high-minded people, especially the women. And especially the South. I do believe the South has produced more high-minded women, women of universal sentiments, than any other section of the country except possibly New England in the last century. Of my six living aunts, five are women of the loftiest theosophical pan-Brahman sentiments. The sixth is still a Presbyterian.

If I had to name a single trait that all these people shared, it is their niceness. Their lives are triumphs of niceness. They like everyone with the warmest and most generous feelings. And as for themselves: it would be impossible for even a dour person not to like them.

Tonight's subject is a playwright who transmits this very quality of niceness in his plays. He begins:

> I believe in people. I believe in tolerance and understanding between people. I believe in the uniqueness and the dignity of the individual—

Everyone on "This I Believe" believes in the uniqueness and the dignity of the individual. I have noticed, however, that the believers are far from unique themselves, are in fact alike as peas in a pod.

> I believe in music. I believe in a child's smile. I believe in love. I also believe in hate.

This is true, I have known a couple of these believers, humanists and lady psychologists who come to my aunt's house. On "This I Believe" they like everyone. But when it comes down to this or that particular person, I have noticed that they usually hate his guts.

I did not always enjoy "This I Believe." While I was living at my aunt's house, I was overtaken by a fit of perversity. But instead of writing a letter to an editor, as was my custom, I recorded a tape which I submitted to Mr Edward R. Murrow. "Here are the beliefs of John Bickerson Bolling, a moviegoer living in New Orleans," it began, and ended, "I believe in a good kick in the ass. This—I believe." I soon regretted it, however, as what my grandfather would have called "a smart-alecky stunt" and I was relieved when the tape was returned. I have listened faithfully to "This I Believe" ever since.

> I believe in freedom, the sacredness of the individual and the brotherhood of man—

concludes the playwright.

I believe in believing. This—I believe.

All my shakiness over Sharon is gone. I switch off my radio and lie in bed with a pleasant tingling sensation in the groin, a tingling for Sharon and for all my fellow Americans.

12. SOMETIME DURING THE NIGHT AND AT THE height of the storm the telephone rings, a dreadful summons, and I find myself in the middle of the floor shaking like a leaf and wondering what is amiss. It is my aunt.

"What's that?" The telephone crackles with static. I listen so hard I can't hear.

My aunt tells me that something has happened to Kate. When Uncle Jules and Walter arrived at the hotel from the Iberia ball, Kate was not to be found. Nell Lovell, herself a former queen, told them that Kate had left abruptly sometime before eleven o'clock. That was three hours ago and she had not come home. But Nell wasn't worried. "You know as well as I do what she's doing, Cousin Em," she told my aunt. "You remember my Christmas party at Empire when she took out up the levee and walked all the way to Laplace? That Kate." But my aunt has her doubts. "Listen to this," she says in a peculiar voice—it is the dry litigious way of speaking of closely knit families in times of trouble: one would imagine she was speaking of a stranger. "Here is the last entry in her diary: Tonight will tell the story—will the new freedom work—if not, no more tight ropes for me, thank you. Now you recall her tight rope."

"Yes." "Tight rope" is an expression Kate used when

she was sick the first time. When she was a child and her mother was alive, she said, it used to seem to her that people laughed and talked in an easy and familiar way and stood on solid ground, but now it seemed that they (not just she but everybody) had become aware of the abyss that yawned at their feet even on the most ordinary occasions—especially on the most ordinary occasions. Thus, she would a thousand times rather find herself in the middle of no-man's-land than at a family party or luncheon club.

"Now I'm not really worried about her," my aunt declares briskly. There is a silence and the wire crackles. Strange to say, my main emotion is a slight social embarrassment. I cast about for something to say. "After all the girl is twenty-five years old," says my aunt.

"That's true."

Lightning strikes somewhere close, a vicious bolt. The clap comes hard upon it, in the very whitening, and shakes the house.

"—finally reached him in his hotel room in Atlanta."

"Who?"

"Sam. He's flying down first thing in the morning, instead of Sunday. He was quite excited."

"About what?"

"He said he had the most extraordinary piece of news. He wouldn't tell me what it was. It seems that by the eeriest sort of coincidence two things happened this very day with a direct bearing on Kate. Anyhow."

"Yes ma'am?"

"I have a hunch she'll wander out your way. If she does, will you drive her home?"

"Yes."

"It isn't as if Kate were another Otey Ann," says my aunt after a moment.

"No, it isn't." She is thinking of two things: one, an acquaintance from Feliciana named Otey Ann Aldridge who went crazy and used to break out of the state hospital in Jackson and come to New Orleans and solicit strangers on Bourbon Street; two, she is thinking of the look in Nell Lovell's eye, the little risible gleam, even as she reassured my aunt.

I awake with a start at three o'clock, put on a raincoat and go outside for a breath of air.

The squall line has passed over. Elysian Fields is dripping and still, but there is a commotion of winds high in the air where the cool heavy front has shouldered up the last of the fretful ocean air. The wind veers around to the north and blows away the storm until the moon swims high, moored like a kite and darting against the fleeing shreds and ragtags of cloud.

I sit in the shelter outside Mrs Schexnaydre's chain link fence. Opposite the school, it is used by those children who catch buses toward the lake. The streetlight casts a blue-black shadow. Across the boulevard, at the catercorner of Elysian Fields and Bons Enfants, is a vacant lot chest high in last summer's weeds. Some weeks ago the idea came to me of buying the lot and building a service station. It is for sale, I learned, for twenty thousand dollars. What with the windfall from Mr Sartalamaccia, it becomes possible to think seriously of the notion. It is easy to visualize the little tile cube of a building with its far flung porches, its apron of silky concrete and, revolving on high, the immaculate bivalve glowing in every inch of its pretty styrene (I have already approached the Shell distributor).

A taxi pulls up under the streetlight. Kate gets out and strides past the shelter, hands thrust deep in her pockets. Her eyes are pools of darkness. There is about her face the rapt almost ugly look of solitary people. When I call out to her, she comes directly over with a lack of surprise, with a dizzy dutiful obedience, which is disquieting. Then I see that she is full of it, one of her great ideas, the sort that occur to people on long walks.

"What a fool I've been!" She lays both hands on my

arm and takes no notice of the smell of the hour. She is nowhere; she is in the realm of her idea. "Do you think it is possible for a person to make a single mistake—not do something wrong, you understand, but make a miscalculation—and ruin his life?"

"Why not?"

"I mean after all. Couldn't a person be miserable because he got one thing wrong and never learned otherwise—because the thing he got wrong was of such a nature that he could not be told because the telling itself got it wrong—just as if you had landed on Mars and therefore had no way of knowing that a Martian is mortally offended by a question and so every time you asked what was wrong, it only grew worse for you?" Catching sight of my sleeve, she seizes it with a curious rough gesture, like a housewife fingering goods. "My stars, pajamas," she says offhandedly. "Well?" She searches my face in the violet shadow.

"I don't know."

"But I do know! I found out, Binx. None of you could have told me even if you wanted to. I don't even know if you know."

I wait gloomily. Long ago I learned to be wary of Kate's revelations. These exalted moments, when she is absolutely certain what course to take for the rest of her life, are often followed by spells of the blackest depression. "No, I swear I don't believe you do," says Kate, peering into my face, into one eye and then the other, like a lover. "And my telling you would do no good."

"Tell me anyhow."

"I am free. After twenty-five years I am free."

"How do you know?"

"You're not surprised?"

"When did you find out?"

"At four thirty this afternoon, yesterday afternoon."

"At Merle's?"

"Yes. I was looking up at his bookshelf and I hadn't said anything for a long time. I saw his book, a book with a sort of burlap cover that always struck me unpleasantly. Yet how hard I had tried to live up to him and his book, live joyfully and as oneself etcetera. There were days when I would come in as nervous as an actress and there were moments when I succeeded—in being myself and brilliantly (look at me, Merle, I'm doing it!), so brilliantly that I think he loved me. Poor Merle. You see, there is nothing he can say. He can't tell me the secret even if he knew it. Do you know what I did? After a minute or so he asked me: what comes to mind? I sat up and rubbed my eyes and then it dawned on me. But I couldn't believe it. It was too simple. My God, can a person live twenty-five years, a life of crucifixion, through a *misunderstanding*? Yes! I stood up. I had discovered that a person does not have to *be* this or *be* that or be anything, not even oneself. One is free. But even if Merle knew this and told me, there is no way in the world I could have taken his advice. How strange to think that you cannot pass along the discovery. So again Merle said: what comes to mind? I got up and told him good-by. He said, it's only four thirty; the hour is not yet over. Then he understood I was leaving. He got interested and suggested we look into the reasons. I said, Merle, how I wish you were right. How good to think that there are reasons and that if I am silent, it means I am hiding something. How happy I would be to be hiding something. And how proud I am when I do find secret reasons for you, your own favorite reasons. But what if there is nothing? That is what I've been afraid of until now—being found out to be concealing nothing at all. But now I know why I was afraid and why I needn't be. I was afraid because I felt that I must *be* such and such a person, even as good a person as your joyous and creative person (I read your articles, Merle). What a discovery! One minute I am straining every nerve to be the sort of person I was expected to be and shaking in my boots for fear I would fail—and the next minute to know with the calmest certitude that even if I could succeed and become your joyous and creative person, that it was not good enough for me and that I had something better. I was free. Now I am saying good-by, Merle. And I walked out, as free as a bird for the first time in my life, twenty-five years old, healthy as a horse, rich as cream, and with the world before me. Ah, don't disapprove, Binx. Binx, Binx. You think I should go back! Oh I will, no doubt. But I know I am right or I would not feel so wonderful.''

She will not feel wonderful long. Already the sky over the Chef is fading and soon the dawn will glimmer about us like the bottom of the sea. I know very well that when the night falls away into gray distances, she will sink into herself. Even now she is overtaking herself: already she is laboring ever so slightly at her exaltation.

I take her cold hands. "What do you think of this for an idea?" I tell her about the service station and Mr Sartalamaccia. "We could stay on here at Mrs Schexnaydre's. It is very comfortable. I may even run the station myself. You could come sit with me at night, if you liked. Did you know you can net over fifteen thousand a year on a good station?"

"You sweet old Binx! Are you asking me to marry you?"

"Sure." I watch her uneasily.

"Not a bad life, you say. It would be the best of all possible lives." She speaks in a rapture—something like my aunt. My heart sinks. It is too late. She has already overtaken herself.

"Don't—worry about it."

"I won't! I won't!"—as enraptured and extinguished in her soul, gone, as a character played by Eva Marie Saint. Leaning over, she hugs herself.

"What's the matter?"

"Ooooh," Kate groans, Kate herself now. "I'm so afraid."

"I know."

"What am I going to do?"

"You mean right now?"

"Yes."

"We'll go to my car. Then we'll drive down to the French Market and get some coffee. Then we'll go home."

"Is everything going to be all right?"

"Yes."

"Tell me. Say it."

"Everything is going to be all right."

III

1. SATURDAY MORNING AT THE OFFICE IS DREARY. THE market is closed and there is nothing to do but get on with the letter writing. But this is no more than I expected. It is a fine day outside, freakishly warm. Tropical air has seeped into the earth and the little squares of St Augustine grass are springy and turgid. Camphor berries pop underfoot; azaleas and Judas trees are blooming on Elysian Fields. There is a sketch of cloud in the mild blue sky and the high thin piping of waxwings comes from everywhere.

As Sharon types the letters, I stand hands in pockets looking through the gold lettering of our window. I think of Sharon and American Motors. It closed yesterday at 30¼.

At eleven o'clock it is time to speak.

"I'm quitting now. I've got sixty miles to go before lunch."

"Where 'bouts you going?"

"To the Gulf Coast."

The clatter of the typewriter does not slacken.

"Would you like to go?"

"M-hm"—absently. She is not surprised. "It just so happens I got work to do."

"No, you haven't. I'm closing the office."

"Well I be dog." There is still no surprise. What I've been waiting to see is how she will go about shedding her secretary manner. She doesn't. The clatter goes on.

"I'm leaving now."

"You gon let me finish this or not!" she cries in a scolding voice. So this is how she does it. She feels her way into familiarity by way of vexations. "You go head."

"Go?"

"I'll be right out. I got to call somebody."

"So do I." I call Kate. Mercer answers the phone. Kate has gone to the airport with Aunt Emily. He believes she is well.

Sharon looks at me with a yellow eye. "Is Miss Cutrer any kin to you?" she cries in her new scolding voice.

"She is my cousin."

"Some old girl told me you were married to her. I said nayo indeed."

"I'm not married to anyone."

"I said you weren't!" She tilts her head forward and goes off into a fit of absent-mindedness.

"Why did you want to know if I was married?"

"I'll tell you one thing, son. I'm not going out with any married man."

But still she has not come to the point of waiting upon my ministrations—like a date. Still very much her own mistress, she sets about tidying up her desk. When she shoulders her Guatemalan bag and walks briskly to the door, it is for me to tag along behind her. Now I see how she will have it: don't think I'm standing around waiting for you to state your business—you said you were closing the office—very well, I am leaving.

I jump ahead of her to open the door.

"Do you want to go home and let me pick you up in half an hour? Put a suit on under your clothes."

"All right!" But it isn't all right. Her voice is a little too bright.

"Meanwhile I'll go get my car and my suit."

"All right." She is openly grudging. It is not right at all! She is just like Linda.

"I have a better idea. Come on and walk home with me to get my car and then I'll take you to your house."

"All right." A much better all right. "Now you wait right here. This won't take me long."

When she comes out, her eyes are snapping.

"Is everything all right?"

"You mighty right it is"—eyes flashing. Uh oh. The boyfriend has torn it.

"I hope you brought your suit down from Eufala."

"Are you kidding?"

"Why no."

"It's some suit. Just an old piece of a suit. I was going to get me one at Maison Blanche but I didn't think I'd be going swimming in March."

"Do you like to swim?"

"Are you kidding?"

"No."

"I'd rather swim than eat. I really would. Where're we going?"

"To the ocean."

"The ocean! I never knew there was an ocean anywhere around here."

"It's the open Gulf. The same thing."

When I put her in the car, she addresses an imaginary third person. "Now this is what I call real service. Your boss not only lets you off to go swimming—he takes you to the beach."

On these terms we set forth: she the girl whose heart's desire is to swim; I, her generous employer, who is nice enough to provide transportation.

Early afternoon finds us spinning along the Gulf Coast. Things have not gone too badly. As luck would have it, no sooner do we cross Bay St Louis and reach the beach drive than we are involved in an accident. Fortunately it is not serious. When I say as luck would have it, I mean good luck. Yet how, you might wonder, can even a minor accident be considered good luck?

Because it provides a means of winning out over the malaise, if one has the sense to take advantage of it.

What is the malaise? you ask. The malaise is the pain of loss. The world is lost to you, the world and the people in it, and there remains only you and the world and you no more able to be in the world than Banquo's ghost.

You say it is a simple thing surely, all gain and no loss, to pick up a good-looking woman and head for the beach on the first fine day of the year. So say the newspaper poets. Well it is not such a simple thing and if you have ever done it, you know it isn't—unless, of course, the woman happens to be your wife or some other everyday creature so familiar to you that she is as invisible as you yourself. Where there is chance of gain, there is also chance of loss. Whenever one courts great happiness, one also risks malaise.

The car itself is all-important, I have discovered. When I first moved to Gentilly, I bought a new Dodge sedan, a Red Ram Six. It was a comfortable, conservative and economical two-door sedan, just the thing, it seemed to me, for a young Gentilly businessman. When I first slid under the wheel to drive it, it seemed that everything was in order—here was I, a healthy young man, a veteran with all his papers in order, a U.S. citizen driving a very good car. All these things were true enough, yet on my first trip to the Gulf Coast with Marcia, I discovered to my dismay that my fine new Dodge was a regular incubator of malaise. Though it was comfortable enough, though it ran like a clock, though we went spinning along in perfect comfort and with a perfect view of the scenery like the American couple in the Dodge ad, the malaise quickly became suffocating. We sat frozen in a gelid amiability. Our cheeks ached from smiling. Either would have died for the other. In despair I put my hand under her dress, but even such a homely little gesture as that was received with the same fearful politeness. I longed to stop the car and bang my head against the curb. We were free, moreover, to do that or anything else, but instead on we rushed, a little vortex of despair moving through the world like the still eye of a hurricane. As it turned out, I should have stopped and banged my head, for Marcia and I returned to New Orleans defeated by the malaise. It was weeks before we ventured out again.

This is the reason I have no use for cars and prefer buses and streetcars. If I were a Christian I would make a pilgrimage by foot, for this is the best way to travel. But girls do not like it. My little red MG, however, is an exception to the rule. It is a miserable vehicle actually, with not a single virtue save one: it is immune to the malaise. You have no idea what happiness Marcia and I experienced as soon as we found ourselves spinning along the highway in this bright little beetle. We looked at each other in astonishment: the malaise was gone! We sat out in the world, out in the thick summer air between sky and earth. The noise was deafening, the wind was like a hurricane; straight ahead the grains of the concrete rushed at us like mountains.

It was nevertheless with some apprehension that I set out with Sharon. What if the malaise had been abated simply by the novelty of the MG? For by now the MG was no novelty. What if the malaise was different with every girl and needed a different cure? One thing was certain. Here was the acid test. For the stakes were very high. Either very great happiness lay in store for us, or malaise past all conceiving. Marcia and Linda were as nothing to this elfin creature, this sumptuous elf from Eufala who moved like a ballerina, hard-working and docile, dreaming in her work, head to the side, cheek downy and spare as a boy's. With her in the bucket seat beside me I spin along the precipice with the blackest malaise below and the greenest of valleys ahead. One great advantage is mine: her boyfriend, the Faubourg Marigny character. The fellow has no better sense than to make demands on her and she has no use for him. Thank God for the macaroni.

Indeed as we pass through the burning swamps of Chef Menteur, it seems to me that I catch a whiff of the malaise. A little tongue of hellfire licks at our heels and the MG jumps ahead, roaring like a bomber through the sandy pine barrens and across Bay St Louis. Sharon sits smiling and silent, her eyes all but closed against the wind, her big golden knees doubled up against the dashboard. "I swear, this is the cutest little car I ever saw!" she yelled at me a minute ago.

By some schedule of proprieties known to her, she did not become my date until she left her rooming house where she put on a boy's shirt and black knee britches. Her roommate watched us from an upper window. "Wave to Joyce," Sharon commands me. Joyce is leaning on the sill, a brown-haired girl in a leather jacket. She has the voluptuous look of roommates left alone. It becomes necessary to look a third time. Joyce shifts her weight and beyond any doubt a noble young ham hikes up under the buckskin. A sadness overtakes me. If only—If only what? If only I could send Sharon on her way and go straight upstairs and see Joyce, a total stranger? Yes. But not quite. If only I could be with both of them, with a house full of them, an old Esplanade rooming house full of strapping American girls with their silly turned heads and their fine big bottoms. In the last split second I could swear Joyce knows what I am thinking, for she gives me a laughing naughty-you look and her mouth forms oh-*ho*! Sharon comes piling into the car and up against me. Now she can touch me.

"Where is Joyce from?"

"Illinois."

"Is she nice?"

"Joyce is a good old girl."

"She seems to be. Are you all good friends?"

"Are you kidding?"

"No."

"Lordy lord, the crazy talks we have. If people could hear us, they would carry us straight to Tuscaloosa."

"What do you talk about?"

"Everybody."

"Me?"

"Why sure."

"What do you say?"

"Do you really want to know?"

"Yes."

"Well I can tell you one thing, son."

"What's that?"

"You're surely not gon find out from me."

"Why not?"

"Larroes catch medloes."

Out Elysian Fields we go, her warm arm lying over mine. All at once she is free with herself, flouncing around on the seat, bumping knee, hip, elbow against me. She is my date (she reminds me a little of a student nurse I once knew: she is not so starchy now but rather jolly and horsy). The MG jumps away from the stop signs like a young colt. I feel fine.

Yes, she is on to the magic of the little car: we are earthbound as a worm, yet we rush along at a tremendous clip between earth and sky. The heavy fragrant air pushes against us, a square hedge of pyrocantha looms dead ahead, we flash past and all of a sudden there is the Gulf, flat and sparkling away to the south.

We are bowling along below Pass Christian when the accident happens. Just ahead of us a westbound green Ford begins a U-turn, thinks it sees nothing, creeps out and rams me square amidships. Not really hard—it makes a hollow metal bang *b-rramp*! and the MG shies like a spooked steer, jumps into the neutral ground, careens into a drain hole and stops, hissing. My bad shoulder has caught it. I think I pass out for a few seconds, but not before I see two things: Sharon, she is all right; and the people who hit me. It is an old couple. Ohio plates. I swear I almost recognize them. I've seen them in the motels by the hundreds. He is old and lean and fit, with a turkey throat and a baseball cap; she is featureless. They are on their way to Florida. He gives me a single terrified look as we buck over the grass, appeals to his wife for help, hesitates, bolts. Off he goes, bent over his wheel like a jockey.

Sharon hovers over me. She touches my chin as if to get my attention. "Jack?"

The pain in my shoulder was past all imagining but is already better.

"How did you know my name was Jack?"

"Mr Daigle and Mr Hebert call you Jack."

"Are you all right?"

"I think so."

"You look scared."

"Why that crazy fool could have killed us."

The traffic has slowed, to feast their eyes on us. A Negro sprinkling a steep lawn under a summer house puts his hose down altogether and stands gaping. By virtue of our misfortune we have become a thing to look at and witnesses gaze at us with heavy-lidded almost seductive expressions. But almost at once they are past and those who follow see nothing untoward. The Negro picks up his hose. We are restored to the anonymity of our little carspace.

Love is invincible. True, for a second or so the pain carried me beyond all considerations, even that of love, but for no more than a second. Already it has been put to work and is performing yeoman service, a lovely checker in a lovely game.

"But what about you?" Sharon asks, coming close. "Honey, you look awful pale."

"He bumped my shoulder."

"Let me see." She comes around and helps me take off my shirt, but the T-shirt is too high and I can't raise my arm. "Wait." She goes after her Guatemalan bag and finds some cuticle scissors and cuts the sleeve through the neck. I feel her stop.

"That's not—"

"Not what?"

"Not from this wreck."

"Sure."

"You got a handkerchief?" She runs down to the beach to wet it in salt water. "Now. We better find a doctor."

I was shot through the shoulder—a decent wound, as decent as any ever inflicted on Rory Calhoun or Tony Curtis. After all it could have been in the buttocks or genitals—or nose. Decent except that the fragment nicked the apex of my pleura and got me a collapsed lung and a big roaring empyema. No permanent damage, however, except a frightening-looking scar in the hollow of my neck and in certain weather a tender joint.

"Come on now, son, where did you get that?" Cold water runs down my side.

"That Ford."

"Why that's terrible!"

"Can't you tell it's a scar?"

"Where did you get it?"

"My razor slipped."

"Come on now!"

"I got it on the Chongchon River."

"In the war?"

"Yes."

"Oh."

O Tony. O Rory. You never had it so good with direction. Nor even you Bill Holden, my noble Will. O ye morning stars together. Farwell forever, malaise. Farewell and good luck, green Ford and old Ohioan. May you live in Tampa happily and forever.

And yet there are fellows I know who would have been

sorry it happened, who would have had no thought for anything but their damned MG. Blessed MG.

I am able to get out creakily and we sit on the grassy bank. My head spins. That son of a bitch really rocked my shoulder. The MG is not bad: a dented door.

"And right exactly where you were sitting," says Sharon holding the handkerchief to my shoulder. "And that old scoun'l didn't even stop." She squats in her black pants like a five year old and peers at me. "Goll—! Didn't that *hurt*?"

"It was the infection that was bad."

"I'll tell you one dang thing."

"What?"

"I surely wouldn't want anybody shooting at me."

"Do you have an aspirin in your bag?"

"Wait."

When she returns, she gives me the aspirin and holds my ruined shoulder in both hands, as if the aspirin were going to hurt.

"Now look behind the seat and bring me the whisky."

She pours me a thumping drink into a paper cup, also from the Guatemalan bag. The aspirin goes down in the burning. I offer her the bottle.

"I swear I believe I will." She drinks, with hardly a face, hand pressed to the middle of her breastbone. We pull on my shirt by stages.

But the MG! We think of her at the same time. What if she suffered a concussion? But she starts immediately, roaring her defiance of the green Ford.

I forget my whisky bottle and when I get out to pick it up, I nearly fall down. She is right there to catch me, Rory. I put both my arms around her.

"Come on now, son, put your weight on me."

"I will. You're just about the sweetest girl I ever knew."

"Ne'mind that. You come on here, big buddy."

"I'm coming. Where're we going?"

"You sit over here."

112

"Can you drive?"

"You just tell me where to go."

"We'll get some beer, then go to Ship Island."

"In this car?"

"In a boat."

"Where is it?"

"There." Beyond the waters of the sound stretches a long blue smudge of pines.

The boat ride is not what I expected. I had hoped for an empty boat this time of year, a deserted deck where we might stretch out in the sun. Instead we are packed in like sardines. We find ourselves sitting bolt upright on a bench in the one little cabin surrounded by at least a hundred children. It is, we learn, a 4-H excursion from Leake County, Mississippi. A dozen men and women who look like Baptist deacons and deaconesses, red-skinned, gap-toothed, friendly—decent folk they are—are in charge. We sit drenched in the smell of upcountry Mississippi, the smell of warm white skins under boiled cotton underwear. How white they are, these farm children, milk white. No sign of sun here, no red necks; not pale are they but white, the rich damp white of skin under clothes.

Out we go like immigrants in the hold, chuffing through the thin milky waters of Mississippi Sound.

The only other couple on the boat is a Keesler Field airman and his girl. His fine silky hair is cropped short as ermine, but his lip is pulled up by the tendon of his nose showing two chipmunk teeth and giving him a stupid look. The girl is a plump little Mississippi armful, fifteen or sixteen; she too could be a Leake County girl. Though they sit holding hands, they could be strangers. Each stares about the cabin as if he were alone. One knows that they would dance and make love the same way, not really mindful of each other but gazing with a mild abiding astonishment at the world around. Surely I have seen them before too, at the zoo or Marineland, him gazing at the animals or fishes noting every creature with the same slow slack wonderment, her gazing at nothing in particular but not bored either, enduring rather and secure in his engrossment.

We land near the fort, a decrepit brick silo left over from the Civil War and littered with ten summers of yellow Kodak boxes and ticket stubs and bottle caps. It is the soul of dreariness, this "historic site" washed by the thin brackish waters of Mississippi Sound. The debris of summers past piles up like archeological strata. Last summer I picked up a yellow scrap of newspaper and read of a Biloxi election in 1948, and in it I caught the smell of history far more pungently than from the metal marker telling of the French and Spanish two hundred years ago and the Yankees one hundred years ago. 1948. What a far-off time.

A plank walk leads across some mudholes and a salt marsh to an old dance pavilion. As we pass we catch a glimpse of the airman and his girl standing bemused at a counter and drinking RC Cola. Beyond, a rise of sand and saw grass is creased by a rivulet of clear water in which swim blue crabs and cat-eye snails. Over the hillock lies the open sea. The difference is very great: first, this sleazy backwater, then the great blue ocean. The beach is clean and a big surf is rolling in; the water in the middle distance is green and lathered. You come over the hillock and your heart lifts up; your old sad music comes into the major.

We find a hole in the rivulet and sink the cans of beer and go down the beach a ways from the children, to a tussock of sand and grass. Sharon is already in, leaving her shirt and pants on the beach like a rag. She wades out ahead of me, turning to and fro, hands outstretched to the water and sweeping it before her. Now and then she raises her hands to her head as if she were placing a crown and combs back her hair with the last two fingers. The green water foams at her knees and sucks out ankle deep and

114

swirling with sand. Out she goes, thighs asuck, turning slowly and sweeping the water before her. How beautiful she is. She is beautiful and brave and chipper as a sparrow. My throat catches with the sadness of her beauty. Son of a bitch, it is enough to bring tears to your eyes. I don't know what is wrong with me. She smiles at me, then cocks her head.

"Why do you look at me like that?"

"Like what?"

"What's the matter with you?"

"I don't know."

"Come on, son. I'm going to give you some beer."

Her suit is of a black sheeny stuff like a swim-meet suit and skirtless. She comes out of the water like a spaniel, giving her head a flirt which slaps her hair around in a wet curl and stooping, brushes the water from her legs. Now she stands musing on the beach, leg locked, pelvis aslant, thumb and forefingers propped along the iliac crest and lightly, propped lightly as an athlete. As the salt water dries and stings, she minds herself, plying around the flesh of her arm and sending fingers along her back.

Down the beach the children have been roped off into two little herds of girls and boys. They wade—evidently they can't swim—in rough squares shepherded by the deacons who wear black bathing suits with high armholes and carry whistles around their necks. The deaconesses watch from bowers which other children are busy repairing with saw grass they have gathered from the ridge.

We swim again and come back to the tussock and drink beer. She lies back and closes her eyes with a sigh. "This really beats typing." Her arm falls across mine and she gives me an affectionate pat and settles herself in the sand as if she really meant to take a nap. But her eyes gleam between her eyelids and I bend to kiss her. She laughs and kisses me back with a friendly passion. We lie embracing each other.

"Whoa now, son," she says laughing.

"What's the matter?"

"Right here in front of God and everybody?"

"I'm sorry."

"Sorry! Listen, you come here."

"I'm here."

She makes a movement indicating both her friendliness and the limit she sets to it. For an hour we swim and drink beer. Once when she gets up, I come up on my knees and embrace her golden thighs, such a fine strapping armful they are.

"What do you think you're doing, boy?"

"Honey, I've been waiting three weeks to grab you like this."

"Well now that you've grabbed me you can turn me loose."

"Sweetheart, I'll never turn you loose." Mother of all living, what an armful.

"All right now, son—"

"What?"

"You can turn me loose."

"No."

"Listen, big buddy. I'm as strong as you are."

"No, you're not."

"I may not be as big as you are—"

"You are here."

"—but I'm just as strong."

"Not really."

"All right, you watch here." She balls up her fist like a man's and smacks me hard on the arm.

"That hurts."

"All right. I won't mess with you."

"Hit me."

"What?"

"You heard me. Hit me." She holds her elbow tight against her body. "Come on, boy."

"What are you talking about? I'm not going to hit you."

"Come on hit me. I'm not kidding. You can't hurt me."

"All right." I hit her.

"Na. I don't mean just playlike. Really hit me."

"You mean it?"

"I swear before God."

I hit just hard enough to knock her over.

"Got dog." She gets up quickly. "That didn't hurt. I got a good mind to hit you right in the mouth, you jackass."

"I believe you," I say laughing. "Now you come here."

"What for? All right now!" She cocks her fist again. "What do you think you're doing?"

"I just want to tell you what's on my mind."

"What?"

"You. You and your sweet lips. Sweetheart, before God I can't think about anything in the world but putting my arms around you and kissing your sweet lips."

"O me."

"Do you care if I do?"

"I don't care if you do."

I hold springtime in my arms, the fullness of it and the rinsing sadness of it.

"I'll tell you something else."

"What?"

"Sweetheart, I can't get you out of my mind. Not since you walked into my office in that yellow dress. I'm crazy about you and you know it, don't you?"

"O me."

I sit back to see her and take her hands. "I can't sleep for thinking of you."

"You swear?"

"I swear."

"We made us some money, didn't we?"

"We sure did. Don't you want some money? I'll give you five thousand dollars."

"No, I don't want any money."

"Let's go down the beach a ways."

"What for?"

"So they can't see us."

"What's the matter with them seeing us?"

"It's all right with me."

"Ho now, you son."

"You're my sweetheart. Do you care if I love you?"

"Nayo indeed. But you're not getting me off down there with those rattlesnakes."

"Rattlesnakes!"

"No sir. We gon stay right here close to those folks and you gon behave yourself."

"All right." I clasp my hands in the hollow of her back. "I'll tell you something else."

"Uh oh." She rears back, laughing, to see me, a little embarrassed by our closeness. "Well you got me."

"I'm sorry you work for me."

"Sorry! Listen, son. I do my work."

"I wouldn't want you to think I was taking advantage of you."

"Nobody's taking advantage of me," she said huffily.

I laugh at her. "No, I mean our business relationship." We sit up and drink our beer. "I have a confession to make to you. I've been planning this all week."

"What?"

"This picnic."

"Well I be dog."

"Don't kid me. You knew."

"I swear I didn't."

"But it's the business part of it that worries me—"

"Business and pleasure don't have to mix."

"Well, all I wanted you to know was that when I acted on impulse—"

"I always act on impulse. I believe in saying what you mean and meaning what you say."

"I can see that."

"You just ask Joyce what I said about you."

"Joyce?"

"My roommate."

"What did you say?"

"You just ask her."

I look up and down the beach. "I don't see her."

"I don't mean now, you jackass."

We swim and lie down together. The remarkable discovery forces itself upon me that I do not love her so wildly as I loved her last night. But at least there is no malaise and we lie drowsing in the sun, hands clasped in the other's back, until the boat whistle blows.

Yet love revives as we spin homewards along the coast through the early evening. Joy and sadness come by turns, I know now. Beauty and bravery make you sad, Sharon's beauty and my aunt's bravery, and victory breaks your heart. But life goes on and on we go, spinning along the coast in a violet light, past Howard Johnson's and the motels and the children's carnival. We pull into a bay and have a drink under the stars. It is not a bad thing to settle for the Little Way, not the big search for the big happiness but the sad little happiness of drinks and kisses, a good little car and a warm deep thigh.

"My mother has a fishing camp at Bayou des Allemands. Would you like to stop there?"

She nods into my neck. She has become tender toward me and now and then presses my cheek with her hand.

Just west of Pearl River a gravel road leaves the highway and winds south through the marshes. All at once we are in the lonely savannah and the traffic is behind us. Sharon still hides her face in my neck.

A lopsided yellow moon sheds a feeble light over the savannah. Faraway hummocks loom as darkly as a flotilla of ships. Awkwardly we walk over and into the marsh and along the boardwalk. Sharon cleaves to me as if, in staying close, she might not see me.

I cannot believe my eyes. It is difficult to understand. We round a hummock and there is the camp ablaze like the *Titanic*. The Smiths are home.

2. MY HALF BROTHERS AND SISTERS ARE EATING CRABS at a sawbuck table on the screened porch. The carcasses mount toward a naked light bulb.

They blink at me and at each other. Suddenly they feel the need of a grown-up. A grown-up must certify that they are correct in thinking that they see me. They all, every last one, look frantically for their mother. Thérèse runs to the kitchen doorway.

"Mother! Jack is here!" She holds her breath and watches her mother's face. She is rewarded. "Yes, Jack!"

"Jean-Paul ate some lungs." Mathilde looks up from directly under my chin.

My half brother Jean-Paul, the son of my mother, is a big fat yellow baby piled up like a Buddha in his baby chair, smeared with crab paste and brandishing a scarlet claw. The twins goggle at us but do not leave off eating.

Lonnie has gone into a fit of excitement in his wheelchair. His hand curls upon itself. I kiss him first and his smile starts his head turning away in a long trembling torticollis. He is fourteen and small for his age, smaller than Clare and Donice, the ten-year-old twins. But since last summer when Duval, the oldest son, was drowned, he has been the "big boy." His dark red hair is nearly always combed wet and his face is handsome and pure when it is not contorted. He is my favorite, to tell the truth. Like me, he is a moviegoer. He will go see anything. But we are good friends because he knows I do not feel sorry for him. For one thing, he has the gift of believing that he can offer his sufferings in reparation for men's indifference to the pierced heart of Jesus Christ. For another thing, I

120

would not mind so much trading places with him. His life is a serene business.

My mother is drying her hands on a dishcloth.

"Well well, look who's here," she says but does not look.

Her hands dry, she rubs her nose vigorously with her three middle fingers held straight up. She has hay fever and crabs make it worse. It is a sound too well known to me to be remembered, this quick jiggle up and down and the little wet wringing noises under her fingers.

We give each other a kiss or rather we press our cheeks together, Mother embracing my head with her wrist as if her hands were still wet. Sometimes I feel a son's love for her, or something like this, and try to give her a special greeting, but at these times she avoids my eye and gives me her cheek and calls on me to notice this about Mathilde or that about Thérèse.

"Mother, I want you to meet Sharon Kincaid."

"Well now!" cries Mother, turning away and inserting herself among the children, not because she has anything against Sharon but because she feels threatened by the role of hostess. "There is nobody here but us children," she is saying.

Sharon is in the best of humors, rounding her eyes and laughing so infectiously that I wonder if she is not laughing at me. From the beginning she is natural with the children. Linda, I remember, was nervous and shifted from one foot to the other and looked over their heads, her face gone heavy as a pudding. Marcia made too much over them, squatting down and hugging her knees like Joan Fontaine visiting an orphanage.

Mother does not ask how I happen to be here or give a sign that my appearance is in any way remarkable—though I have not seen them for six months. "Tessie, tell Jack about your class's bus trip." —and she makes her escape to the kitchen. After a while her domesticity will begin to get on my nerves. By the surest of instincts she steers clear of all that is exceptional or "stimulating." Any event or idea which does not fall within the household regimen, she stamps at once with her own brand of the familiar. If, as a student, I happened to get excited about Jackson's Valley Campaign or Freud's *Interpretation of Dreams*, it was not her way to oppose me. She approved it as a kind of wondrous Rover boy eccentricity: "Those? Oh those are Jack's books. The stacks and stacks of books that boy brings home! Jack, do you know everything in those books?" "No'm." Nevertheless I became Dick Rover, the serious-minded Rover boy.

It is good to see the Smiths at their fishing camp. But not at their home in Biloxi. Five minutes in that narrow old house and dreariness sets into the marrow of my bones. The gas logs strike against the eyeballs, the smell of two thousand Sunday dinners clings to the curtains, voices echo round and round the bare stairwell, a dismal Sacred Heart forever points to itself above the chipped enamel mantelpiece. Everything is white and chipped. The floors, worn powdery, tickle the nostrils like a schoolroom. But here on Bayou des Allemands everybody feels the difference. Water laps against the piling. The splintered boards have secret memories of winter, the long dreaming nights and days when no one came and the fish jumped out of the black water and not a soul in sight in the whole savannah; secrets the children must find out and so after supper they are back at their exploring, running in a gang from one corner to another. Donice shows me a muskrat trap he had left last August and wonder of wonders found again. They only came down this morning, Mother explains, such a fine day it was, and since the children have a holiday Monday, will stay through Mardi Gras if the weather holds. With Roy away, Mother is a member of the gang. Ten minutes she will spend in the kitchen working with her swift cat-efficiency, then out and away with the children, surging to and fro in their light inconstant play, her eyes fading in a fond infected look.

Thérèse is telling about her plans to write her Congressman about the Rivers and Harbors bill. Thérèse and Mathilde are something like Joan and Jane in the Civics reader.

"Isn't that Tessie a *case*?" my mother cries as she disappears into the kitchen, signifying that Tessie is smart but also that there is something funny about her precocity.

"Where's Roy? We didn't see a car. We almost didn't walk over."

"Playing poker!" they all cry. This seems funny and everybody laughs. Lonnie's hand curls. If our arrival had caused any confusion, we are carried quickly past by the strong current of family life.

"Do you have any more crabs, Mother?"

"Any more crabs! Ask Lonnie if we weren't just wondering what to do with the rest. You haven't had your supper?"

"No'm."

Mother folds up the thick layer of newspaper under the crab carcasses, making a neat bundle with her strong white hands. The whole mess comes away leaving the table dry and clean. Thérèse spreads fresh paper and Mathilde fetches two cold bottles of beer and two empty bottles for hammering the claws and presently we have a tray apiece, two small armies of scarlet crabs marching in neat rows. Sharon looks queer but she pitches in anyhow and soon everybody is making fun of her. Mathilde shows her how to pry off the belly plate and break the corner at the great claw so that the snowy flesh pops out in a fascicle. Sharon affects to be amazed and immediately the twins must show her how to suck the claws.

Outside is the special close blackness of night over water. Bugs dive into the tight new screen and bounce off with a guitar thrum. The children stand in close, feeling the mystery of the swamp and the secrecy of our cone of light. Clairain presses his stomach against the arm of my chair. Lonnie tries to tune his transistor radio; he holds it in the crook of his wrist, his hands bent back upon it.

Once his lip falls open in the most ferocious leer. This upsets Sharon. It seems to her that a crisis is at hand, that Lonnie has at last reached the limit of his endurance. When no one pays any attention to him, she grows fidgety—why doesn't somebody help him?—then, after an eternity, Mathilde leans over carelessly and tunes in a station loud and clear. Lonnie turns his head, weaving, to see her, but not quite far enough.

Lonnie is dressed up, I notice. It turns out that Aunt Ethel, Roy's sister, was supposed to take him and the girls to a movie. It was not a real date, Mother reminds him, but Lonnie looks disappointed.

"What is the movie?" I ask him.

"*Fort Dobbs*." His speech is crooning but not hard to understand.

"Where is it?"

"At the Moonlite."

"Let's go."

Lonnie's head teeters and falls back like a dead man's.

"I mean it. I want to see it."

He believes me.

I corner my mother in the kitchen.

"What's the matter with Lonnie?"

"Why nothing."

"He looks terrible."

"That child won't drink his milk!" sings out my mother.

"Has he had pneumonia again?"

"He had the five day virus. And it was bad bad bad bad bad. Did you ever hear of anyone with virus receiving extreme unction?"

"Why didn't you call me?"

"He wasn't in danger of death. The extreme unction was his idea. He said it would strengthen him physically as well as spiritually. Have you ever heard of that?"

"Yes. But is he all right now?"

She shrugs. My mother speaks of such matters in a light

allusive way, with the overtones neither of belief nor disbelief but rather of a general receptivity to lore.

"Dr Murtag said he'd never seen anything like it. Lonnie got out of bed in half an hour."

Sometimes when she mentions God, it strikes me that my mother uses him as but one of the devices that come to hand in an outrageous man's world, to be put to work like all the rest in the one enterprise she has any use for: the canny management of the shocks of life. It is a bargain struck at the very beginning in which she settled for a general belittlement of everything, the good and the bad. She is as wary of good fortune as she is immured against the bad, and sometimes I seem to catch sight of it in her eyes, this radical mistrust: an old knowledgeable gleam, as old and sly as Eve herself. Losing Duval, her favorite, confirmed her in her election of the ordinary. No more heart's desire for her, thank you. After Duval's death she has wanted everything colloquial and easy, even God.

"But now do you know what he wants to do? Fast and abstain during Lent." Her eyes narrow. Here is the outrage. "He weighs eighty pounds and he has one foot in the grave and he wants to fast." She tells it as a malignant joke on Lonnie and God. For a second she is old Eve herself.

Fort Dobbs is good. The Moonlite Drive-In is itself very fine. It does not seem too successful and has the look of the lonesome pine country behind the Coast. Gnats swim in the projection light and the screen shimmers in the sweet heavy air. But in the movie we are in the desert. There under the black sky rides Clint Walker alone. He is a solitary sort and a wanderer. Lonnie is very happy. Thérèse and Mathilde, who rode the tops of the seats, move to the bench under the projector and eat snowballs. Lonnie likes to sit on the hood and lean back against the windshield and look around at me when a part comes he knows we both like. Sharon is happy too. She thinks I am a nice fellow to take Lonnie to the movies like this. She thinks I am being unselfish. By heaven she is just like the girls in the movies who won't put out until you prove to them what a nice unselfish fellow you are, a lover of children and dogs. She holds my hand on her knee and gives it a squeeze from time to time.

Clint Walker rides over the badlands, up a butte, and stops. He dismounts, squats, sucks a piece of mesquite and studies the terrain. A few decrepit buildings huddle down there in the canyon. We know nothing of him, where he comes from or where he goes.

A good night: Lonnie happy (he looks around at me with the liveliest sense of the secret between us; the secret is that Sharon is not and never will be onto the little touches we see in the movie and, in the seeing, know that the other sees—as when Clint Walker tells the saddle tramp in the softest easiest old Virginian voice: "Mister, I don't believe I'd do that if I was you"—Lonnie is beside himself, doesn't know whether to watch Clint Walker or me), this ghost of a theater, a warm Southern night, the Western Desert and this fine big sweet piece, Sharon.

A good rotation. A rotation I define as the experiencing of the new beyond the expectation of the experiencing of the new. For example, taking one's first trip to Taxco would not be a rotation, or no more than a very ordinary rotation; but getting lost on the way and discovering a hidden valley would be.

The only other rotation I can recall which was possibly superior was a movie I saw before the war called *Dark Waters*. I saw it in Lafitte down on Bayou Barataria. In the movie Thomas Mitchell and Merle Oberon live in a decaying mansion in a Louisiana swamp. One night they drive into the village—to see a movie! A repetition within a rotation. I was nearly beside myself with rotatory emotion. But *Fort Dobbs* is as good as can be. My heart sings like Octavian and there is great happiness between me and

Lonnie and this noble girl and they both know it and have the sense to say nothing.

3. THREE O'CLOCK AND SUDDENLY AWAKE AMID THE smell of dreams and of the years come back and peopled and blown away again like smoke. A young man am I, twenty-nine, but I am as full of dreams as an ancient. At night the years come back and perch around my bed like ghosts.

My mother made up a cot in my corner of the porch. It is a good place, with the swamp all around and the piles stirring with every lap of water.

But, good as it is, my old place is used up (places get used up by rotatory and repetitive use) and when I awake, I awake in the grip of everydayness. Everydayness is the enemy. No search is possible. Perhaps there was a time when everydayness was not too strong and one could break its grip by brute strength. Now nothing breaks it—but disaster. Only once in my life was the grip of everydayness broken: when I lay bleeding in a ditch.

In a sudden rage and, as if I had been seized by a fit, I roll over and fall in a heap on the floor and lie shivering on the boards, worse off than the miserablest muskrat in the swamp. Nevertheless I vow: I'm a son of a bitch if I'll be defeated by the everydayness.

(The everydayness is everywhere now, having begun in the cities and seeking out the remotest nooks and corners of the countryside, even the swamps.)

For minutes at a stretch I lie rigid as a stick and breathe the black exhalation of the swamp.

Neither my mother's family nor my father's family understands my search.

My mother's family thinks I have lost my faith and they pray for me to recover it. I don't know what they're talking about. Other people, so I have read, are pious as children and later become skeptical (or, as they say on "This I Believe": "In time I outgrew the creeds and dogmas of organized religion"). Not I. My unbelief was invincible from the beginning. I could never make head or tail of God. The proofs of God's existence may have been true for all I know, but it didn't make the slightest difference. If God himself had appeared to me, it would have changed nothing. In fact, I have only to hear the word God and a curtain comes down in my head.

My father's family thinks that the world makes sense without God and that anyone but an idiot knows what the good life is and anyone but a scoundrel can lead it.

I don't know what either of them are talking about. Really I can't make head or tail of it. The best I can do is lie rigid as a stick under the cot, locked in a death grip with every-dayness, sworn not to move a muscle until I advance another inch in my search. The swamp exhales beneath me and across the bayou a night bittern pumps away like a diesel. At last the iron grip relaxes and I pull my pants off the chair, fish out a notebook and scribble in the dark:

REMEMBER TOMORROW
Starting point for search:

It no longer avails to start with creatures and prove God.

Yet it is impossible to rule God out.

The only possible starting point: the strange fact of one's own invincible apathy—that if the proofs were proved and God presented himself, nothing would be changed. Here is the strangest fact of all.

Abraham saw signs of God and believed. Now the only sign is that all the signs in the world make no difference. Is this God's ironic revenge? But I am onto him.

4. *CHEPPITY CHEPPITY CHEP CHEP. CHEP. SILENCE. Cheppity chep chep. Chep.*

It starts as an evil turn of events. There is a sense of urgency. Something has to be done. Let us please do something about it. Then it is a color, a very bad color that needs tending to. Then a pain. But there is no use: it is a sound and it is out there in the world and nothing can be done about it. Awake.

Cheppity cheppity chep chep. Chep. Silence.

"Shtfire and save matches."

Not ten feet below, two men try to start an outboard motor clamped to a handsome blue hull. The boat drifts into a miniature dock, knocks. The world is milk: sky, water, savannah. The thin etherlike water vaporizes; tendrils of fog gather like smoke; a white shaft lies straight as a ruler over the marsh.

"Why don't you tighten up on your needle valve?"

"Why don't you kiss my ass?"

The voices sound reedy and old in the wan white world. One of them must be my stepfather, Roy Smith. Yes, the helmsman. The green visor of his hat covers his face, all but a lip heavy with anger, but I recognize his arms. The muscle curves out far beyond the dimple of the elbow; his forearms are like little hams. Black-burnished hair sprouts through the links of his watchband. He sits embracing the red cowl of the motor, his abdomen strong and heavy between his legs.

Roy leans back, poises, pulls the rope with a short powerful chop. It catches with a throaty roar and this changes everything. The pleasant man in the bow is taken by surprise and knocked off balance as the boat skews against the dock. But now the boat seeks open water and the fishermen sit quickly about and settle themselves, their faces serene now and full of hope. Roy Smith is seen to be a cheerful florid man, heavy-set but still youngish. The water of the bayou boils up like tea and disgorges bubbles of smoke. The hull disappears into a white middle distance and the sound goes suddenly small as if the boat had run into cotton.

A deformed live oak emerges from the whiteness, stands up in the air, like a tree in a Chinese print. Minutes pass. An egret lets down on his light stiff wings and cocks one eye at the water. Behind me the screen door opens softly and my mother comes out on the dock with a casting rod. She props the rod against the rail, puts down a wax-paper bundle, scratches both arms under the sleeves and looks about her, yawning. "Hinh-honh," she says in a yawn-sigh as wan and white as the morning. Her blouse is one of Roy's army shirts and not much too big for her large breasts. She wears blue Keds and ladies' denims with a flyless front pulled high over her bulky hips. With her baseball cap pressed down over her wiry hair she looks like the women you see fishing from highway bridges.

Mother undoes the bundle, takes out a scout knife and pries loose the frozen shrimp. She chops off neat pink cubes, slides them along the rail with her blade, stopping now and then to jiggle her nose and clear her throat with the old music. To make sure of having room, she goes out to the end of the dock, lays back her arm to measure, and casts in a big looping straight-arm swing, a clumsy yet practiced movement that ends with her wrists bent in, in a womanish angle. The reel sings and the lead sails far and wide with its gyrating shrimp and lands with hardly a splash in the light etherish water. Mother holds still for a second, listening intently as if she meant to learn what the fishes thought of it, and reels in slowly, twitching the rod from time to time.

I pull on my pants and walk out barefoot on the dock. The sun has cleared the savannah but it is still a cool milky world. Only the silvery wood is warm and raspy underfoot.

"Isn't it mighty early for you!" Her voice is a tinkle over the water.

My mother is easy and affectionate with me. Now we may speak together. It is the early morning and our isolation in the great white marsh.

"Can I fix you some breakfast?"

"No'm. I'm not hungry." Our voices go ringing around the empty room of the morning.

Still she puts me off. I am only doing a little fishing and it is like any other day, she as much as says to me, so let us not make anything remarkable out of it. She veers away from intimacy. I marvel at her sure instinct for the ordinary. But perhaps she knows what she is doing.

"I *wish* I had known you were going to get up so early," she says indignantly. "You could have gone over to the Rigolets with Roy and Kinsey. The reds are running."

"I saw them."

"Why didn't you go!"—in the ultimate measure of astonishment.

"You know I don't like to fish."

"I had another rod!"

"It's just as well."

"That's true," she says after a while. "You never did. You're just like your father." She gives me a swift look, which is unusual for her. "I noticed last night how much you favor him." She casts again and again holds still.

"He didn't like to fish?"

"He thought he did!"

I stretch out at full length, prop my head on a two-by-four. It is possible to squint into the rising sun and at the same time see my mother spangled in rainbows. A crab spider has built his web across a finger of the bayou and the strands seem to spin in the sunlight.

"But he didn't really?"

"Unh un—" she says, dragging it out to make up for her inattention. Every now and then she wedges the rod between her stomach and the rail and gives her nose a good wringing.

"Why didn't he?"

"Because he didn't. He would say he did. And once he did! I remember one day we went down Little Bayou Sara. He had been sick and Dr Wills told him to work in the morning and take off in the afternoons and take up fishing or an interesting hobby. It was the prettiest day, I remember, and we found a hole under a fallen willow—a good place for *sac au lait* if I saw one. So I said, go ahead, drop your line right there. Through the *tree*? he said. He thought it was a lot of humbug—he wasn't much of a fisherman; Dr Wills and Judge Anse were big hunters and fishermen and he pretended he liked it but he didn't. So I said, go ahead, right down through the leaves—that's the way you catch *sac au lait*. I be John Brown if he didn't pull up the fattest finest *sac au lait* you ever saw. He couldn't believe his eyes. Oh he got himself all wound up about it. Now isn't this an ideal spot, he would say over and over again, and: Look at such and such a tree over there, look how the sunshine catches the water in such and such a way—we'll have to come back tomorrow and the next day and all summer—that's all we have to do!" My mother gives her rod a great spastic jerk, reels in quickly and frowns at the mangled shrimp. "Do you see what that scoun'l beast—! Do you know that that ain't anything in the world but some old hardhead sitting right on the bottom."

"Did he go back the next day?"

"Th. No indeed. No, in, deed," she says, carving three cubes of shrimp. Again she lays back her arm. The shrimp gyrates and Mother holds still. "What do you think he says when I mention *sac au lait* the next morning?"

"What?"

" 'Oh no. Oh no. You go ahead.' And off he goes on his famous walk."

"Walk?"

"Up the levee. Five miles, ten miles, fifteen miles. Winter or summer. I went with him one Christmas morning I remember. Mile after mile and all of it just the same. Same old brown levee in front, brown river on one side, brown fields on the other. So when he got about a half a mile ahead of me, I said, shoot. What am I doing out here humping along for all I'm worth when all we going to do is turn around and hump on back? So I said, good-by, Mister, I'm going home—you can walk all the way to Natchez if you want to." It is my mother's way to see life, past and present, in terms of a standard comic exaggeration. If she had spent four years in Buchenwald, she would recollect it so: "So I said to him: listen, Mister, if you think I'm going to eat this stuff, you've got another think coming."

The boards of the dock, warming in the sun, begin to give off a piney-winey smell. The last tendril of ground fog burns away, leaving the water black as tea. The tree is solitary and mournful, a poor thing after all. Across the bayou the egret humps over, as peaked and disheveled as a buzzard.

"Was he a good husband?" Sometimes I try, not too seriously, to shake her loose from her elected career of the commonplace. But her gyroscope always holds her on course.

"Good? Well I'll tell you one thing—he was a good walker!"

"Was he a good doctor?"

"Was he! And what hands! If anyone ever had the hands of a surgeon, he did." My mother's recollection of my father is storied and of a piece. It is not him she remem-

133

bers but an old emblem of him. But now something occurs to her. "He was smart, but he didn't know it all! I taught him a thing or two once and I can tell you he thanked me for it."

"What was that?"

"He had lost thirty pounds. He wasn't sick—he just couldn't keep anything down. Dr Wills said it was amoeba (that year he thought everything was amoeba; another year it was endometritis and between you and me he took out just about every uterus in Feliciana Parish). At the breakfast table when Mercer brought in his eggs and grits, he would just sit there looking at it, white as a sheet. Me, it was all I could do not to eat, my breakfast and his. He'd put a mouthful of grits in his mouth and chew and chew and he just couldn't swallow it. So one day I got an idea. I said listen: you sat up all night reading a book, didn't you? Yes, I did, he said, what of it? You enjoyed it, didn't you? Yes, I did. So I said: all right. Then we'll read it. The next morning I told Mercer to go on about his business. I had my breakfast early and I made his and brought it to him right there in his bed. I got his book. I remember it—it was a book called *The Greene Murder Case*. Everybody in the family read it. I began to read and he began to listen, and while I read, I fed him. I told him, I said, you can eat, and I fed him. I put the food in his mouth and he ate it. I fed him for six months and he gained twenty-five pounds. And he went back to work. Even when he ate by himself downstairs, I had to read to him. He would get downright mad at me if I stopped. 'Well go on!' he would say."

I sit up and shade my eyes to see her.

Mother wrings her nose. "It was because—"

"Because of what?" I spit over into the water. The spit unwinds like a string.

She leans on the rail and gazes down into the tea-colored bayou. "It was like he thought eating was not—

important enough. You see, with your father, everything, every second had to be—"

"Be what, Mother?"

This time she gives a real French shrug. "I don't know. Something."

"What was wrong with him?"

"He was overwrought," she replies at once and in her regular mama-bee drone and again my father disappears into the old emblem. I can hear echoes of my grandfather and grandmother and Aunt Emily, echoes of porch talk on the long summer evenings when affairs were settled, mysteries solved, the unnamed named. My mother never got used to our porch talk with its peculiar license. When someone made a spiel, one of our somber epic porch spiels, she would strain forward in the dark, trying to make out the face of the speaker and judge whether he meant to be taken as somberly as he sounded. As a Bolling in Feliciana Parish, I became accustomed to sitting on the porch in the dark and talking of the size of the universe and the treachery of men; as a Smith on the Gulf Coast I have become accustomed to eating crabs and drinking beer under a hundred and fifty watt bulb—and one is as pleasant a way as the other of passing a summer night.

"How was he overwrought?"

She plucks the hook clean, picks up a pink cube, pushes the barb through, out, and in again. Her wrists are rounded, not like a young girl's but by a deposit of hard fat.

"It was his psychological make-up."

Yes, it is true. We used to talk quite a bit about psychological make-ups and the effect of glands on our dismal dark behavior. Strangely, my mother sounds more like my aunt than my aunt herself. Aunt Emily no longer talks of psychological make-ups.

"His nervous system was like a high-powered radio. Do you know what happens if you turn up the volume and tune into WWL?"

"Yes," I say, unspeakably depressed by the recollection of the sad little analogies doctors like to use. "You mean he wasn't really cut out to be an ordinary doctor, he really should have been in research."

"That's right!" My mother looks over in surprise, but not much surprise, then sends her lead off like a shot. "Now Mister—!" she addresses an unknown fish and when he does not respond, falls to musing. "It's peculiar though. You're so much like your father and yet so different. You know, you've got a little of my papa in you—you're easy-going and you like to eat and you like the girls."

"I don't like to fish."

"You're too lazy, if you ask me. Anyhow, Papa was not a fisherman, as I have told you before. He owned a fleet of trawlers at Golden Meadow. But did he love pretty girls. Till his dying day."

"Does it last that long?"

"Anh anh anh anh anh!" In the scandal of it, Mother presses her chin into her throat, but she does not leave off watching her float. "Don't you get risque with me! This is your mother you're talking to and not one of your little hotsy-totsies."

"Hotsy-totsies!"

"Yes."

"Don't you like Sharon?"

"Why yes. But she's not the one for you." For years my mother has thrown it out as a kind of proverb that I should marry Kate Cutrer, though actually she has also made an emblem out of Kate and does not know her at all. "But do you know a funny thing?"

"What?"

"It's not you but Mathilde who is moody like your father. Sister Regina says she is another Alice Eberle."

"Who is Alice Eberle?"

"You know, the Biloxi girl who won the audition with Horace Heidt and His Musical Knights."

"Oh."

Mother trills in her throat with the old music. I squint up at her through the rainbows.

"But when he got sick the next time, I couldn't help him."

"Why not?"

She smiles. "He said my treatment was like horse serum: you can only use it once."

"What did happen?"

"The war came."

"That helped?"

"He helped himself. He had been in bed for a month, up in your room—you were off at school. He wouldn't go to the clinic, he wouldn't eat, he wouldn't go fishing, he wouldn't read. He'd just lie there and watch the ceiling fan. Once in a while he would walk down to the Chinaman's at night and eat a po-boy. That was the only way he could eat—walk down to the Chinaman's at midnight and eat a po-boy. That morning I left him upstairs as usual. I sent Mercer up with his paper and his tray and called Clarence Saunders. Ten minutes later I look up and here he comes down the steps, all dressed up. He sits himself down at the dining room table as if nothing had happened, orders breakfast and eats enough to kill a horse—all the while reading his paper and not even knowing he was eating. I ask him what has happened. What has happened! Why, Germany has invaded Poland, and England and France have declared war! I'm here to tell you that in thirty minutes he had eaten his breakfast, packed a suitcase and gone to New Orleans."

"What for?"

"To see the Canadian consul."

"Yes, I remember him going to Windsor, Ontario."

"That was two months later. He gained thirty pounds in two months."

"What was he so excited about?"

"He knew what it meant! He told us all at supper: this

is it. We're going to be in it sooner or later. We should be in it now. And I'm not waiting. They were all so proud of him—and especially Miz Cutrer. And when he came home that spring in his blue uniform and the gold wings of a flight surgeon, I swear he was the best-looking man I ever saw in my life. And so—cute! We had the best time.''

Sure he was cute. He had found a way to do both: to please them and please himself. To leave. To do what he wanted to do and save old England doing it. And perhaps even carry off the grandest coup of all: to die. To win the big prize for them and for himself (but not even he dreamed he would succeed not only in dying but in dying in Crete in the wine dark sea).

''Then before that he was lazy too.''

''He was not!''

''It is not laziness, Mother. Partly but not all. I'll tell you a strange thing. During the war a bad thing happened to me. We were retreating from the Chongchon River. We had stopped the Chinese by setting fire to the grass with tracer bullets. What was left of a Ranger company was supposed to be right behind us. Or rather we thought we were retreating, because we got ambushed on the line of retreat and had to back off and head west. I was supposed to go back to the crossroad and tell the Ranger company about the change. I got back there and waited half an hour and got so cold I went to sleep. When I woke up it was daylight.''

''And you didn't know whether the Rangers had come by or not?''

''That wasn't it. For a long time I couldn't remember anything. All I knew was that something was terribly wrong.''

''Had the Rangers gone by during the night?'' asks my mother, smiling and confident that I had played a creditable role.

''Well no, but that's not—''

''What happened to them?''

138

"They got cut off."

"You mean they were all killed?"

"There wasn't much left to them in the first place."

"What a terrible thing. We'll never know what you boys went through. But at least your conscience was clear."

"It was not my conscience that bothered me. What I am trying to tell you is that nothing seemed worth doing except something I couldn't even remember. If somebody had come up to me and said: if you will forget your preoccupation for forty minutes and get to work, I can assure you that you will find the cure of cancer and compose the greatest of all symphonies—I wouldn't have been interested. Do you know why? Because it wasn't good enough for me."

"That's selfish."

"I know."

"I'll tell you one thing. If they put me up there and said, Anna, you hold your ground and start shooting, you know what I would do?"

"What?"

"I'd be long gone for the rear."

I summon up the vision of my mother in headlong retreat before the Chinese and I have to laugh.

"We'll never know what it was like though," Mother adds, but she is not paying much attention, to tell the truth. I really have to laugh at her. She kneads a pink cube so the fish can smell it. "You know what, Jack?" Her eyes brim with fondness, a fondness carefully guarded against the personal, the heartfelt, a fondness deliberately rendered trite. "It's funny you should mention that. Believe it or not, Roy and I were talking the other day and Roy, not me, said you would be wonderful in something like that."

"Like what?"

"Cancer research."

"Oh."

Fishing is poor. The egret pumps himself up into the

air and rows by so close I can hear the gristle creak in his wings.

5. AFTER BREAKFAST THERE IS A COMMOTION ABOUT Mass. The Smiths, except Lonnie, would never dream of speaking of religion—raising the subject provokes in them the acutest embarrassment: eyes are averted, throats are cleared, and there occurs a murmuring for a minute or two until the subject can be changed. But I have heard them argue forty-five minutes about the mechanics of going to Mass and with all the ardor of relief, as if in debating the merits of the nine o'clock Mass in Biloxi as against the ten thirty in Bay St Louis they were indeed discussing religion and who can say they weren't? But perhaps they are right: certainly if they spoke to me of God, I would jump in the bayou.

I suggest to Roy Smith, who has just returned from the Rigolets, that Sharon and I stay home and mind Jean-Paul. "Oh no," says my mother under drooping lids. "Jean-Paul can go. We'll all go. Sharon's going too, aren't you, Sharon?" Sharon laughs and says she will. They've been talking together.

The church, an old one in the rear of Biloxi, looks like a post office. It is an official-looking place. The steps are trodden into scallops; the brass rail and doorplate are worn bright as gold from hard use. We arrive early so Lonnie can be rolled to a special place next to a column. By the time Mass begins we are packed in like sardines. A woman comes up the aisle, leans over and looks down our pew. She gives me an especially hard look. I do not budge. It is like the subway. Roy Smith, who got home just in time to change to a clean perforated shirt, gives up his seat to a little girl and kneels in the aisle with several other men, kneels on one knee like a tackle, elbow propped on his upright knee, hands clasped sideways. His face is dark with blood, his breath whistles in his nose as he studies the chips in the terrazzo floor.

Sharon is good: she has a sweet catholic wonder peculiar to a certain type of Protestant girl—once she is put at her ease by the heroic unreligiousness of the Smiths (what are they doing here? she thinks); she gazes about yellow-eyed. (She thinks: how odd they all are, and him too—all that commotion about getting here and now that they are here, it is as if it were over before it began—each has lapsed into his own blank-eyed vacancy and the priest has turned his back.)

When the bell rings for communion, Roy gets heavily to his feet and pilots Lonnie to the end of the rail. All I can see of Lonnie is a weaving tuft of red hair. When the priest comes to him, Roy holds a hand against Lonnie's face to steady him. He does this in a frowning perfunctory way, eyes light as an eagle's.

6. THE WOMEN ARE IN THE KITCHEN, MY MOTHER cleaning redfish and Sharon sitting at a window with a lapful of snap beans. The board sash opens out over the swamp where a flock of redwings rattle like gourds and ride down the cattails, wings sprung out to show their scarlet epaulets. Jean-Paul swings over the floor, swiveling around on his fat hip, his sharklike flesh whispering over the rough boards, and puts his finger into the cracks to get at the lapping water. There comes to me on the porch the voices of the morning, the quarreling late eleven o'clock sound of the redwings and the talk of the women, easy in its silences, come together, not in their likenesses (for how different they are: Sharon's studied upcountry exclamations—"I surely didn't know people ate crawfish!"—by which she means that in Eufala only Negroes eat crawfish; and my mother's steady catarrhal hum—"If Roy wants bisque this year, he'd better buy it—do you know how long it takes to make bisque?") but come together rather in their womanness and under the easy dispensation of the kitchen.

The children are skiing with Roy. The blue boat rides up and down the bayou, opening the black water like a knife. The gear piled at the end of the dock, yellow nylon rope and crimson lifebelt, makes aching phosphor colors in the sunlight.

Lonnie finds me and comes bumping his chair into my cot. On Sundays he wears his suit and his snap-brim felt hat. He has taken off his coat but his tie is still knotted tightly and fastened by a chain-and-bar clasp. When Lonnie gets dressed up, he looks like a little redneck come to a wedding.

"Do you want to renew your subscriptions?"

"I might. How many points do you have?"

"A hundred and fourteen."

"Doesn't that make you first?"

"Yes, but it doesn't mean I'll stay first."

"How much?"

"Twelve dollars, but you don't have to renew."

The clouds roll up from Chandeleur Island. They hardly seem to move, but their shadows come racing across the grass like a dark wind. Lonnie has trouble looking at me. He tries to even his eyes with mine and this sets his head weaving. I sit up.

Lonnie takes the money in his pronged fingers and sets about putting it into his wallet, a bulky affair with an album of plastic envelopes filled with holy cards.

"What is first prize this year?"

"A Zenith Trans-World."

"But you have a radio."

"Standard band." Lonnie gazes at me. The blue stare holds converse, has its sentences and periods. "If I get the Zenith, I won't miss television so much."

"I would reconsider that. You get a great deal of pleasure from television."

Lonnie appears to reconsider. But he is really enjoying the talk. A smile plays at the corner of his mouth. Lonnie's monotonous speech gives him an advantage, the same advantage foreigners have: his words are not worn out. It is like a code tapped through a wall. Sometimes he asks me straight out: do you love me? and it is possible to tap back: yes, I love you.

"Moreover, I do not think you should fast," I tell him.

"Why not?"

"You've had pneumonia twice in the past year. It would not be good for you. I doubt if your confessor would allow it. Ask him."

"He is allowing it."

"On what grounds?"

"To conquer an habitual disposition." Lonnie uses the peculiar idiom of the catechism in ordinary speech. Once he told me I needn't worry about some piece of foolishness he heard me tell Linda, since it was not a malicious lie but rather a "jocose lie."

"What disposition is that?"

"A disposition to envy."

"Envy who?"

"Duval."

"Duval is dead."

"Yes. But envy is not merely sorrow at another's good fortune: it is also joy at another's misfortune."

"Are you still worried about that? You accused yourself and received absolution, didn't you?"

"Yes."

"Then don't be scrupulous."

"I'm not scrupulous."

"Then what's the trouble?"

"I'm still glad he's dead."

"Why shouldn't you be? He sees God face to face and you don't."

Lonnie grins at me with the liveliest sense of our complicity: let them ski all they want to. We have something better. His expression is complex. He knows that I have entered the argument as a game played by his rules and he knows that I know it, but he does not mind.

"Jack, do you remember the time Duval went to the field meet in Jackson and won first in American history and the next day made all-state guard?"

"Yes."

"I hoped he would lose."

"That's not hurting Duval."

"It is hurting me. You know what capital sin does to the life of the soul."

"Yes. Still and all I would not fast. Instead I would concentrate on the Eucharist. It seems a more positive thing to do."

"That is true." Again the blue eyes engage mine in lively converse, looking, looking away, and looking again. "But Eucharist is a sacrament of the living."

"You don't wish to live?"

"Oh sure!" he says laughing, willing, wishing even, to lose the argument so that I will be sure to have as much fun as he.

It is a day for clouds. The clouds come sailing by, swelled out like clippers. The creamy vapor boils up into great thundering ranges and steep valleys of cloud. A green snake swims under the dock. I can see the sutures between the plates of its flat skull. It glides through the water without a ripple, stops mysteriously and nods against a piling.

"Jack?"

"Yes?"

144

"Are we going for a ride?"

For Lonnie our Sundays together have a program. First we talk, usually on a religious subject; then we take a ride; then he asks me to do him like Akim.

The ride is a flying trip over the boardwalk and full tilt down the swamp road. Lonnie perches on the edge of his chair and splits the wind until tears run out of his eyes. When the clouds come booming up over the savannah, the creatures of the marsh hush for a second then set up a din of croaking and pumping.

Back on the porch he asks me to do him like Akim. I come for him in his chair. It has to be a real beating up or he won't be satisfied. During my last year in college I discovered that I was picking up the mannerisms of Akim Tamiroff, the only useful thing, in fact, that I learned in the entire four years.

"I must get those plans."

"Come on now Jack don't." Lonnie shrinks back fearfully-joyfully. His hand curls like a burning leaf.

My mother sticks her head out of the kitchen.

"Now aren't those two a case?" She turns back to Sharon. "I tell you, that Lonnie and Jack are one more *case*."

After I kiss him good-by, Lonnie calls me back. But he doesn't really have anything to say.

"Wait."

"What?"

He searches the swamp, smiling.

"Do you think that Eucharist—"

"Yes?"

He forgets and is obliged to say straight out: "I am still offering my communion for you."

"I know you are."

"Wait."

"What?"

"Do you love me?"

"Yes."

"How much?"

"Quite a bit."

"I love you too." But already he has the transistor in the crook of his wrist and is working at it furiously.

7. ON ITS WAY HOME THE MG BECOMES INFESTED with malaise. It is not unexpected, since Sunday afternoon is always the worst time for malaise. Thousands of cars are strung out along the Gulf Coast, whole families, and all with the same vacant headachy look. There is an exhaust fume in the air and the sun strikes the water with a malignant glint. A fine Sunday afternoon, though. A beautiful boulevard, ten thousand handsome cars, fifty thousand handsome, well-fed and kindhearted people, and the malaise settles on us like a fallout.

Sorrowing, hoping against hope, I put my hand on the thickest and innerest part of Sharon's thigh.

She bats me away with a new vigor.

"Son, don't you mess with me."

"Very well, I won't," I say gloomily, as willing not to mess with her as mess with her, to tell the truth.

"That's all right. You come here."

"I'm here."

She gives me a kiss. "I got your number, son. But that's all right. You're a good old boy. You really tickle me." She's been talking to my mother. "Now you tend to your business and get me on home."

"Why?"

"I have to meet someone."

IV

1. SAM YERGER IS WAITING FOR ME ON THE SIDE-
walk, bigger than life. Really his legs are as big
and round as an elephant's in their heavy cylindrical linens
and great flaring brogues. Seeing him strikes a pang to the
marrow; he has the urgent gentle manner of an emissary
of bad news. Someone has died.

Beyond a doubt he is waiting for me. At the sight of my
MG, he makes an occult sign and comes quickly to the
curb.

"Meet me in the basement," he actually whispers and
turns and goes immediately up the wooden steps, his footsteps echoing like pistol shots.

Sam looks very good. Though he is rumpled and red-
eyed, he is, as always, of a piece, from his bearish-big
head and shoulders and his soft collar riding up like a ruff
into the spade of hair at the back of his neck to his elephant legs and black brogues. It would be a pleasure to
be red-eyed and rumpled if one could do it with Sam's
style. His hair makes two waves over his forehead in the
Nelson Eddy style of a generation ago.

Sam Yerger's mother, Aunt Mady, was married to Judge
Anse's law partner, old man Ben Yerger. After college in
the East, Sam left Feliciana Parish for good and worked

on the old New Orleans *Item*. In the 1930s he wrote a humorous book about the French-speaking Negroes called *Yambilaya Ya-Ya* which was made into a stage show and later a movie. During the war Sam was chief of the Paris bureau of a wire service. I remember hearing a CBS news analyst call him "an able and well-informed reporter." For a while he was married to Joel Craig, a New Orleans beauty (Joel's voice, a throaty society voice richened, it always seemed to me, cured, by good whisky—took on for me the same larger-than-life plenitude as Sam himself). They lived first in the Quarter and then in the Mexican state of Chiapas, where I visited them in 1954. There he wrote a novel called *The Honored and the Dishonored* which dealt, according to the dust jacket, with "the problem of evil and the essential loneliness of man." Sam broke his leg in search of some ruins in a remote district and nearly died before some Indians found the two of them. He and Joel were very fond of each other and liked to joke in a way that at first seemed easy-going. For example, Sam liked to say that Joel was just the least little bit pregnant, and before they were married Joel liked to say that she was sick and tired of being Sam's bawd; I liked hearing her say *bawd* in that big caramel voice. She liked to call me Leftenant: "Leftenant, it has at long last dawned on me what it is about you that attracts me." "What?" I asked, shifting around uneasily. "You've got dignidad, Leftenant." It was not a good thing to say because thereafter I could never say or do anything without a consciousness of my dignity. When I visited them in Mexico, each spoke highly of the other and in the other's presence, which was slightly embarrassing. "He's quite a guy," Joel told me. "Do you know what he told me after lying under a cliff for thirty-six hours with two inches of his femur sticking out? He said: Queenie, I think I'm going to pass out and before I do, I'm going to give you a piece of advice—God, I thought he was going to die and knew and was telling me what to do with his book—and he said quite solemnly: Queenie, always stick to Bach and the early Italians—and passed out cold as a mackerel. And by God, it's not bad advice." Sam would say of Joel: "She's a fine girl. Always cherish your woman, Binx." I told him I would. That summer I had much to thank him for. At the City College of Mexico I had met this girl from U.C.L.A. named Pat Pabst and she had come down with me to Chiapas. "Always cherish your woman," Sam told me and stomped around in very good style with his cane. I looked over at Pat Pabst who, I knew, was in Mexico looking for the Real Right Thing. And here it was: old Sam, a regular bear of a writer with his black Beethoven face, pushing himself around with a stoic sort of gracefulness; and I in my rucksack and with just the hint of an old Virginian voice. It was all her little California heart desired. She clave to me for dear life. After leaving Mexico—he had been overtaken by nostalgia, the characteristic mood of repetition—Sam returned to Feliciana where he wrote a nostalgic book called *Happy Land* which was commended in the reviews as a nice blend of a moderate attitude toward the race question and a conservative affection for the values of the agrarian South. An earlier book, called *Curse upon the Land*, which the dust jacket described as "an impassioned plea for tolerance and understanding," had not been well received in Feliciana. Now and then Sam turns up in New Orleans on a lecture tour and visits my aunt and horses around with Kate and me. We enjoy seeing him. He calls me Brother Andy and Kate Miss Ruby.

"We've got to get Kate out of here and to do it, I need your help."

Sam comes bursting through Kate's new shutters and starts pacing up and down the tiny courtyard where I sit hunched over and bemused by the malaise. I notice that Kate has begun peeling plaster from the wall of the basement, exposing more plantation brick. "Here's the story. She's going to New York and you're going to take her there. Take her there today and wait for me—I'll be back in ten days. She is to see Étienne Suë—you know who he is: one of those fabulous continental geniuses who is as well known for his work in Knossan antiquities as his clinical researches. The man is chronically ill himself and sees no more than a handful of patients, but he'll see Kate. I've already called him. But here is the master stroke. I've already made arrangements for her to stay with the Princess.''

''The Princess?''

There is a noise above us. I blink up into the thin sunlight. Bessie Coe—so called to distinguish her from Bessie Baham the laundress—a speckle-faced Negress with a white lip, leans out from the servants' walk to shake a mop. Since she is kitchen help, she can allow herself to greet me in the old style. ''Mist Binx,'' she declares hoarsely, hollering it out over my head to the neighborhood in a burlesque of a greeting yet good-naturedly and even inviting me to join in the burlesque.

''She is seventy-five years old, a little bitty dried-up old thing and next to Em the most charming, the wittiest and the wisest woman I ever knew. She has been of more service to us in the U.N. than the entire American delegation. Her place is always electric with excitement. Kate—who in my opinion is already a great lady—would find herself for the first time. The long and the short of it is she needs a companion. The very night I left New York she said to me: now you listen here—while you are in your American South, you make it your business to find me a nice Southern girl—you know the kind I have in mind. Of course the kind she had in mind is the Southerner who is so curiously like the old-style Russian gentry. I thought no more about it until last night as I watched Kate go up the steps. My God, I said, there goes Natasha Rostov. Have you ever noticed it?''

''Natasha?'' I say blinking. ''What has happened? Has something happened to Kate?''

"I am not sure what happened." Sam places heel to toe and, holding his elbow in his hand and his arm straight up and down in front of him—himself gathered to a point, aimed—puffs a cigarette. "Certainly there was nothing wrong when Kate went to bed at two o'clock this morning. On the contrary. She was exalted. We had had, she and I and Em, four hours of the best talk I ever had anywhere. She was the most fascinating woman in New Orleans and she damn well knew it."

(Aye, sweet Kate, and I know too. I know your old upside-down trick: when all is lost, when they despair of you, then it is, at this darkest hour, that you emerge as the gorgeous one.)

"Emily and I talked for a little while longer and went up to bed. It was not later than two thirty. At four o'clock something woke me. What it was I can't for the life of me recall but I awoke with the most importunate sense of something wrong. I went into the hall. There was a light under Kate's door but I heard nothing. So I went back to bed and slept until eight." Sam speaks in a perfunctory voice, listing items rapidly and accurately in a professional style. "When Kate had not appeared for breakfast by ten o'clock, Emily sent Mercer up with a tray. Meanwhile Jules had left for church. Mercer knocked at Kate's door and called out loudly enough to be heard downstairs and received no answer. Now Emily was visibly alarmed and asked me to come up with her. For ten minutes we knocked and called (do you know how very long ten minutes is?). So what the hell, I kicked the door down. Kate was in bed and deeply asleep, it seemed to me. But her breathing was quite shallow and there was a bottle of capsules open on the table. But it was by no means empty— I judge that it was just over one-third filled. Anyhow, Emily could not wake her up. Whereupon she, Emily, became extremely agitated and asked me to call Dr Mink. By the time he arrived, of course, Kate had waked up and was lashing out with a particularly malevolent and drunken

151

sort of violence. Toward Emily she exhibited a cold fury which was actually frightening. When she told us to get the hell out, I can assure you that I obeyed at once. Dr Mink lavaged her stomach and gave her a stimulant—'' Sam looks at his watch, ''—that was an hour ago. Now that fellow has pretty good nerve. He wouldn't put her in the hospital which would have been the cagey thing to do. Emily asked him what he proposed to do. He said Kate had promised to see him Monday and that was good enough for him—and as for the pentobarbital, no one could really keep anybody else from swallowing any number any time he wanted to. He's a great admirer of Suë, by the way. We did manage to get the bottle, however—''

"Sam!" My aunt's voice, low and rich in overtones of meaning, comes down to us.

Sam looks down past his arm to see that his heel is aligned properly. I start up nervously, uneasy that Sam might have missed the warning in my aunt's voice.

"One more thing. Oscar and Edna are here. Now wouldn't you know they'd be? But perhaps it is just as well. For it is an awkward moment for Kate. The trick is for her to show herself. Here's what we hit upon: you show up, knowing nothing, come looking for her and fetch her down to dinner.''

My aunt catches my eye from the dining room and I go in to kiss her and speak to the Oscar Bollings. Things seem calm enough. Uncle Jules is laughing with Aunt Edna about something. Though Aunt Emily is abstracted, temple propped on three fingers, she speaks cheerfully, and I can't help but wonder if Sam's story is not exaggerated. Uncle Oscar and Aunt Edna have come down from Feliciana Parish for Carnival and the Spring Pilgrimage, an annual tour of old houses and patios. Aunt Edna is a handsome stoutish woman with snapping black eyes and a near-mustache. Though she is at least sixty-five, her hair is still black and loops back over her ears in a way that makes me think of "raven tresses." Uncle Oscar is all dressed up, but you can tell he is countrified. The fourth of the elder Bolling brothers, he elected to be neither soldier nor lawyer nor doctor but storekeeper—that is, until his recent success in exhibiting Lynwood to tourists at a dollar a head. In certain quirks of expression and waggings of head, he is startlingly like Judge Anse, but there is a flattening of the nosebridge and a softening of the forehead and a giddy light-blue amiability about the eyes. Upon the death of the brothers and the emigration of the girls, Uncle Oscar and Aunt Edna fell heir to the old place. It is not much of a showplace, to be honest (it never occurred to anyone to give it a name until Aunt Edna thought of Lynwood), being a big old rambling pile and having no special virtue save only its deep verandas and its avenue of oaks. But Uncle Oscar and Aunt Edna managed to fix it up wonderfully well and even win a permanent place on the Azalea Trail. Strangely enough, it was not Uncle Oscar, the old settler, who restored the house in the best Natchez style—adding a covered walk to the outkitchen, serving mint juleps where the Bollings had never drunk anything but toddies, and even dressing up poor old Shad in a Seagram's butler suit and putting him out on the highway with a dinner bell—it was not Uncle Oscar but Aunt Edna, the druggist's daughter from upstate New York whom Uncle Oscar met and married while she was training at Plattsburg in the first world war.

When I bend to kiss her, my aunt gives me no sign whatever, beyond her usual gray look and the usual two quick pats on the cheek—no sign, unless it is a certain depth of irony, a gray under gray.

There comes to me in the ascent a brief annunciatory syllable in the throat stopped in the scrape of a chair as if, having signaled me and repenting of it, it had then to pass itself off as but one of the small day noises of the house. Off the landing is a dark little mezzanine arranged as a

153

room of furniture. It is a place one passes twenty times a
day and no more thinks of entering than of entering a
picture, nor even of looking at, but having entered, enters
with all the oddness of entering a picture, a tableau in
depth wherein space is untenanted and wherefrom the view
of the house, the hall and dining room below, seems at
once privileged and strange. Kate is there in the shadows.
She sits beside the porcelain fireplace with its glassed-in
cases of medals and tufted Bohemian slippers and gold-
encrusted crystal and the ambrotype of Captain Alex Bolling of the 2nd Louisiana Infantry not merely locked in but
sealed in forever by glass set into the wall, an immurement
which used to provoke in me the liveliest speculation by
virtue of its very permanence—to think of the little objects
closeted away forever in the same sequestered air of 1938—
Kate sits, herself exempt from the needs and necessaries
of all passers-by, and holds her arms in her hands and
cheerfully makes room for me in the love seat. Not until
later do I think why it is she looks so well: she is all
dressed up, for the first time since Christmas. It is the
scent of her perfume, her nylon-whispering legs, the white
dress against her dark skin, a proper dress fluted and
flounced and now gathered by her and folded away from
me.

The angle is such that we can see the dining room and
its company, except my aunt. There is only her right wrist
and hand curving out and under the chair arm to rub the
lion's face with its cloven leprous nose.

"Tell Mother that I am fine and that I will be down
later. I am not hungry." Then I will indeed be fine, Kate
as good as says. It is her sense of their waiting upon her
and that alone that intrudes itself into her mezzanine.

When I return (my aunt received me with a single grave
nod), Kate is smoking, inhaling deeply and blowing
plumes of lung smoke into the air. Her knees are crossed
and she swings her leg and holds her Zippo and pack in
her lap.

"Have you seen Sam?" she asks me.

"Yes."

"What did he tell you?"

"That you had a bad night and that Merle had been here." I tell her the truth because I have not the wit to tell her anything else. Kate knows it: I am the not-quite-bright one whom grown-ups take aside to question.

"Hm. Do you want to know the truth? I had a very good night. Possibly the best night of my life."

Sam touches knife to goblet. As is his custom, he speaks down the table to my aunt but with a consciousness of the others as listeners-in. At his right, Uncle Jules is content to listen in and look on with an expression of almost besotted amiability. This is one of Em's "dinners," Sam is speaking at the Forum, Em is president. Long ago he, Uncle Jules, and with the same shrewdness with which he recognizes signs of corporate illness and corporate health, made out a certain pattern in Emily's lectures. Persons of the most advanced views on every subject and of the most exquisite sensitivity to minorities (except Catholics, but this did not bother Uncle Jules), they were nevertheless observed by him to observe the same taboos and celebrate the same rites. Not so Uncle Oscar. Sitting there rared back and gazing up at the chandelier, he too is aware that he has fallen in with pretty high-flown company, but he will discover no such thing; any moment now he will violate a taboo and blaspheme a rite by getting off on niggers, Mrs Roosevelt, dagos and Jews, and all in the same breath. But Uncle Jules will neither trespass nor be trespassed upon. His armor is his unseriousness. It would never occur to him to take their, Aunt Emily's lecturers', irreverent sallies as an assault upon his own deep dumb convictions. The worst they can do is live up to themselves, behave just as he has come to expect "Em's people" to behave.

Sam tolls his goblet. "Last Thursday, Em, Eric got back

from Geneva and I met him at the airport. His face was white as chalk—''

Kate, who has been sitting back and peering down her cheek at Sam like a theatergoer in the balcony, begins smoothing out the cellophane of her cigarette pack.

"We talked like that last night. I was very happy—"

Aunt Edna leans out to intercept Sam's monologue. She has not yet caught on to Sam's way of talking, so she is upset. "But what can a person *do*?"—and she actually wrings her hands. Aunt Edna is as nice as can be, but she is one of our kinfolks I avoid. Her soul is in her eyes and when we meet, she shoots me deep theosophical soul-glances, and though I shoot them back and am quite sympathetic on the whole, it is an uneasy business.

"Sam is a very gentle person and a very kind person," says Kate.

"I know."

"He is very fond of you. Are you going to hear his lecture?"

"I would like to, but I have to get up early tomorrow morning and go to Chicago."

"What for?"

"Business."

"We had a wonderful evening, but when I went to bed, I was somewhat apprehensive. You know how you have to guard against Sam's flights?"

"Yes."

"Whatever goes up must come down and I was ten miles high."

"I know."

"But I was on guard and I did not fall. I went straight to bed and to sleep. Then some hours later I awoke suddenly. There was nothing wrong. I was wide awake and completely alert. I thought about your proposal and it seemed to me that it might be possible after all. If only I did not ruin everything."

Mercer passes a dish of sweet potatoes. At each place

he stops breathing, head thrown back and eyes popping out, then lets out his breath with a strangling sound.

Uncle Oscar has hiked an arm back over his chair and says something to Sam. I can't make it out but I recognize the voice, the easy garrulity wheezing off into a laughter which solicits your agreement and threatens reprisal if you withhold it. Yet I used to like Uncle Oscar's store in Feliciana—to hear his voice now is almost to smell the floorboards soured by wet Growena. But even then, to be there and to be solicited by him was a perilous thing. It was a perilous thing to see him do battle in the deadly arena of a country store, see him gird himself to annihilate his opponent and, to insure himself against counterattack, go wheezing off into easy laughter and so claim the victory.

"Oscar!" cries Aunt Edna, pretending to be in a buzzing good humor. Already she can hear Sam in Dallas: "I heard a delightful commentary on the mind of the South last week—" Leaning over, she gives Uncle Oscar a furious affectionate pat which signifies that he is a good fellow and we all love him. It also signifies that he can shut up.

"There was no question of sleep," says Kate. "I came downstairs and found one of Father's mysteries and went back to bed and read the whole thing. It was about some people in Los Angeles. The house was dark and still and once in a while a boat whistle blew on the river. I saw how my life could be—living as a neat little person like Della Street, doing my stockings every night. But then I remembered what happened in Memphis. Did you know I lived in Memphis once?"

My aunt pays as little attention to Uncle Oscar as to Sam. Her thumbnail methodically combs the grooves which represent the lion's mane.

"It was in 1951—you were in the army. Father and I were warring over politics. Come to think of it, I might actually have been kicked out of the house. Anyhow Mother suggested it might be a good thing if I went to visit an old classmate of hers in Memphis, a lady named Mrs Boykin Lamar. She was really quite a person, had sung in the Civic Opera in New York and wrote quite a funny book about her travels in Europe as a girl. They were as kind to me as anyone could be. But no one could think of anything to say. Night after night we sat there playing operas on the phonograph and dreading the moment when the end came and someone had to say something. I became so nervous that one night I slipped on the hearth and fell into the fire. Can you believe it was a relief to suffer extreme physical pain? Hell couldn't be fire— there are worse things than fire. I moved to a hotel and for a while I was all right. I had a job doing casework and I had plenty of dates. But after a while the room began to reproach me. When I came home from work every afternoon, the sun would be setting across the river in Arkansas and every day the yellow light became sadder and sadder. And Arkansas over there in the yellow West—O my God, you have no idea how sad it looked. One afternoon I packed my suitcase and caught the Illinois Central for home.''

Sam is spieling in pretty good style, all the while ironing out the tablecloth into shallow gutters with the blade of his knife. A new prefatory note creeps into his voice. It is like a symphony when the ''good'' part is coming, and I know that Sam is working up to one of his stories. These stories of Sam used to arouse in me an appreciation so keen and pleasurable that it bordered on the irritable. On the dark porch in Feliciana he told us once of the time when he made a journey up the headwaters of the Orinoco and caught a fever and lay ill for weeks. One night he heard an incredibly beautiful voice sing the whole of *Winterreise*. He was sure it was delirium until the next morning when he met the singer, an Austrian engineer who sang lieder better than Lotte Lehmann, etc. When he finished I was practically beside myself with irritable pleasure and became angry with the others because they were not sufficiently moved by the experience.

"Emily, do you remember the night we saw *There Shall Be No Night* and you were so moved that you insisted on walking all the way back to the Carlyle?"

But Kate pays no attention. She holds her feathered thumb to the light and inspects it minutely. "Last night everything was fine until I finished the book. Then it became a matter of waiting. What next, I thought. I began to get a little scared—for the first time I had the feeling of coming to the end of my rope. I became aware of my own breathing. Things began to slip a little. I fixed myself a little drink and took two nembutals and waited for the lift."

It is the first time she has spoken of her capsules. My simplemindedness serves her well.

"You know what happened then? What did Sam say? Never mind. Did you see Merle? No? Hm. What happened was the most trivial thing imaginable, nothing grand at all, though I would like to think it was. I took six or eight capsules altogether. I knew that wouldn't kill me. My Lord, I didn't want to die—not at that moment. I only wanted to—break out, or off, off dead center— Listen. Isn't it true that the only happy men are wounded men? Admit it! Isn't that the truth?" She breaks off and goes off into a fit of yawning. "I felt so queer. Everything seemed so—no 'count somehow, you know?" She swings her foot and hums a little tune. "To tell you the truth, I can't remember too well. How strange. I've always remembered every little thing."

"—and you spoke to me for the first time of your messianic hopes?" Sam smiles at my aunt. In Feliciana we used to speculate on the new messiah, the scientist-philosopher-mystic who would come striding through the ruins with the *Gita* in one hand and a Geiger counter in the other. But today Sam miscalculates. My aunt says nothing. The thumbnail goes on combing the lion's mane.

Dinner over, Uncle Oscar waits in the dining room until the others have left, then seizes his scrotum and gives his leg a good shake.

I rise unsteadily, sleepy all at once to the point of drunkenness.

"Wait." Kate takes my arm urgently in both hands. "I am going with you."

"All right. But first I think I'll take a little nap on the porch."

"I mean to Chicago."

"Chicago?"

"Yes. Do you mind if I go?"

"No."

"When are you leaving?"

"Tomorrow morning."

"Could you change it to tonight and get two tickets on the train?"

"Why the train?" I begin to realize how little I have slept during the past week.

"I'll tell you what. You go lie down and I'll take care of it."

"All right."

"After Chicago do you think there is a possibility we might take a trip out west and stay for a while in some little town like Modesto or Fresno?"

"It is possible."

"I'll fix everything." She sounds very happy. "Do you have any money?"

"Yes."

"Give it to me."

It is a matter for astonishment, I think drowsily in the hammock, that Kate should act with such dispatch—out she came, heels popping, arm in arm with her stepmother, snapped her purse and with Sam looking on, somewhat gloomily it struck me, off she went in her stiff little Plymouth—and then I think why. It is trains. When it comes to a trip, to the plain business of going, just stepping up into the Pullman and gliding out of town of an evening, she is as swift and remorseless as Della Street.

Now later, on Prytania, Uncle Oscar hands Aunt Edna into the station wagon—they are bound for their Patio-by-Candlelight tour—and goes huffing around to his door, rared back and with one hand pressed into his side. Sam tiptoes to the screen. "Well now look ahere, Brother Andy. Ain't that the Kingfish and Madame Queen? Sho 'tis."

In this vertigo of exhaustion, laughter must be guarded against like retching.

"Brother Andy, is you getting much?"

"No." My stomach further obliges Sam with a last despairing heave. Oh Lord.

Later there seems to come into my hand—and with it some instructions from Sam of which there is no more to be remembered than that they were delivered in the tone of one of my aunt's grand therapeutic schemes—a squarish bottle, warmed by Sam's body and known to my fingers through the ridge of glass left by the mold and the apothecary symbol *oz* or $\mathfrak{z}$ or $\mathfrak{z}$.

2. SURE ENOUGH, THREE HOURS LATER WE ARE ROCKing along an uneven roadbed through the heart of the Ponchitoula swamp.

No sooner do we open the heavy door of Sieur Iberville and enter the steel corridor with its gelid hush and the stray voices from open compartments and the dark smell of going high in the nostrils—than the last ten years of my life take on the shadowy aspect of a sojourn between train rides. It was ten years ago that I last rode a train, from San Francisco to New Orleans, and so ten years since I last enjoyed the peculiar gnosis of trains, stood on the eminence from which there is revealed both the sorry litter of the past and the future bright and simple as can be, and the going itself, one's privileged progress through the world. But trains have changed. Gone are the uppers and lowers, partitions and cranks, and the green velour; only the porter remains, the same man, I think, a black man with palms the color of shrimp and a neck swollen with dislike. Our roomettes turn out to be little coffins for a single person. From time to time, I notice, people in roomettes stick their heads out into the corridor for some sight of humankind.

Kate is affected by the peculiar dispensation of trains. Her gray jacket comes just short of her wide hips and the tight skirt curves under her in a nice play on vulgarity. On the way to the observation car she pulls me into the platform of the vestibule and gives me a kiss, grabbing me under the coat like a waitress. In celebration of Mardi Gras, she has made up her eyes with a sparkle of mascara and now she looks up at me with a black spiky look.

"Are we going to live in Modesto?"

"Sure," I say, uneasy at her playfulness. She is not as well as she makes out. She is not safe on a train after all; it is rather that by a kind of bravado she can skim along in the very face of the danger.

The observation car is crowded, but we find seats together on a sofa where I am jammed against a fellow reading a newspaper. We glide through the cottages of Carrollton cutting off backyards in odd trapezoids, then through the country clubs and cemeteries of Metaire. In the gathering dusk the cemeteries look at first like cities, with their rows of white vaults, some two- and three-storied and forming flats and tenements, and the tiny streets and corners and curbs and even plots of lawn, all of such a proportion that in the very instant of being mistaken and from the eye's own necessity, they set themselves off into the distance like a city seen from far away. Now in the suburbs we ride at a witch's level above the gravelly roofs.

It gradually forces itself upon me that a man across the aisle is looking at me with a strange insistence. Kate nudges me. It is Sidney Gross and his wife, beyond a doubt bound also for the convention. The son of Sidney Gross of Danziger and Gross, Sidney is a short fresh-faced crinkle-haired boy with the bright beamish look Southern Jews sometimes have. There has always been a special cordiality between us. He married a pretty Mississippi girl; she, unlike Sidney, is wary of such encounters—she would know which of us spoke first at our last encounter—so she casts sleepy looks right past us, pausing, despite herself on Kate's white face and black spiky eyes. But Sidney hunches over toward us, beaming, a stalwart little pony back with his head well set on his shoulders and his small ears lying flat.

"Well well well. Trader Jack. So you slipped up on your plane reservations too."

"Hello, Sidney, Margot. This is Kate Cutrer."

Margot becomes very friendly, in the gossipy style of the Mississippi Delta.

"So you forgot about it being Mardi Gras and couldn't get a plane."

"No, we like the train."

Sidney is excited, not by the trip as I am, but by the convention. Leaning across the aisle with a program rolled up in his hand, he explains that he is scheduled for a panel on tax relief for bond funds. "What about you?"

"I think I am taking part in something called a Cracker Barrel Session."

"You'll like it. Everybody talks right off the top of their heads. You can take your coat off, get up and stretch. Anything. Last year we had this comical character from Georgia." Sidney casts about for some way of conveying just how comical and failing, passes on without minding. "What a character. Extremely comical. What's the topic?"

"Competing with the variable endowments."

"Oh yass," says Sidney with a wry look of our trade. "I don't worry about it." He slides the cylinder of paper to and fro. "Do you?"

"No."

Sidney suggests a bridge game, but Kate begs off. The Grosses move to a table in the corner and start playing gin rummy.

Kate, who has been fumbling in her purse, becomes still. I feel her eyes on my face.

"Do you have my capsules?"

"What?"

"My capsules."

"Why yes, I do. I forgot that I had them."

Not taking her eyes from my face, she receives the bottle, puts it in her purse, snaps it.

"That's not like you."

"I didn't take them."

"Who did?"

"Sam gave them to me. It was while I was in the hammock. I hardly remember it."

"He took them from my purse?"

"I don't know."

For a long moment she sits, hands in her lap, fingers curling up and stirring a little. Then abruptly she rises and leaves. When she returns, her face is scrubbed and pale, the moisture still dark at the roots of her hair. What has upset her is not the incident of the capsules but meeting the Grosses. It spoils everything, this prospect of making pleasant talk, of having a delightful time, as Sidney would put it ("There we were moping over missing the plane, when Jack Bolling shows up and we have ourselves a ball")—when we might have gone rocking up through dark old Mississippi alone together in the midst of strangers. Still she is better. Perhaps it is her reviving hope of losing the Grosses to gin rummy or perhaps it is the first secret promise of the chemicals entering her blood.

Now, picking up speed, we gain the swamp. Kate and I sway against each other and watch the headlights of the cars on the swamp road, winking through the moss like big yellow lightning bugs.

The drowsiness returns. It is unwelcome. I recognize it as the sort of fitful twilight which has come over me of late, a twilight where waking dreams are dreamed and sleep never comes.

The man next to me is getting off in St Louis. When the conductor comes to collect our tickets, he surrenders a stub: he is going home. His suit is good. He sits with his legs crossed, one well-clad haunch riding up like a ham, his top leg held out at an obtuse angle by the muscle of his calf. His brown hair is youthful (he himself is thirty-eight or forty) and makes a cowlick in front. With the cowlick and the black eyeglasses he looks quite a bit like the actor Gary Merrill and has the same certified permission to occupy pleasant space with his pleasant self. In ruddy good health, he muffles a hearty belch in a handkerchief. This very evening, no doubt, he has had an excellent meal at Galatoire's, and the blood of his portal vein bears away a golden harvest of nutrient globules. When he first goes through his paper, he opens it like a book and I have no choice but to read the left page with him. We pause at an advertisement of a Bourbon Street nightclub which is a picture of a dancer with an oiled body. Her triceps arch forward like a mare's. For a second we gaze heavy-lidded and pass on. Now he finds what he wants and folds his paper once, twice and again, into a neat packet exactly two columns wide, like a subway rider in New York. Propping it against his knee, he takes out a slender gold pencil, makes a deft one-handed adjustment, and underlines several sentences with straight black lines (he is used to underlining). Dreaming at his shoulder, I can make out no more than

In order to deepen and enrich the marital—

It is a counseling column which I too read faithfully.

The train sways through the swamp. The St Louisan, breathing powerfully through the stiff hairs of his nose, succeeds in sitting in such a manner, tilted over on his right hip and propped against himself, that his thigh forms a secure writing platform for the packet.

The voices in the car become fretful. It begins to seem that the passengers have ridden together for a long time and have developed secret understandings and old grudges. They speak crossly and elliptically to each other.

Staying awake is a kind of sickness and sleep is forever guarded against by a dizzy dutiful alertness. Waking wide-eyed dreams come as fitfully as swampfire.

Dr and Mrs Bob Dean autograph copies of their book *Technique in Marriage* in a Canal Street department store. A pair of beauties. I must have come in all the way from Gentilly, for I stand jammed against a table which supports a pyramid of books. I cannot take my eyes from the Deans: an oldish couple but still handsome and both, rather strangely, heavily freckled. As they wait for the starting time, they are jolly with each other and swap banter in the professional style of show people (I believe these preliminaries are called the warm-up). "No, we never argue," says Bob Dean. "Because whenever an argument starts, we consult the chapter I wrote on arguments." "No, dear," says Jackie Dean. "It was I who wrote the chapter—" etc. Everyone laughs. I notice that nearly all the crowd jamming against me are women, firm middle-aged one-fifty pounders. Under drooping lids I watch the Deans, peculiarly affected by their routine which is staged so effortlessly that during the exchange of quips, they are free to cast business-like looks about them as if no one were present. But when they get down to business, they become as sober as Doukhobors and effuse an air of dedicated almost evangelical helpfulness. A copy of the book lies open on the table. I read: "Now with a tender regard for your partner remove your hand from the nipple and gently manipulate—" It is impossible not to imagine them at their researches, as solemn as a pair of brontosauruses, their heavy old freckled limbs about each other, hands probing skillfully for sensitive zones, pigmented areolas, out-of-the-way mucous glands, dormant vascular nexuses. A wave of prickling passes over me such as I have never experienced before.

My head, nodding like a daffodil, falls a good three inches toward the St Louisan before it jerks itself up. Kate sits shivering against me, but the St Louisan is as warm and solid as roast beef. As the train rocks along on its unique voyage through space-time, thousands of tiny thing-events bombard us like cosmic particles. Lying in a ditch outside is a scrap of newspaper with the date May 3, 1954. My Geiger counter clicks away like a teletype. But no one else seems to notice. Everyone is buried in his magazine. Kate is shaking like a leaf because she longs to be an anyone who is anywhere and she cannot.

The St Louisan reads a headline

SCIENTIST PREDICTS FUTURE IF NUCLEAR ENERGY IS NOT MISUSED

Out comes the gold pencil to make a neat black box. After reading for a moment he comes back to the beginning and is about to make a second concentric box, thinks better of it, takes from his pocket a silver knife, undoes the scissors and clips the whole article, folds it and places it in his wallet. It is impossible to make out any of the underlined passages except the phrase: "the gradual convergence of physical science and social science."

A very good phrase. I have to admire the St Louisan for his neat and well-ordered life, his gold pencil and his scissors-knife and his way of clipping articles on the convergence of the physical sciences and the social sciences;

it comes over me that in the past few days my own life has gone to seed. I no longer eat and sleep regularly or write philosophical notes in my notebook and my fingernails are dirty. The search has spoiled the pleasure of my tidy and ingenious life in Gentilly. As late as a week ago, such a phrase as "hopefully awaiting the gradual convergence of the physical sciences and the social sciences" would have provoked no more than an ironic tingle or two at the back of my neck. Now it howls through the Ponchitoula swamp, the very sound and soul of despair.

Kate has stopped shivering and when she lights up and starts smoking, I am certain she is better. But I am mistaken. "Oooh," she says in a perfunctory workaday voice and starts forward again. The car lurches and throws her against Sidney's chair; there the train holds her fast: for three seconds she might be taken for a rapt onlooker of the gin-rummy game. Sidney rocks the deck against the polished wood until the cards are perfectly aligned. The gold ring on his little finger seems to serve as a device, a neat little fastening by means of which his hand movements are harnessed and made trim.

Half an hour passes and Kate does not return. I find her in her roomette, arms folded and face turned to the dark glass. We sit knee to knee.

"Are you all right?"

She nods slowly to the window, but her cheek is against me. Outside a square of yellow light flees along an embankment, falls away to the woods and fields, comes roaring back good as new. Suddenly a perky head pops up. Kate is leaning forward hugging herself.

"I am all right. I am never too bad with you."

"Why?"

"No thanks to you. On the contrary. The others are much more sympathetic than you, especially Mother and Sam."

"What about Merle?"

"Merle! Listen, with Merle I could break wind and he would give me that same quick congratulatory look. But you. You're nuttier than I am. One look at you and I have to laugh. Do you think that is sufficient ground for marriage?''

"As good as any. Better than love.''

"Love! What do you know about love?''

"I didn't say I knew anything about it.''

She is back at her window, moving her hand to see it move in the flying yellow square. We hunch up knee to knee and nose to nose like the two devils on the Rorschach card. Something glitters in the corner of her eye. Surely not a tear.

"Quite a Carnival. Two proposals in one Mardi Gras.''

"Who else?''

"Sam.''

"No kidding.''

"No kidding. And I'll tell you something else. Sam is quite a person behind that façade. An essentially lonely person.''

"I know.''

"You're worse than Sam.'' She is angry.

"How?''

"Sam is a schemer. He also likes me. He knows that someday I will be quite rich. But he also likes me. That isn't so bad. Scheming is human. You have to be human to be a schemer. Whenever I see through one of Sam's little schemes, I feel a sensation of warmth. Ah ha, think I to myself, so it must have been in the world once—men and women wanting something badly and scheming away like beavers. But you—''

"Yes?''

"You're like me. So let us not deceive one another.''

Her voice is steadier. Perhaps it is the gentle motion of the train with which we nod ever so slightly, yes, yes, yes.

She says: "Can't you see that for us it is much too late for such ingenious little schemes?''

"As marrying?''

"The only way you could carry it off is as another one of your ingenious little researches. Admit it.''

169

"Then why not do it?"

"You remind me of a prisoner in the death house who takes a wry pleasure in doing things like registering to vote. Come to think of it, all your gaiety and good spirits have the same death house quality. No thanks. I've had enough of your death house pranks."

"What is there to lose?"

"Can't you see that after what happened last night, it is no use. I can't play games now. But don't you worry. I'm not going to swallow all the pills at once. Losing hope is not so bad. There's something worse: losing hope and hiding it from yourself."

"Very well. Lose hope or not. Be afraid or not. But marry me anyhow, and we can still walk abroad on a summer night, hope or no hope, shivering or not, and see a show and eat some oysters down on Magazine."

"No no."

"I don't understand—"

"You're right. You don't understand. It is not some one thing, as you think. It is everything. It is all so monstrous."

"What is monstrous?"

"I told you," she says irritably. "Everything. I'm not up to it. Having a little hubby—you would be hubby, dearest Binx, and that is ridiculous—did I hurt your feelings? Seeing hubby off in the morning, having lunch with the girls, getting tight at Eddie's and Nell's house and having a little humbug with somebody else's hubby, wearing my little diaphragm and raising my two lovely boys and worrying for the next twenty years about whether they will make Princeton."

"I told you we would live in Gentilly. Or Modesto."

"I was being ingenious like you."

"Do you want to live like Sam and Joel?"

"Binx Binx. You're just like your aunt. When I told her how I felt, she said to me: Katherine, you're perfectly right. Don't ever lose your ideals and your enthusiasm for ideas—she thought I was talking about something literary or political or Great Books, for God's sake. I thought to myself: is that what I'm doing?—and ran out and took four pills. Incidentally they're all wrong about that. They all think any minute I'm going to commit suicide. What a joke. The truth of course is the exact opposite: suicide is the only thing that keeps me alive. Whenever everything else fails, all I have to do is consider suicide and in two seconds I'm as cheerful as a nitwit. But if I could *not* kill myself—ah then, I would. I can do without nembutal or murder mysteries but not without suicide. And that reminds me." And off she goes down the steel corridor, one hand held palm out to the wall.

None of this is new, of course. I do not, to tell the truth, pay too much attention to what she says. It is her voice that tells me how she is. Now she speaks in her "bold" tone and since she appears more composed, to the point of being cheerful, than her words might indicate, I am not seriously concerned about her.

But the roomette soon becomes suffocating and, not feeling up to talking business with Sidney Gross, I head in the opposite direction, stop in the first vestibule and have a long drink from my Mardi Gras bottle. We must be pulling into Jackson. The train screeches slowly around a curve and through the back of town. Kate comes out and stands beside me without a word. She smells of soap and seems in vaulting good spirits.

"Have a drink?"

"Do you remember going up to Baton Rouge on the train to see the football games?"

"Sure." Balancing there, her oval face aglow in the dark vestibule, hair combed flat on her head and down into the collar of her suit, she looks like a college girl. She drinks, pressing fingers to her throat. "Lord, how beautiful."

The train has stopped and our car stands high in the air, squarely above a city street. The nearly full moon swims through streaming ragtags of cloud and sheds a brilliant light on the Capitol dome and the spanking new glass-and-steel office buildings and the empty street with its glittering streetcar track. Not a soul is in sight. Far away, beyond the wings of the Capitol building stretch the dark tree-covered hills and the twinkling lights of the town. By some trick of moonlight the city seems white as snow and never-tenanted; it sleeps away on its hilltop like the holy city of Zion.

Kate shakes her head slowly in the rapt way she got from her stepmother. I try to steer her away from beauty. Beauty is a whore.

"You see that building yonder? That's Southern Life and Accident. If you had invested a hundred dollars in 1942, you'd now be worth twenty-five thousand. Your father bought a good deal of the original stock." Money is a better god than beauty.

"You don't know what I *mean*," she cries in the same soft rapture.

I know what she means all right. But I know something she doesn't know. Money is a good counterpoise to beauty. Beauty, the quest of beauty alone, is a whoredom. Ten years ago I pursued beauty and gave no thought to money. I listened to the lovely tunes of Mahler and felt a sickness in my very soul. Now I pursue money and on the whole feel better.

"I see how I could live in a city!" Kate cries. She turns to face me and clasps her hands behind my waist.

"How?"

"Only one way. By your telling me what to do. It is as simple as that. Why didn't I see it before?"

"That I should tell you what to do?"

"Yes. It may not be the noblest way of living, but it is one way. It is my way! Oh dear sweet old Binx, what a joy it is to discover at last what one is. It doesn't matter what you are as long as you *know*!"

"What are you?"

"I'll gladly tell you because I just found out and I never want to forget. Please don't let me forget. I am a religious person."

"How is that?"

"Don't you see? What I want is to believe in someone completely and then do what he wants me to do. If God were to tell me: Kate, here is what I want you to do; you get off this train right now and go over there to that corner by the Southern Life and Accident Insurance Company and stand there for the rest of your life and speak kindly to people—you think I would not do it? You think I would not be the happiest girl in Jackson, Mississippi? I would."

I have a drink and look at her corner. The moonlight seems palpable, a dense pure matrix in which is embedded curbstone and building alike.

She takes the bottle. "Will you tell me what to do?"

"Sure."

"You can do it because you are not religious. God is not religious. You are the unmoved mover. You don't need God or anyone else—no credit to you, unless it is a credit to be the most self-centered person alive. I don't know whether I love you, but I believe in you and I will do what you tell me. Now if I marry you, will you tell me: Kate, this morning do such and such, and if we have to go to a party, will you tell me: Kate, stand right there and have three drinks and talk to so and so? Will you?"

"Sure."

Kate locks her arms around my chest, wrist in hand, and gives me a passionate kiss.

Later, just as I knew it would, her precious beauty leaves her flat and she is frightened. Another trip to the washroom and now she stands swaying against me as Sieur Iberville rocks along through north Mississippi. We leave spring behind. The moon hangs westering and yellow over winter fields as blackened and ancient and haunted as battlegrounds.

"Oh oh oh," Kate moans and clings to me. "I feel awful. Let's go to your roomette."

"It's been made up."

"Then we'll lie down."

We have to lie down: the door opens onto the bed. Feeling tender toward her, I embrace her and tell her that I love her.

"Oh no," says Kate and takes hold of me coarsely. "None of that, bucko."

"None of what?"

"No love, please."

I misunderstand her and pull away.

"No no. Don't leave either," she says, holding me and watching me still.

"All right."

"Just don't speak to me of love, bucko."

"All right, but don't call me bucko."

Her black spiky eyes fall full upon me, but not quite seeing, I think. Propped on one hand, she bites her lip and lets the other fall on me heavily, as if I were an old buddy. "I'll tell you something."

"What?"

"The other day I said to Merle." Again the hand falls heavily and takes hold of me. "What would you say to me having a little fling? He misunderstood me and gave me the business about a mature and tender relation between adults etcetera etcetera—you know. I said, no no, Merle, you got it wrong. I'm talking about some plain old monkey business—" she gives me a shake, "—like a comic book one of your aunt's maids showed me last week in which Tillie the Toiler and Mac—not the real Tillie, you understand, but a Frenchy version of Tillie—go to an office party and Tillie has a little set-to with Mac in the stockroom and gets caught by Whipple. I told Merle about it and said: that's what I mean, Merle, how about that?"

"What did Merle say?"

Kate doesn't seem to hear. She drums her fingers on the sill and gazes out at the rushing treetops.

"So—when all is said and done, that is the real thing, isn't it? Admit it. You and the little Hondurian on the second floor with her little book, in the morning, in the mid-morning, and there in the linen closet with the mops and pails—"

"It is your Hondurian and your comic book—"

"Now I'll tell you what you can do, Whipple. You get out of here and come back in exactly five minutes. Oh you're a big nasty Whipple and you're only fit for one thing."

I'll have to tell you the truth, Rory, painful though it is. Nothing would please me more than to say that I had done one of two things. Either that I did what you do: tuck Debbie in your bed and, with a show of virtue so victorious as to be ferocious, grab pillow and blanket and take to the living-room sofa, there to lie in the dark, hands clasped behind head, gaze at the ceiling and talk through the open door of your hopes and dreams. Or—do what a hero in a novel would do: he too is a seeker and a pilgrim of sorts and he is just in from Guanajuato or Sambuco where he has found the Real Right Thing or from the East where he apprenticed himself to a wise man and became proficient in the seventh path to the seventh happiness. Yet he does not disdain this world either and when it happens that a maid comes to his bed with a heart full of longing for him, he puts down his book in a good and cheerful spirit and gives her as merry a time as she could possibly wish for. Whereupon, with her dispatched into as sweet a sleep as ever Scarlett enjoyed the morning of Rhett's return, he takes up his book again and is in an instant ten miles high and on the Way.

No, Rory, I did neither. We did neither. We did very badly and almost did not do at all. Flesh poor flesh failed us. The burden was too great and flesh poor flesh, neither hallowed by sacrament nor despised by spirit (for despising is not the worst fate to overtake the flesh), but until this moment seen through and canceled, rendered null by the cold and fishy eye of the malaise—flesh poor flesh now at this moment summoned all at once to be all and everything, end all and be all, the last and only hope—quails and fails. The truth is I was frightened half to death by her bold (not really bold, not whorish bold but theorish bold) carrying on. I reckon I am used to my blushing little Lindas from Gentilly. Kate too was scared. We shook like leaves. Kate was scared because it seemed now that even Tillie the Toiler must fail her. I never worked so hard in my life, Rory. I had no choice: the alternative was unspeakable. Christians talk about the horror of sin, but they have overlooked something. They keep talking as if everyone were a great sinner, when the truth is that nowadays one is hardly up to it. There is very little sin in the depths of the malaise. The highest moment of a malaisian's life can be that moment when he manages to sin like a proper human (Look at us, Binx—my vagabond friends as good as cried out to me—we're sinning! We're succeeding! We're human after all.).

"Good night, sweet Whipple. Now you tuck Kate in. Poor Kate." She turns the pillow over for the cool of the underside. "Good night, sweet Whipple, good night, good night, good night."

3. IT TURNS OUT THAT MY MISGIVINGS ABOUT CHI-cago were justified. No sooner do we step down from the train than the genie-soul of Chicago flaps down like a buzzard and perches on my shoulder. During the whole of our brief sojourn I am ridden by it—brief sojourn, I say, briefer even than it was planned to be, since it was cut abruptly short by the catastrophe Monday night, the very night of our arrival. All day long before the catastrophe I stand sunk in thought, blinking and bemused, on street corners. Kate looks after me. She is strangely at home in the city, wholly impervious to the five million personal rays of Chicagoans and the peculiar smell of existence here, which must be sniffed and gotten hold of before taking a single step away from the station (if only somebody could tell me who built the damn station, the circumstances of the building, details of the wrangling between city officials and the railroad, so that I would not fall victim to it, the station, the very first crack off the bat. Every place of arrival should have a booth set up and manned by an ordinary person whose task it is to greet strangers and give them a little trophy of local space-time stuff—tell them of his difficulties in high school and put a pinch of soil in their pockets—in order to insure that the stranger shall not become an Anyone). Oh son of a bitch but I am in a sweat. Kate takes charge with many a cluck and much fuss, as if she had caught sight in me of a howling void and meant to conceal it from the world. All of a sudden she is a regular city girl not distinguishable from any other little low-browed olive-skinned big-butted Mediterranean such as populates the streets and subways of the North.

I am consoled only to see that I was not mistaken: Chicago is just as I remembered it. I was here twenty-five years ago. My father brought me and Scott up to see the Century of Progress and once later to the World Series. Not a single thing do I remember from the first trip but this: the sense of the place, the savor of the genie-soul of the place which every place has or else is not a place. I could have been wrong: it could have been nothing of the sort, not the memory of a place but the memory of being a child. But one step out into the brilliant March day and there it is as big as life, the genie-soul of the place which, wherever you go, you must meet and master first thing or be met and mastered. Until now, one genie-soul and only one ever proved too strong for me: San Francisco—up and down the hills I pursued him, missed him and was pursued, by a presence, a powdering of fall gold in the air, a trembling brightness that pierced to the heart, and the sadness of coming at last to the sea, the coming to the end of America. Nobody but a Southerner knows the wrenching rinsing sadness of the cities of the North. Knowing all about genie-souls and living in haunted places like Shiloh and the Wilderness and Vicksburg and Atlanta where the ghosts of heroes walk abroad by day and are more real than people, he knows a ghost when he sees one, and no sooner does he step off the train in New York or Chicago or San Francisco than he feels the genie-soul perched on his shoulder.

Here is Chicago. Now, exactly as twenty-five years ago, the buildings are heavy and squarish and set down far apart and at random like monuments on a great windy plain. And the Lake. The Lake in New Orleans is a backwater glimmering away in a pleasant lowland. Not here. Here the Lake is the North itself: a perilous place from which the spirit winds come pouring forth all roused up and crying out alarm.

The wind and the space—they are the genie-soul. Son of a bitch, how can I think about variable endowments, feeling the genie-soul of Chicago perched on my shoulder?

But the wind and the space, they are the genie-soul. The wind blows in steady from the Lake and claims the space for its own, scouring every inch of the pavements and the cold stony fronts of the buildings. It presses down between buildings, shouldering them apart in skyey fields of light and air. The air is windpressed into a lens, magnifying and sharpening and silencing—everything is silenced in the uproar of the wind that comes ransacking down out of the North. This is a city where no one dares dispute the claim of the wind and the skyey space to the out-of-doors. This Midwestern sky is the nakedest loneliest sky in America. To escape it, people live inside and underground. One other thing I remember: my father took me down into one of these monuments to see the pool where

Tarzan-Johnnie-Weissmuller used to swim—an echoing underground place where a cold gray light filtered down from a three-story skylight and muscular men wearing metal discs swam and shouted, their voices ringing against the wet tile walls.

Some years later, after Scott's death, we came my father and I to the Field Museum, a long dismal peristyle dwindling away into the howling distance, and inside stood before a tableau of Stone Age Man, father, mother and child crouched around an artificial ember in postures of minatory quiet—until, feeling my father's eye on me, I turned and saw what he required of me—very special father and son we were that summer, he staking his everything this time on a perfect comradeship—and I, seeing in his eyes the terrible request, requiring from me his very life; I, through a child's cool perversity or some atavistic recoil from an intimacy too intimate, turned him down, turned away, refused him what I knew I could not give.

Prepared then for the genie-soul of Chicago, we take the city in stride at first and never suffer two seconds of malaise. Kate is jolly. Straight to the Stevens to register for rooms and the Cracker Barrel—there is Sidney standing by the reception table, princely-looking in his way of standing not like the others in friendly head-down-to-listen attitudes, but rared back in his five and a half feet, hand in pocket and coat hiked open at the vent, forehead faceted and flashing light.

Sidney fastens a plastic name card to my lapel and, before I know it, has hustled me off upstairs to a blue ballroom, leaving Kate and Margot to trail along, somewhat stony-faced, behind us.

"What is this, Sidney?" I say dismayed and hanging back. I begin to sweat and can only think of hitting the street and having three drinks in the first bar. Trapped in this blue cave, the genie-soul of Chicago will surely catch up with us. "I didn't think there were any doings till tomorrow."

"That's right. This is only the Hot Stove League."

"Oh Lord, what is that?" I say sweating.

"We get acquainted, talk over last year's business, kick around the boners of the funds. You'll like it."

Sure enough, there in the middle of the floor is a ten-foot potbellied stove made of red cellophane. Waiters pass by with trays of martinis and a salon orchestra plays "Getting to Know You."

The delegates are very decent fellows. I find myself talking to half a dozen young men from the West Coast and liking them very much—one in particular, a big shy fellow from Spokane named Stanley Kinchen, and his wife, a fine-looking woman, yellow-haired and bigger than Sharon, lips curling like a rose petal, head thrown back like a queen and a tremendous sparkle in the eye. What good people they are. It is not at all bad being a businessman. There is a spirit of trust and cooperation here. Everyone jokes about such things, but if businessmen were not trusting of each other and could not set their great projects going on credit, the country would collapse to-morrow and be no better off than Saudi Arabia. It strikes me that Stanley Kinchen would actually do anything for me. I know I would for him. I introduce Kate as my fiancée and she pulls down her mouth. I can't tell whether it is me she is disgusted with or my business colleagues. But these fellows: so friendly and—? What, dejected? I can't be sure.

Kinchen asks me if I am going to be in the Cracker Barrel. He is very nervous: it seems he is program chairman and somebody defected on him. He takes me aside.

"Would you do me a favor? Would you kick off with a ten minute talk on Selling Aids?"

"Sure."

We shake hands and part good comrades.

But I have to get out of here, good fellows or no good fellows. Too much fellow feeling makes me nervous, to tell the truth. Another minute and the ballroom will itself grow uneasy. Already the cellophane stove has begun to glow ominously.

"I have to find Harold Graebner," I tell Kate.

I grab her hand and slip out and away into the perilous out-of-doors, find the tiniest bar in the busiest block of the Loop. There I see her plain, see plain for the first time since I lay wounded in a ditch and watched an Oriental finch scratching around in the leaves—a quiet little body she is, a tough little city Celt; no, more of a Rachel really, a dark little Rachel bound home to Brooklyn on the IRT. I give her a pat on the leg.

"What?" she says, hardly paying attention—she is busy finding Harold's address on the map and adding up the bar bill. I never noticed how shrewd and parsimonious she is—a true Creole.

"Sweet Kate," say I patting her.

"All right, let's go." But she does not leave immediately. We have six drinks in two bars, catch buses, cross a hundred miles of city blocks, pass in the neighborhood of millions of souls, and come at last to a place called Wilmette which turns out not to be a place at all since it has no genie, where lives Harold Graebner the only soul known to me in the entire Midwest. Him, one soul in five million, we must meet and greet, wish good luck and bid farewell—else we cannot be sure we are here at all—before hopping off again into the maze of a city set down so unaccountably under the great thundering-lonesome Midwestern sky.

Off the bus and hopping along Wilmette happy as jaybirds, pass within a few feet of noble Midwestern girls with their clear eyes and their splendid butts and never a thought for them. What an experience, Rory, to be free of it for once. Rassled out. What a sickness it is, Rory, this latter-day post-Christian sex. To be pagan it would be one thing, an easement taken easily in a rosy old pagan world; to be Christian it would be another thing, fornication forbidden and not even to be thought of in the new life, and

I can see that it need not be thought of if there were such a life. But to be neither pagan nor Christian but this: oh this is a sickness, Rory. For it to be longed after and dreamed of the first twenty years of one's life, not practiced but not quite prohibited; simply longed after, longed after as a fruit not really forbidden but mock-forbidden and therefore secretly prized, prized first last and always by the cult of the naughty nice wherein everyone is nicer than Christians and naughtier than pagans, wherein there are dreamed not one but two American dreams: of Ozzie and Harriet, nicer-than-Christian folks, and of Tillie and Mac and belly to back.

We skip on by like jaybirds in July.

Harold lives in a handsome house in a new suburb back of Wilmette. His father left him a glass business in South Chicago and Harold has actually gotten rich. Every Christmas he sends a card with a picture of his wife and children and a note something like: "Netted better than thirty-five thou this year—now ain't that something?" You would have to know Harold to understand that this is not exactly a boast. It is a piece of cheerful news from a cheerful and simple sort of a fellow who can't get over his good fortune and who therefore has to tell you about it. "Now ain't that something, Rollo?" he would say and put up his hands in his baby-claw gesture. I know what he means. Every time American Motors jumps two dollars, I feel the same cheerful and expanding benevolence.

Since Kate and I can hardly wait to be back on our rambles, we visit with Harold about twenty minutes. As I said before, Harold loves me because he saved my life. I love him because he is a hero. I have a boundless admiration for heroes and Harold is the real thing. He got the DSC for a patrol action in the Chongchon Valley. Another lieutenant leading the fix patrol—I, you may as well know—got himself hung up; Lieutenant Graebner, who had the support patrol, came roaring up through the mortar fire like old Pete Longstreet himself and, using his three five rocket launcher like a carbine, shot a hole through the concertina (we were hung up on a limestone knob encircled by the concertina) and set fire to an acre or so of Orientals. When I say he is an unlikely hero, I don't mean he is a modest little fellow like Audie Murphy—Audie Murphy is a hero and he looks like a hero. Harold is *really* unheroic—to such a degree that you can't help but feel he squanders his heroism. Not at all reticent about the war, he speaks of it in such a flat unlovely way that his own experiences sound disappointing. With his somewhat snoutish nose and his wavy hair starting halfway back on his head and his singsongy way of talking, he reminds me of a TV contestant:

M.C.: Lieutenant, I bet you were glad to see the fog roll in that particular night.
HAROLD (unaccountably prissy and singsongy): Mr Marx, I think I can truthfully say that was one time I didn't mind being in a fog about something (looking around at the audience).
M.C.: Hey! I'm supposed to make the jokes around here!

Harold's wife is a thin hump-shouldered girl with a beautiful face. She stands a ways off from us holding her baby, my godson, and hesitates between a sort of living room and a peninsula bar; she seems on the point of asking us to sit down in one place or the other but she never does. I keep thinking she is going to get tired herself, holding the big baby. Looking at her, I know just how Harold sees her: as beeyoutiful. He used to say that so-and-so, Veronica Lake maybe, was beeyoutiful—Harold is originally from Indiana and he called me peculiar Midwestern names like "heller" and "turkey"—and his wife is beautiful in just the same way: blond hair waving down her cheeks like a madonna, heavenly blue eyes, but stooped so that her shoulder-blades flare out in back like wings.

Harold walks up and down with both hands lifted up in the baby-claw gesture he uses when he talks, and there stands his little madonna-wife sort of betwixt and between us and the kids around the TV. But Harold is glad to see me. "Old Rollo," he says, looking at the middle of my chest. "This is great, Rollo," and he is restless with an emotion he can't identify. Rollo is a nickname he gave me in the Orient—it evidently signifies something in the Midwest which is not current in Louisiana. "Old Rollo"—and he would be beside himself with delight at the aptness of it. Now it comes over him in the strongest way: what a good thing it is to see a comrade with whom one has suffered much and endured much, but also what a wrenching thing. Up and down he goes, arms upraised, restless with it and not knowing what it is.

"Harold, about the baby's baptism—"

"He was baptized yesterday," says Harold absently.

"I'm sorry."

"You were godfather-by-proxy."

"Oh."

The trouble is there is no place to come to rest. We stand off the peninsula like ships becalmed—unable to move.

Turning my back on Harold, I tell Kate and Veronica how Harold saved my life, telling it jokingly with only one or two looks around at him. It is too much for Harold, not my gratitude, not the beauty of his own heroism, but the sudden confrontation of a time past, a time so terrible and splendid in its arch-reality; and so lost—cut adrift like a great ship in the flood of years. Harold tries to parse it out, that time and the time after, the strange ten years intervening, and it is too much for him. He shakes his head like a fighter.

We stand formally in the informal living area.

"Harold, how long have you been here?"

"Three years. Look at this, Rollo." Harold shoves along the bar-peninsula a modernistic horsehead carved out of white wood, all flowing mane and arching neck. "Who do you think made it?"

"It's very good."

"Old Rollo," says Harold, eying the middle of my chest. Harold can't parse it out, so he has to do something. "Rollo, how tough are you? I bet I can take you." Harold wrestled at Northwestern. "I could put you down right now." Harold is actually getting mad at me.

"Listen, Harold," I say, laughing. "Do you go into the city every day?"

Harold nods but does not raise his eyes.

"How did you decide to live here?"

"Sylvia's family live in Glencoe. Rollo, how do you like it way down yonder in New Orleans?"

Harold would really like to wrestle and not so playfully either. I walked in and brought it with me, the wrenching in the chest. It would be better for him to be rid of it and me.

Ten minutes later he lets us out at the commuter station and tears off into the night.

"What a peculiar family," says Kate, gazing after the red turrets of Harold's Cadillac.

Back to the Loop where we dive into the mother and Ur-womb of all moviehouses—an Aztec mortuary of funeral urns and glyphs, thronged with the spirit-presences of another day, William Powell and George Brent and Patsy Kelly and Charley Chase, the best friends of my childhood—and see a movie called *The Young Philadelphians*. Kate holds my hand tightly in the dark.

Paul Newman is an idealistic young fellow who is disillusioned and becomes cynical and calculating. But in the end he recovers his ideals.

Outside, a new note has crept into the wind, a black williwaw sound straight from the terrible wastes to the north. "Oh oh oh," wails Kate as we creep home to the hotel, sunk into ourselves and with no stomach even for hand-holding. "Something is going to happen."

Something does. A yellow slip handed across the hotel desk commands me to call operator three in New Orleans.

This I accordingly do, and my aunt's voice speaks to the operator, then to me, and does not change its tone. She does not bother to add a single overtone of warmth or cold, love or hate, to the monotone of her notification—and this is more ominous than ten thousand williwaws.

"Is Kate with you?"

"Yes ma'am."

"Would you like to know how we found you?"

"Yes."

"The police found Kate's car at the terminal."

"The police?"

"Kate did not tell anyone she was leaving. However, her behavior is not unexplainable and therefore not inexcusable. Yours is."

I am silent.

"Why didn't you tell me?"

I think. "I can't remember."

4. IT IS IMPOSSIBLE TO FIND A SEAT ON A FLIGHT TO New Orleans the night before Mardi Gras. No trains are scheduled until Tuesday morning. But buses leave every hour or so. I send my aunt a telegram and call Stanley Kinchen and excuse myself from the talk on Selling Aids—it is all right: the original speaker has recovered. Stanley and I part even more cordially than we met. It is a stratospheric cordiality such as can only make further meetings uneasy. But I do not mind. At midnight we are bound for New Orleans on a Scenicruiser which takes a more easterly course than the Illinois Central, down along the Wabash to Memphis by way of Evansville and Cairo.

It is good to be leaving; Chicago is fit for no more than a short rotation. Kate is well. The summons from her stepmother has left her neither glum nor fearful. She speaks at length to her stepmother and, with her sure instinct for such matters, gets her talking about canceling reservations and return tickets, wins her way, decides we'll stay, then changes her mind and insists on coming home to ease their minds. Now she gazes curiously about the bus station, giving way every few seconds to tremendous face-splitting yawns. Once on the bus she collapses into a slack-jawed oblivion and sleeps all the way to the Ohio River. I doze fitfully and wake for good when the dawn breaks on the outskirts of Terre Haute. When it is light enough, I take out my paperback *Arabian Deserta* and read until we stop for breakfast in Evansville. Kate eats heartily, creeps back to the bus, takes one look at the black waters of the Ohio River and the naked woods of the bottom lands where winter still clings like a violet mist, and falls heavily to sleep, mouth mashed open against my shoulder.

Today is Mardi Gras, fat Tuesday, but our bus has left Chicago much too late to accommodate Carnival visitors. The passengers are an everyday assortment of mothers-in-law visiting sons-in-law in Memphis, school teachers and telephone operators bound for vacations in quaint old Vieux Carré. Our upper deck is a green bubble where, it turns out, people feel themselves dispensed from the conventional silence below as if, in mounting with others to see the wide world and the green sky, they had already established a kind of freemasonry and spoken the first word among themselves. I surrender my seat to Kate's stretchings out against me and double up her legs for her and for the rest of the long day's journey down through Indiana and Illinois and Kentucky and Tennessee and Mississippi hold converse with two passengers—the first, a romantic from Wisconsin; the second, a salesman from a small manufacturing firm in Murfreesboro, Tennessee, who wrecked his car in Gary.

Now in the fore seat of the bubble and down we go plunging along the Illinois bank of the Mississippi through a region of sooty glens falling steeply away to the west and against the slope of which are propped tall frame houses with colored windows and the spires of Polish churches. I read:

> We mounted in the morrow twilight; but long after daybreak the heavens seemed shut over us, as a tomb, with gloomy clouds. We are engaged in horrid lava beds.

The romantic sits across the aisle, slumped gracefully, one foot propped on the metal ledge. He is reading *The Charterhouse of Parma*. His face is extraordinarily well-modeled and handsome but his head is too small and, arising as it does from the great collar of his car coat, it makes him look a bit dandy and dudish. Two things I am curious about. How does he sit? Immediately graceful and not aware of it or mediately graceful and aware of it? How does he read *The Charterhouse of Parma*? Immediately as a man who is in the world and who has an appetite for the book as he might have an appetite for peaches, or mediately as one who finds himself under the necessity of sticking himself into the world in a certain fashion, of slumping in an acceptable slump, of reading an acceptable book on an acceptable bus? Is he a romantic?

He is a romantic. His posture is the first clue: it is too good to be true, this distillation of all graceful slumps. To clinch matters, he catches sight of me and my book and goes into a spasm of recognition and shyness. To put him out of his misery, I go over and ask him how he likes his book. For a tenth of a second he eyes me to make sure I am not a homosexual; but he has already seen Kate with me and sees her now, lying asleep and marvelously high in the hip. (I have observed that it is no longer possible for one young man to speak unwarily to another not known to him, except in certain sections of the South and West, and certainly not with a book in his hand.) As for me, I have already identified him through his shyness. It is pure heterosexual shyness. He is no homosexual, but merely a romantic. Now he closes his book and stares hard at it as if he would, by dint of staring alone, tear from it its soul in a word. "It's—very good," he says at last and blushes. The poor fellow. He has just begun to suffer from it, this miserable trick the romantic plays upon himself: of setting just beyond his reach the very thing he prizes. For he prizes just such a meeting, the chance meeting with a chance friend on a chance bus, a friend he can talk to, unburden himself of some of his terrible longings. Now having encountered such a one, me, the rare bus friend, of course he strikes himself dumb. It is a case for direct questioning.

He is a senior at a small college in northern Wisconsin where his father is bursar. His family is extremely proud of the educational progress of their children. Three sisters have assorted PhDs and MAs, piling up degrees on into the middle of life (he speaks in a rapid rehearsed way, a way he deems appropriate for our rare encounter, and when he is forced to use an ordinary word like "bus"—having no other way of conferring upon it a vintage flavor, he says it in quotes and with a wry expression). Upon completion of his second trimester and having enough credits to graduate, he has lit out for New Orleans to load bananas for a while and perhaps join the merchant marine. Smiling tensely, he strains forward and strikes himself dumb. For a while, he says. He means that he hopes to find himself a girl, the rarest of rare pieces, and live the life of Rudolfo on the balcony, sitting around on the floor and experiencing soul-communions. I have my doubts. In the first place, he will defeat himself, jump ten miles ahead of himself, scare the wits out of some girl with his great choking silences, want her so desperately that by his own peculiar logic he can't have her; or having her, jump another ten miles beyond both of them and end by fleeing to the islands where, propped at the rail of his ship in some rancid port, he will ponder his own loneliness.

In fact, there is nothing more to say to him. The best one can do is deflate the pressure a bit, the terrible romantic pressure, and leave him alone. He is a moviegoer, though of course he does not go to movies.

The salesman has no such trouble. Like many businessmen, he is a better metaphysician than the romantic. For example, he gives me a sample of his product, a simple ell of tempered and blued steel honed to a two-edged blade. Balancing it in his hand, he tests its heft and temper. The hand knows the blade, practices its own metaphysic of the goodness of the steel.

"Thank you very much," I say, accepting the warm blade.

"You know all in the world you have to do?"

"No."

"Walk into the office—" (He sells this attachment to farm implement stores) "—and ask the man how much is his bush hog blade. He'll tell you about nine and a half a pair. Then all you do is drop this on his desk and say thirty-five cents and you can't break it."

"What does it do?"

"Anything. Clears, mulches, peas, beans, saplings so big, anything. That little sombitch will go now." He strikes one hand straight out past the other, and I have a sense of the storied and even legendary properties of the blade, attested in the peculiar Southern esteem of the excellence of machinery: the hot-damn beat-all risible accolade conferred when some new engine sallies forth in its outlandish scissoring side-winding foray.

We sit on the rear seat, the salesman with his knee crocked up, heel under him, arm levered out over his knee.

He wears black shoes and white socks for his athlete's foot and now and then sends down a finger to appease the itching. It pleases him to speak of his cutter and of his family down in Murfreesboro and speak all the way to Union City and not once to inquire of me and this pleases me since I would not know what to say. Businessmen are our only metaphysicians, but the trouble is, they are one-track metaphysicians. By the time the salesman gets off in Union City, my head is spinning with facts about the thirty-five cent cutter. It is as if I had lived in Murfreesboro all my life.

Canal Street is dark and almost empty. The last parade, the Krewe of Comus, has long since disappeared down Royal Street with its shuddering floats and its blazing flambeau. Street cleaners sweep confetti and finery into soggy heaps in the gutters. The cold mizzling rain smells of sour paper pulp. Only a few maskers remain abroad, tottering apes clad in Spanish moss, Frankenstein monsters with bolts through their necks, and a neighborhood gang or two making their way arm and arm, wheeling and whip-popping, back to their trucks.

Kate is dry-eyed and abstracted. She stands gazing about as if she had landed in a strange city. We decide to walk up Loyola Avenue to get our cars. The romantic is ahead of us, at the window of a lingerie shop, the gay sort where black net panties invest legless torsos. Becoming aware of us before we pass and thinking to avoid the embarrassment of a greeting (what are we to say, after all, and suppose the right word fails us?), he hurries away, hands thrust deep in his pockets, his small well-modeled head tricking to and fro above the great collar of his car coat.

V

1. "I AM NOT SAYING THAT I PRETEND TO UNDERstand you. What I am saying is that after two days of complete mystification it has at last dawned on me what it is I fail to understand. That is at least a step in the right direction. It was the novelty of it that put me off, you see. I do believe that you have discovered something new under the sun."

It is with a rare and ominous objectivity that my aunt addresses me Wednesday morning. In the very violence of her emotion she has discovered the energy to master it, so that now, in the flush of her victory, she permits herself to use the old forms of civility and even of humor. The only telltale sign of menace is the smile through her eyes, which is a bit too narrow and finely drawn.

"Would you verify my hypothesis? Is not that your discovery? First, is it not true that in all of past history people who found themselves in difficult situations behaved in certain familiar ways, well or badly, courageously or cowardly, with distinction or mediocrity, with honor or dishonor. They are recognizable. They display courage, pity, fear, embarrassment, joy, sorrow, and so on. Such anyhow has been the funded experience of the race for two or three thousand years, has it not? Your discovery, as best as I can determine, is that there is an alternative which no one has hit upon. It is that one finding oneself in one of life's critical situations need not after all respond in one of the traditional ways. No. One may simply default. Pass. Do as one pleases, shrug, turn on one's heel and leave. Exit. Why after all need one act humanly? Like all great discoveries, it is breathtakingly simple.'' She smiles a quizzical-legal sort of smile which reminds me of Judge Anse.

The house was no different this morning. The same chorus of motors, vacuum cleaners, dishwasher, laundromat, hum and throb against each other. From an upper region, reverberating down the back stairwell, comes the muted hollering of Bessie Coe, as familiar and querulous a sound as the sparrows under the eaves. Nor was Uncle Jules different, except only in his slight embarrassment, giving me wide berth as I passed him on the porch and saying his good morning briefly and sorrowfully as if the farthest limit of his disapproval lay in the brevity of his greeting. Kate was nowhere to be seen. Until ten o'clock my aunt, I know, is to be found at her rolltop desk where she keeps her ''accounts.'' There is nothing to do but go directly in to her and stand at ease until she takes notice of me. Now she looks over, as erect and handsome as the Black Prince.

''Yes?''

''I am sorry that through a misunderstanding or thoughtlessness on my part you were not told of Kate's plans to go with me to Chicago. No doubt it was my thoughtlessness. In any case I am sorry and I hope that your anger—''

''Anger? You are mistaken. It was not anger. It was discovery.''

''Discovery of what?''

''Discovery that someone in whom you had placed great hopes was suddenly not there. It is like leaning on what seems to be a good stalwart shoulder and feeling it go all mushy and queer.''

We both gaze down at the letter opener, the soft iron

sword she has withdrawn from the grasp of the helmeted figure on the inkstand.

"I am sorry for that."

"The fact that you are a stranger to me is perhaps my fault. It was stupid of me not to believe it earlier. For now I do believe that you are not capable of caring for anyone, Kate, Jules, or myself—no more than that Negro man walking down the street—less so, in fact, since I have a hunch he and I would discover some slight tradition in common." She seems to notice for the first time that the tip of the blade is bent. "I honestly don't believe it occurred to you to let us know that you and Kate were leaving, even though you knew how desperately sick she was. I truly do not think it ever occurred to you that you were abusing a sacred trust in carrying that poor child off on a fantastic trip like that or that you were betraying the great trust and affection she has for you. Well?" she asks when I do not reply.

I try as best I can to appear as she would have me, as being, if not right, then wrong in a recognizable, a right form of wrongness. But I can think of nothing to say.

"Do you have any notion of how I felt when, not twelve hours after Kate attempted suicide, she vanishes without a trace?"

We watch the sword as she lets it fall over the fulcrum of her forefinger; it goes *tat't't* on the brass hinge of the desk. Then, so suddenly that I almost start, my aunt sheathes the sword and places her hand flat on the desk. Turning it over, she flexes her fingers and studies the nails, which are deeply scored by longitudinal ridges.

"Were you intimate with Kate?"

"Intimate?"

"Yes."

"Not very."

"I ask you again. Were you intimate with her?"

"I suppose so. Though intimate is not quite the word."

"You suppose so. Intimate is not quite the word. I wonder what is the word. You see—'' she says with a sort of humor, ''—there is another of my hidden assumptions. All these years I have been assuming that between us words mean roughly the same thing, that among certain people, gentlefolk I don't mind calling them, there exists a set of meanings held in common, that a certain manner and a certain grace come as naturally as breathing. At the great moments of life—success, failure, marriage, death—our kind of folks have always possessed a native instinct for behavior, a natural piety of grace, I don't mind calling it. Whatever else we did or failed to do, we always had that. I'll make you a little confession. I am not ashamed to use the word class. I will also plead guilty to another charge. The charge is that people belonging to my class think they're better than other people. You're damn right we're better. We're better because we do not shirk our obligations either to ourselves or to others. We do not whine. We do not organize a minority group and blackmail the government. We do not prize mediocrity for mediocrity's sake. Oh I am aware that we hear a great many flattering things nowadays about your great common man—you know, it has always been revealing to me that he is perfectly content so to be called, because that is exactly what he is: the common man and when I say common I mean common as hell. Our civilization has achieved a distinction of sorts. It will be remembered not for its technology nor even its wars but for its novel ethos. Ours is the only civilization in history which has enshrined mediocrity as its national ideal. Others have been corrupt, but leave it to us to invent the most undistinguished of corruptions. No orgies, no blood running in the street, no babies thrown off cliffs. No, we're sentimental people and we horrify easily. True, our moral fiber is rotten. Our national character stinks to high heaven. But we are kinder than ever. No prostitute ever responded with a quicker spasm of sentiment when our hearts are touched. Nor is there anything new about thievery, lewdness, lying, adultery. What is new is that in our time liars and thieves and whores and adulterers wish also to be congratulated and are congratulated by the great public, if their confession is sufficiently psychological or strikes a sufficiently heartfelt and authentic note of sincerity. Oh, we are sincere. I do not deny it. I don't know anybody nowadays who is not sincere. Didi Lovell is the most sincere person I know: every time she crawls in bed with somebody else, she does so with the utmost sincerity. We are the most sincere Laodiceans who ever got flushed down the sinkhole of history. No, my young friend, I am not ashamed to use the word class. They say out there we think we're better. You're damn right we're better. And don't think they don't know it—" She raises the sword to Prytania Street. "Let me tell you something. If he out yonder is your prize exhibit for the progress of the human race in the past three thousand years, then all I can say is that I am content to be fading out of the picture. Perhaps we are a biological sport. I am not sure. But one thing I am sure of: we live by our lights, we die by our lights, and whoever the high gods may be, we'll look them in the eye without apology." Now my aunt swivels around to face me and not so bad-humoredly. "I did my best for you, son. I gave you all I had. More than anything I wanted to pass on to you the one heritage of the men of our family, a certain quality of spirit, a gaiety, a sense of duty, a nobility worn lightly, a sweetness, a gentleness with women—the only good things the South ever had and the only things that really matter in this life. Ah well. Still you can tell me one thing. I know you're not a bad boy—I wish you were. But how did it happen that none of this ever meant anything to you? Clearly it did not. Would you please tell me? I am genuinely curious."

I cannot tear my eyes from the sword. Years ago I bent the tip trying to open a drawer. My aunt looks too. Does she suspect?

"That would be difficult for me to say. You say that none of what you said ever meant anything to me. That is not true. On the contrary. I have never forgotten anything you ever said. In fact I have pondered over it all my life. My objections, though they are not exactly objections, cannot be expressed in the usual way. To tell the truth, I can't express them at all."

"I see. Do you condone your behavior with Kate?"

"Condone?" Condone. I screw up an eye. "I don't suppose so."

"You don't suppose so." My aunt nods gravely, almost agreeably, in her wry legal manner. "You knew that Kate was suicidal?"

"No."

"Would you have cared if Kate had killed herself?"

"Yes."

After a long silence she asks: "You have nothing more to say?"

I shake my head.

Mercer opens the door and sticks his head in, takes one whiff of the air inside, and withdraws immediately.

"Then tell me this. Yes, tell me this!" my aunt says, brightening as, groping, she comes at last to the nub of the matter. "Tell me this and this is all I shall ever want to know. I am assuming that we both recognize that you had a trust toward Kate. Perhaps my assumption was mistaken. But I know that you knew she was taking drugs. Is that not correct?"

"Yes."

"Did you know that she was taking drugs during this recent trip?"

"Yes."

"And you did what you did?"

"Yes."

"That is all you have to say?"

I am silent. Mercer starts the waxer. It was permission for this he sought. I think of nothing in particular. A cry goes up in the street outside, and there comes into my sight the Negro my aunt spoke of. He is Cothard, the last of the chimney sweeps, an outlandish blueblack Negro dressed in a frock coat and bashed-in top hat and carrying over his shoulder a bundle of palmetto leaves and brown straw. The cry comes again. *"R-r-r-ramonez la cheminée du haut en bas!"*

"One last question to satisfy my idle curiosity. What has been going on in your mind during all the years when we listened to music together, read the *Crito*, and spoke together—or was it only I who spoke—good Lord, I can't remember—of goodness and truth and beauty and nobility?"

Another cry and the *ramoneur* is gone. There is nothing for me to say.

"Don't you love these things? Don't you live by them?"

"No."

"What do you love? What do you live by?"

I am silent.

"Tell me where I have failed you."

"You haven't."

"What do you think is the purpose of life—to go to the movies and dally with every girl that comes along?"

"No."

A ledger lies open on her desk, one of the old-fashioned kind with a marbled cover, in which she has always kept account of her properties, sundry service stations, Canadian mines, patents—the peculiar business accumulation of a doctor—left to her by old Dr Wills. "Well." She closes it briskly and smiles up at me, a smile which, more than anything which has gone before, marks an ending. Smiling, she gives me her hand, head to one side, in her old party style. But it is her withholding my name that assigns me my new status. So she might have spoken to any one of a number of remotely connected persons, such as a Spring Fiesta tourist encountered by accident in her own hall.

We pass Mercer who stands respectfully against the wall. He murmurs a greeting which through an exquisite calculation expresses his affection for me and at the same time declares his allegiance to my aunt. Out of the corner of my eye, I see him hop nimbly into the dining room, full of fizzing good spirits. We find ourselves on the porch.

"I do thank you so much for coming by," says my aunt, fingering her necklace and looking past me at the Vaudrieul house.

Kate hails me at the corner. She leans into my MG, tucking her blouse, as brisk as a stewardess.

"You're stupid stupid stupid," she says with a malevolent look.

"What?"

"I heard it all, you poor stupid bastard." Then, appearing to forget herself, she drums her nails rapidly upon the windshield. "Are you going home now?"

"Yes."

"Wait for me there."

2. IT IS A GLOOMY DAY. GENTILLY IS SWEPT FITFULLY by desire and by an east wind from the burning swamps at Chef Menteur.

Today is my thirtieth birthday and I sit on the ocean wave in the schoolyard and wait for Kate and think of nothing. Now is the thirty-first year of my dark pilgrimage on this earth and knowing less than I ever knew before, having learned only to recognize merde when I see it, having inherited no more from my father than a good nose for merde, for every species of shit that flies—my only talent—smelling merde from every quarter, living in fact in the very century of merde, the great shithouse of scientific humanism where needs are satisfied, everyone becomes an anyone, a warm and creative person, and prospers like a dung beetle, and one hundred percent of people are humanists and ninety-eight percent believe in God, and men are dead, dead, dead; and the malaise has settled like a fallout and what people really fear is not that the bomb will fall but that the bomb will not fall—on this my thirtieth birthday, I know nothing and there is nothing to do but fall prey to desire.

Nothing remains but desire, and desire comes howling down Elysian Fields like a mistral. My search has been abandoned; it is no match for my aunt, her rightness and her despair, her despairing of me and her despairing of herself. Whenever I take leave of my aunt after one of her serious talks, I have to find a girl.

Fifty minutes of waiting for Kate on the ocean wave and I am beside myself. What has happened to her? She has spoken to my aunt and kicked me out. There is nothing to do but call Sharon at the office. The little pagoda of aluminum and glass, standing in the neutral ground of Elysian Fields at the very heart of the uproar of a public zone, is trim and pretty on the outside but evil-smelling within. Turning slowly around, I take note of the rhymes in pencil and the sad cartoons of solitary lovers; the wire thrills and stops and thrills and in the interval there comes into my ear my own breath as if my very self stood beside me and would not speak. The phone does not answer. Has she quit?

Some children have come into the playground across the street; two big boys give them a ride on the ocean wave. Ordinarily the little children ride only the merry-go-round which is set close to the ground and revolves in a fixed orbit.

I've got to find her, Rory. It is certain now that my aunt is right and that Kate knows it and that nothing is left but Sharon. The east wind whistles through the eaves of my pagoda and presses the glass against its fittings. I try the apartment. She is out. But Joyce is there, Joyce-in-the-window, Joyce of the naughty-you mouth and the buckskin jacket.

"This is Jack Bolling, Joyce," says a voice from old Virginia.

"Well well."

"Is Sharon there?"

"She is out with her mother and Stan." Joyce's voice has a Middle West snap. Moth-errr, she says and: we-ull we-ull. "I don't know when shill be back." She sounds like Pepper Young's sister.

"Who is Stan?"

"Stan Shamoun, her fiancé."

"Oh yes, that's right." What's right? She's not only quit. She's marrying the macaroni. "What about you? Are you getting married?"

"What's that?"

"I've been wanting to meet you for some time."

"I just thot of something."

"What?"

"The Lord of Misrule reigned yesterday—"

"Who?" Is she starting out on some sort of complicated Midwestern joke? Grinning like a lunatic, I hold on for dear life.

Joyce goes on talking in a roguish voice about the Lord of Misrule and a fellow down from Purdue, a dickens if she ever saw one.

The two big boys on the playground have got the ocean wave going fast enough so they can jump on and keep up speed by kicking the ground away on the low passes. *Iii-oorrr iii-oorrr* goes the dry socket on its pole in a faraway childish music and the children embrace the iron struts and lay back their heads to watch the whirling world.

"Joyce. I wonder if I may be frank with you"—the voice comes into my ear and I myself am silent.

"Please do. I like frank people."

"I thought you were that kind of person—" Old confederate Marlon Brando—a reedy insinuating voice, full of winks and leers and above all pleased with itself. What a shock. On and on it goes. "—I know some folks might think it was a little unconventional but I'm gon tell you anyway. I know you don't remember it but I saw you last Saturday—" It is too much trouble to listen.

"I remember!"

Round and round goes the ocean wave screeching out its Petrouchka music *iii-oorrr iii-oorrr* and now belling out so far that the inner bumper catches the pole and slings around in a spurt so outrageously past all outrage that the children embrace the iron struts for dear life.

"I'm only home for lunch," says Joyce. "But why don't you come over Saturday night. Some of the kids will be there. Praps we could all go to Pat O'Brien's." Joyce makes herself out to be a big girl child, one of the kids, and all set for high jinks.

"No praps about it."

A watery sunlight breaks through the smoke of the Chef and turns the sky yellow. Elysian Fields glistens like a vat of sulfur; the playground looks as if it alone had survived the end of the world. At last I spy Kate; her stiff little Plymouth comes nosing into my bus stop. There she sits like a bomber pilot, resting on her wheel and looking sideways at the children and not seeing, and she could be I myself, sooty-eyed and nowhere.

Is it possible that— For a long time I have secretly hoped for the end of the world and believed with Kate and my aunt and Sam Yerger and many other people that only after the end could the few who survive creep out of their holes and discover themselves to be themselves and to live as merrily as children among the viny ruins. Is it possible that—it is not too late?

Iii-oorrr goes the ocean wave, its struts twinkling in the golden light, its skirt swaying to and fro like a young dancing girl.

"I'd like to very much, Joyce. May I bring along my

own fiancée, Kate Cutrer? I want you and Sharon to meet her."

"Why shore, why shore," says Joyce in peculiar Midwest take-off of her roommate Sharon and sounding somewhat relieved, to tell the truth.

The playground is deserted. I notice that the school itself is locked and empty. Traffic goes hissing along Elysian Fields and the jaybirds jeer in the camphor trees. People turn in now and then at the school gate but they make for the church next door. At first I suppose it is a wedding or a funeral, but they leave by twos and threes and more arrive. Then, as a pair of youths come ambling along the sidewalk, I catch sight of the smudge at the hair roots. Of course. It is Ash Wednesday. Sharon has not quit me. All Cutrer branch offices close on Ash Wednesday.

We sit in Kate's car, a 1951 Plymouth which, with all her ups and downs, Kate has ever cared for faithfully. It is a tall gray coupe and it runs with a light gaseous sound. When she drives, head ducked down, hands placed symmetrically on the wheel, the pale underflesh of her arms trembling slightly, her paraphernalia—straw seat, Kleenex dispenser, magnetic tray for cigarettes—all set in order about her, it is easy to believe that the light stiff little car has become gradually transformed by its owner until it is hers herself in its every nut and bolt. When it comes fresh from the service station, its narrow tires still black and wet, the very grease itself seems not the usual muck but the thrifty amber sap of the slender axle tree.

"Why didn't you tell her about our plans?" Kate still holds the steering wheel and surveys the street. "I was in the library and heard every word. You *idiot*."

Kate is pleased. She is certain that I have carried off a grand stoic gesture, like a magazine hero.

"Did you tell her?" I ask.

"I told her we are to be married."

"Are we?"

"Yes."

"What did she say to that?"

"She didn't. She only hoped that you might come to see her this afternoon."

"I have to anyway."

'Why?"

"I promised her one week ago I would tell her what I planned to do."

"What do you plan to do?"

I shrug. There is only one thing I can do: listen to people, see how they stick themselves into the world, hand them along a ways in their dark journey and be handed along, and for good and selfish reasons. It only remains to decide whether this vocation is best pursued in a service station or—

"Are you going to medical school?"

"If she wants me to."

"Does that mean you can't marry me now?"

"No. You have plenty of money."

"Then let us understand each other."

"All right."

"I don't know whether I can succeed."

"I know you don't."

"It seems the wildest sort of thing to do."

"Yes."

"We had better make it fast."

"All right."

"I am so afraid."

Kate's forefinger begins to explore the adjacent thumb, testing the individual spikes of the feathered flesh. A florid new Mercury pulls up behind us and a Negro gets out and goes up into the church. He is more respectable than respectable; he is more middle-class than one could believe: his Archie Moore mustache, the way he turns and, seeing us see him, casts a weather eye at the sky; the way he plucks a handkerchief out of his rear pocket with a flurry of his coattail and blows his nose in a magic placative gesture (you see, I have been here before: it is a routine matter).

"If I could be sure you knew how frightened I am, it would help a great deal."

"You can be sure."

"Not merely of marriage. This afternoon I wanted some cigarettes, but the thought of going to the drugstore turned me to jelly."

I am silent.

"I am frightened when I am alone and I am frightened when I am with people. The only time I'm not frightened is when I'm with you. You'll have to be with me a great deal."

"I will."

"Do you want to?"

"Yes."

"I will be under treatment for a long time."

"I know that."

"And I'm not sure I'll ever change. Really change."

"You might."

"But I think I see a way. It seems to me that if we are together a great deal and you tell me the simplest things and not laugh at me—I beg you for pity's own sake never to laugh at me—tell me things like: Kate, it is all right for you to go down to the drugstore, and give me a kiss, then I will believe you. Will you do that?" she says with her not-quite-pure solemnity, her slightly reflected Sarah Lawrence solemnity.

"Yes, I'll do that."

She has started plucking at her thumb in earnest, tearing away little shreds of flesh. I take her hand and kiss the blood.

"But you must try not to hurt yourself so much."

"I will try! I will!"

The Negro has already come outside. His forehead is an ambiguous sienna color and pied: it is impossible to be sure that he received ashes. When he gets in his Mercury, he does not leave immediately but sits looking down at something on the seat beside him. A sample case? An insurance manual? I watch him closely in the rearview mirror. It is impossible to say why he is here. Is it part and parcel of the complex business of coming up in the world? Or is it because he believes that God himself is present here at the corner of Elysian Fields and Bons Enfants? Or is he here for both reasons: through some dim dazzling trick of grace, coming for the one and receiving the other as God's own importunate bonus?

It is impossible to say.

EPILOGUE

So ENDED MY THIRTIETH YEAR TO HEAVEN, AS THE POET called it.

In June Kate and I were married. It was practicable to wind up my business affairs in Gentilly and to accompany my aunt to North Carolina sooner than I expected, since Sharon, now Mrs Stanley Shamoun, had become so competent that she was able to transact the light summer business without assistance, at least until my replacement could be found. In August Mr Sartalamaccia purchased my duck club for twenty-five thousand dollars. When medical school began in September, Kate found a house near her step-mother, one of the very shotgun cottages done over by my cousin Nell Lovell and very much to Kate's taste with its saloon doors swinging into the kitchen, its charcoal-gray shutters and its lead St Francis in the patio.

My aunt has become fond of me. As soon as she accepted what she herself had been saying all those years, that the Bolling family had gone to seed and that I was not one of her heroes but a very ordinary fellow, we got along very well. Both women find me comical and laugh a good deal at my expense.

On Mardi Gras morning of the next year, my Uncle

Jules suffered a second heart attack at the Boston Club, from which he later died.

The following May, a few days after his fifteenth birthday, my half-brother Lonnie Smith died of a massive virus infection which was never positively identified.

As for my search, I have not the inclination to say much on the subject. For one thing, I have not the authority, as the great Danish philosopher declared, to speak of such matters in any way other than the edifying. For another thing, it is not open to me even to be edifying, since the time is later than his, much too late to edify or do much of anything except plant a foot in the right place as the opportunity presents itself—if indeed asskicking is properly distinguished from edification.

Further: I am a member of my mother's family after all and so naturally shy away from the subject of religion (a peculiar word this in the first place, *religion*; it is something to be suspicious of).

Reticence, therefore, hardly having a place in a document of this kind, it seems as good a time as any to make an end.

The day before Lonnie died, Kate took a notion to pay him a visit. Ordinarily I pick her up at Merle's office, drop her off at her stepmother's and drive downtown where I transact a few odds and ends of business for her, my aunt, at Uncle Jules's office. But today we have only to walk across the street from Merle's office to Touro Infirmary.

I had my doubts about Kate's idea. It was an extravagant womanish sort of whim, what I call privately a doubling, or duplication: like the time she took a notion to fly to Dallas in a state of rapture and hear Marian Anderson; it sounded to her like the sort of thing one might well do. I don't mean she worries about what is the fashionable thing to do; no, it just sounded like a good thing to do—what one does under the circumstances if one is the sort of

208

person who etc etc—so she did it. Also: she had not seen Lonnie since the onset of his illness and although I tried to prepare her for the change, she was not prepared.

Afterwards in the street, she went stumbling ahead of me, knuckles in her mouth and blind with tears.

"Oh my God, how dreadful."

"I shouldn't have let you go."

"It was like a blow in the face."

"I'm sorry."

"That poor little boy—he's so hideously thin and yellow, like one of those wrecks lying on a flatcar at Dachau. Why is he so *yellow*?"

"He's got hepatitis."

"How can you be so cold-blooded? Are you going to be thick-skinned and bumptious like a medical student? How I hate that! He's dying, Binx!"

"I know."

"What was that he whispered to you?"

"He told me he had conquered an habitual disposition."

"What is that?"

"He also said you were a very good-looking girl."

"He breaks my *heart*!" We walk in silence. "And his poor parents. Did you see the way Mr Smith stepped out into the hall and dashed the tears from his eyes like a countryman?"

"Yes."

"It is so *pitiful*."

She stops to blow her nose. Her heavy gunmetal hair is separated by a wide ragged part. I kiss the thick white skin of her scalp. "You are very good-looking today." In the past year, she has fattened up; her shoulders are sleek as a leopard.

Kate is horrified. "Please don't." She plucks at her thumb. "There is something grisly about you."

"I have to find the children." When Lonnie took a turn for the worse early this morning, my mother had to bring all the children with her, all but Jean-Paul. They've been sitting in the car since eight o'clock.

Thérèse catches sight of me and sticks her sharp little face out the window. "How is Lonnie?" she asks, trying a weaving motion.

"He is very sick."

"Is he going to die?" Thérèse asks in her canny smart-girl way.

"Yes." I sit around backwards to see them. Kate smiles in at them and stands a ways off. "But he wouldn't want you to be sad. He told me to give you a kiss and tell you that he loved you."

They are not sad. This is a very serious and out-of-the-way business. Their eyes search out mine and they cast about for ways of prolonging the conversation, this game of serious talk and serious listening.

"We love him too," says Mathilde with a sob.

"Kiss us first!" cry Donice and Clare from the back seat.

Mathilde sobs in my neck and Thérèse eyes me shrewdly. "Was he anointed?" she asks in her mama-bee drone.

"Yes."

"Very good."

Only the two girls are sad, but they are also secretly proud of having caught onto the tragedy.

Donice casts about. "Binx," he says and then appears to forget. "When Our Lord raises up on the last day, will Lonnie still be in a wheelchair or will he be like us?"

"He'll be like you."

"You mean he'll be able to ski?" The children cock their heads and listen like old men.

"Yes."

"Hurray!" cry the twins, but somewhat abstractly and more or less attentive to the sound of their own voices.

"Listen," I say, laughing at them. "How would you like to go up to Audubon Park and ride the train?"

"Yes! Yes!"

"Then wait a minute. I'll be right back."

"Binx, we love you too!" cries Donice for the fun of it and leans way out the window. "Will you come to see us?"

"Sure. Now hush up. I want to talk to Kate."

Kate looks back at the car. "You were very sweet with them."

"Thanks."

"What's the matter?"

"Nothing. Will you do me a favor?"

"What?"

"I'll be up here all day with Lonnie and the children. Will you go downtown for me and pick up some governments at the office? Your mother has decided again to keep them at home. She thinks that if war comes, her desk is safer than the vault. Will you go?"

"Alone?"

"Yes. You can ride the streetcar down St Charles. It is nice sitting by an open window."

"I wouldn't know what to ask for!"

"You don't have to. I'll call Mr Klostermann and he'll hand you an envelope. Here's what you do: take the streetcar, get off at Common, walk right into the office. Mr Klostermann will give you an envelope—you won't have to say a word—then catch the streetcar at the same place. It will go on down to Canal and come back up St Charles."

"I don't have any money."

"Here."

She considers the quarter in her palm. "Here's the only thing. It's not that I'm afraid." She looks at a cape jasmine sticking through an iron fence. I pick it and give it to her.

"You're sweet," says Kate uneasily. "Now tell me . . ."

"What?"

"While I am on the streetcar—are you going to be thinking about me?"

"Yes."

"What if I don't make it?"

"Get off and walk home."

"I've got to be sure about one thing."

"What?"

"I'm going to sit next to the window on the Lake side and put the cape jasmine in my lap?"

"That's right."

"And you'll be thinking of me just that way?"

"That's right."

"Good-by."

"Good-by."

Twenty feet away she turns around.

"Mr Klostermann?"

"Mr Klostermann."

I watch her walk toward St Charles, cape jasmine held against her cheek, until my brothers and sisters call out behind me.

About the Author

WALKER PERCY himself went to medical school and interned at Bellevue, intending to be a psychiatrist. After a three-year bout with tuberculosis, he married, converted to Catholicism, and became a writer, first of essays, then of fiction. His first novel, THE MOVIE-GOER, won the National Book Award and has never been out of print since its publication in 1961. His other novels are THE LAST GENTLEMAN, LOVE IN THE RUINS, LANCELOT, and THE SECOND COMING. His nonfiction books are THE MESSAGE IN THE BOTTLE and LOST IN THE COSMOS. He and his wife, Mary Bernice, live in Covington, Louisiana.